Tea & Whiskey

Angela Jablonski

Cover designed by Selfpubbookcovers.com/thrillerauthor

This book is a work of fiction. Names, characters, places, and incidents either are products of the author's imagination or are used fictitiously. Any resemblance to actual persons, living or dead, events, or locales is entirely coincidental.

Angela Jablonski

Printed in the United States of America

Second Printing: April 2019
Amazon.com

ISBN- 1981081976

Dedication

I would like to dedicate this book to my mother, Bonna Beitler, who always supported me in my writing and gave me the inspiration for this story. If it weren't for her, Tea & Whiskey would never have been written.

Wagon Trails

They left their father's hearth, those stalwart pioneers, to follow their dreams to the west seeking new frontiers. They laded Conestoga wagons and without a backwards glance, with faith and fortitude, ventured into that vast expanse.

They gathered at Independence to form a wagon train, then ferried the Mighty MO to trek the featureless plains. They followed the rutted Oregon Trail of those who'd gone before, never sensing the hazards and trials that were to be in store.

They were met with savages, mud, dust and howling gales, trudging westward, ever westward over endless hills and vales. With visions of virgin homestead lands, they followed the sun. They wouldn't be deterred from the migration they had begun.

'Prairie schooners' were crammed with goods and vital tools and were drawn by plodding oxen and cantankerous mules. The caravan was under the command of a crusty wagon master. Not to obey his ever bidding, was sure to court disaster.

Alas, they left many desolate graves along the rutted track, victims of exhaustion, disease, and fearful Indian attacks. They conquered interminable valleys and towering crests, to fulfil their aspirations and complete their western quests.

Robert L. Hinshaw
CMSgt, USAF, Retired

Prologue

Seaford, England: November 1849

Nightfall happened to be black as the Earl of Hell's waist coat. It was cold and crisp, and snowflakes fell like lace in the evening breeze. The winter night was a dream to look upon, yet for Elizabeth Cornwall, it was becoming a nightmare.

"Let me go," she screamed at the man holding her around her waist, his arm muscles bulging to their breaking point. She needed to get away, but he held her too tight. This couldn't be happening, not to her. She had a wonderful life, why was it being taken away from her?

Elizabeth struck his forearm and kicked at his legs, doing everything she could to get away, but he was too strong. *How did it come to this*? One minute she was in her father's tea shop tallying the evening's receipts and the next, she was being pulled roughly against her will.

"Let me go," she yelled, but he refused to hear her terrified wailing. Her body tensed, and she could hear her heartbeat thrashing in her ears. He was going

to regret doing this to her. She struggled even harder, headbutting him in the face and kicking him in the shin. He grunted and cursed in her ear while continuing to drag her down the street.

"Damnit all to hell!" Blood dripped from his nose as he pulled her farther from the small building, she was in. He gripped her harder around the waist, trying to stop her flailing arms. "Stop it," he murmured, holding her tight.

"Release me at once!" She strained as hard as she could against his steel grip, causing harm to herself, but not noticing the pain. She wrenched away from him, but he seized her arm and pulled her hard against his body.

"Elizabeth!" he gasped, panting in terror, and holding her close to him, trying to shield her with his body.

She stared in horror at the gigantic flames that roared from shattered windows and shot through the roof of her father's tea shop; causing the entire building she was just in, to be engulfed in a ghastly inferno. Black smoke billowed into the night sky, shading the glittering stars from sight as timbers burned and a shower of sparks were drifting and swirling as a stairway collapsed. A large bucket brigade of local townsmen fought to extinguish the blaze, but to no avail. The heat was so intense, it caused several men to step back and merely watch. Timbers creaked and cracked in the winter wind before the roof caved in, causing sparks to fly in every direction, many landing on the roofs of other buildings.

"Mother! Father!" Elizabeth coughed, feeling as if a hand had closed around her throat. She reached out to the burning building, her legs giving way and she fell to the street. She pressed her fists to the sides of her head and could feel her heart racing as though it would explode. The fire light reflected across her face as a hot tear slowly made its way down her soot-covered cheek. She couldn't believe what she was witnessing.

"I'm sorry, Elizabeth, but they're gone," Ellis squatted in front of her and gripped her trembling shoulders. "No one could survive that blaze," he said with sadness and pulled her gently to him. Softly stroking her raven hair, he could feel her body shudder as she cried.

A large crowd formed in the street watching the dreadful sight. More men volunteered to put out the blaze, while women tried shielding the eyes of their children from the terrible scene. All around her, she could hear men shouting orders above the roar of the fire. Ellis rose and quickly made his way back to the bucket brigade. Elizabeth lay there watching her father's tea shop go up in flames. Tears of black soot streamed down her face and her yellow dress that her mother had made, was scorched, and torn. There was pain in her lungs and throat, as though they too, were on fire. Turning away, she closed her eyes to the carnage that lay before her.

"You, poor dear." An old woman in a brown dress took off her wool shawl and wrapped it around Elizabeth's shoulders. She shivered, her legs chilled from the snow. She pulled the shawl tight around her and gazed up at the woman, her lower lip trembling. *'How could they be gone? Her parents were her whole life. What was to become of her now?'*

"Dear God," she whispered while the old woman helped her to her feet. Snow mixed with ash fell quietly on the cobblestone street.

Elizabeth froze and shook violently, but not from the cold. She recalled the terrible look in her mother's eyes as the flames engulfed the storage room. Before she could get near the doorway, Ellis had grabbed her and pulled her to safety. She was alive, but her parents had perished, and there was nothing she could have done to help them. The building shifted, and timbers fell, crashing to the ground. Black smoke and sparks whooshed into the air and the crowd stepped back, staring at the devastation.

"You, men, start throwing water on the other buildings. We don't want this bastard to start

8

spreading," Elizabeth heard Ellis shout to the volunteers.

The old woman wrapped her arm around Elizabeth's shoulders and gently led her away. She didn't dare look back, there was nothing left to do now, but go home. All her life, she'd been safe and protected, but now she had no one. Her family was gone.

∞ ∞ ∞

Later that night, Elizabeth sat curled in her father's brown, leather chair, wrapped in her mother's blanket, staring at the crackling blaze in the fireplace. She didn't want to build a fire, but it was too cold to go without one. Tears glistened in her puffy eyes and rolled down her flushed cheeks; she hugged her arms to herself.

"Mother, why? Why did this happen?" she whispered in a voice that seemed to echo.

She had to do something, but what? She couldn't stay in Seaford; her entire life had just gone up in flames. She watched the firewood shift and pop and clapped her hands over her ears and thought of the tea shop's roof collapsing on her parents. How could it be only that evening, so much tragedy had occurred? That just a few minutes of a single day could shatter her life forever.

I've seen too much, witnessed too many painful scenes. I must leave, she thought wrapping the blanket tighter around herself. The scent of her mother's perfume assaulted her senses as a tear dropped onto the coverlet.

While she mauled over her options, there came a gentle knock at the front door. It creaked open and Ellis' head peered around the corner, his face and hair streaked with black soot.

Ellis Hawkins was a tall, good-looking man, thick tawny-gold hair with just a hint of grey and smoky hazel eyes. He loved Elizabeth more than life itself and would do anything for her even though he was older than her, at least twice her age. He intended to make her his wife.

"Elizabeth?" he asked, gazing around the dark room, the flickering orange glow of the fireplace giving off the only light.

"I'm here," she said, lifting her arm, then tucked it back under the blanket.

His cream-colored sweater was tattered and black from the fire and his pants had a hole in the knee. He sat on the edge of her mother's rocking chair, the knitting she had been working on still lay across the arm. Hunched over, his arms resting on his thighs, he gazed at the floor for a moment, not quite knowing what to say. He coughed and cleared his throat.

"Everything has been arranged for your parents' funeral, there's nothing you need to do," he said quietly, almost a whisper.

"Thank you, Ellis," her voice was monotone. Fatigue burdened her body, and she lacked the energy to think straight.

He leaned over and took her fine-boned hand in his. "Do you know what you'll do now?" His thumb slowly brushed over her knuckles.

She shook her head, not saying a word. He let her hand drop, stood, and stepped to the fireplace. With his back to her, he leaned against the mantle and played with a porcelain figurine.

"You need to figure out your next move, Elizabeth. The shop is gone and the only money you have is in the safe," he said matter-of-factly.

"I know," she spoke at the air rather than making eye contact and stared at the shadows playing on the far wall of the cottage.

The snow had gathered on the ledge of the windowsill, ice crystals collected on the pane and snow fell in gentle waves in front of the window. How dare it be so beautiful and peaceful. How could life continue as though tonight never happened? This was a nightmare and when she woke up, her mother would be in the kitchen making black pudding, eggs, and potatoes and her father would be sitting at his secretary filling out ledgers. *Wake up, please wake up*! She put her fists against her temples and squeezed her eyes shut.

Ellis closed his eyes and took a calming breath then placed the figurine back on the mantle, knelt in front of her and took both her hands. His love for her was strong and he knew he'd make her a good husband. Though he wasn't as wealthy as her father, he could give her a comfortable life full of loyalty and happiness. The touch of her hands sent tingling shocks up his arms and made his heart beat quicker. God, how he wanted to kiss her and pull her hard against his chest.

"Marry me," he spoke with quiet, but desperate, firmness.

"What?" she gasped. She took a double take, clearly surprised at what he had asked her. A sudden coldness hit her very core. Her mouth turned down and her brows curved together.

"I know it's rather soon, but you know how I feel about you. I promise to take care of you, and you would never want for anything. Please, Elizabeth, become my wife." He kissed her knuckles and gazed lovingly at her. She withdrew her hands and placed them against her chest.

"Ellis," she stood up, dumbfounded, "what are you saying?" He was an ever-changing mystery. She paced back and forth, her fingers touching her parted lips. "I can't marry you. Bloody hell, you're my father's best friend and twice my age. Ellis, I don't love you in that way."

How could he ask such a thing and the night of her parent's death of all things? This can't be happening. How could he be so insensitive to her feelings? She paced around the room in her night dress, shaking her head; the blanket forgotten and laying in a heap near the chair. The fire began to die so Ellis threw a few logs on the blaze and stood watching her. She wrung her hands and continued to move about the room, her bare feet padding across the wooden floor. Her heart fell at the thought of marrying Ellis. She never thought of him as anything more than a friend and how could he mistake her feelings for him as more than friendship. She never gave him any indication that she felt *that way* toward him. Where did he get the idea, she was in love with him? She drew her hands into fists and began to stomp around the room, her anger swelling deep inside her chest.

"Elizabeth, we could grow to love one another." He stopped her and placed his hands on her shoulders, gently pushing a strand of hair behind her ear.

"I'm sorry, Ellis, I can't." She glanced at him and shook her head, her fists balled at her sides. She was so angry – not so much at him – but at the situation. Her parents were dead, and he was offering a marriage proposal all in one night.

With an odd twinge of disappointment, he nodded and took her in his arms, resting his chin on top of her head. "I figured you would say that. It was worth a try. You know, I'll always be here if you need me."

"Yes, I know," she nodded, her hands falling to her sides.

He released her and stepped back. "Alright then, get some sleep and I'll see you tomorrow morning." He kissed her forehead, and left the little, stone cottage.

Slumping back into her father's chair, she pondered what to do next. She couldn't stay in Seaford. She needed to get as far away from England as possible. As she sat gazing at the fireplace, she thought of her father's tea shop. It was a quaint little establishment stocked with the finest teas from all around the world.

Elizabeth impatiently pulled her drifting thoughts together. She would have to leave England, maybe America and open a tea shop like her father's. She had once read a dime novel about America and how wonderful it was. It talked about its cities such as New York and Boston, the war between the Colonies and her native land, the culture, and the wilds, and about the wagon trains moving west to settle in California, the Territories of Oregon, and Washington. That might be something she could do, take a wagon there, and she could start fresh in a new land with new people… a new life.

She made her way from the fireplace to her father's secretary. Opening the top drawer, she found the secret compartment and popped it open. Pulling out a small piece of paper with several numbers on it, she strolled over to a painting of her mother and looked at it affectionately.

"I love you so much, but I can't stay. I'm sorry, mother," she said, touching the painting, a quivering smile crossed her face.

Her father, Charles, always compared her to the woman in the portrait. Alice Cornwall seemed to gaze down at her daughter with a hint of a smile. Her raven hair hung in long, graceful curves over her slender shoulders while her gentle, loving hands sat lightly on her lap. Her lilac-colored dress trimmed with white lace brought out her soft, violet eyes. She seemed content with her life.

Elizabeth lifted the portrait off the wall and sat it gingerly against her father's secretary. Holding the small piece of paper, she dialed the lock of the safe until it clicked. Grabbing the handle, she swung the door open and looked inside. There were a great deal of papers, ledgers, and contracts, but under it, lay a large money bag. She picked it up, shut the safe door and replaced the portrait then sitting at the secretary, she opened the bag and counted the money.

∞ ∞ ∞

A week later, Elizabeth, fingering her necklace, stood at the white cliffs gazing out over the water, her black mourning dress blowing in the bitterly, cold wind. Dark, gloomy clouds hovered overhead, matching her melancholy heart. She had sold her cottage and most of her property, except for her mother's tea set and her father's bible. The funeral was over, and her parents were gone. There was nothing keeping her in Seaford. It was best she leave the pain in the past and look toward the future.

"Elizabeth?" Ellis called out above the bitter wind. "It's time to go or you'll miss your boat."

She took one last look at the white caps and, with a heavy heart, strolled over to where Ellis stood, holding the reins to a horse and buggy. She gazed up at him with tear filled eyes, her lower lip quivering. He pulled out a white handkerchief from his coat pocket and dabbed the corner of her eyes then took her arm and helped her into the buggy. He pulled a thick blanket over her lap, climbed in himself then snapping the reins, they were off.

"I think you're just being foolish, Elizabeth, traveling all by yourself. I believe I should be escorting you to Oregon," Ellis said with a heavy sigh. He held the reins tight in his hands and his body tensed. Though she had refused him, the feel of her body so close to his was driving him mad. How could he say good-bye to her – to let her go like this?

"I told you, Ellis, this is something I must do alone," she proclaimed, trying to put up a brave front. Her eyes began to tear up, but she wouldn't let them fall. She had to show courage or Ellis would never let her leave and this was something she had to do. Ellis would just have to learn to live with her decision. She was a grown woman of twenty and could do what she thought was best for her and America was what she needed.

Elizabeth took a deep breath and let it out slowly. She was terrified yet exuberated. Her heart began to beat faster, and she thought of the adventure waiting for her across the ocean and the whole new world before her.

Chapter One

Independence Missouri: Late April 1850

Elizabeth wandered around the general store, gazing at all the beautiful luxuries she could never afford. There were several dresses in many different colors of plaid, gingham, and calico. She strolled over to a shelf filled with books and gazed at the titles with a smile. She loved to read and had brought a few with her on her travels. She moved around the room, spotting a pretty, white nightgown with delicate lace and a pink ribbon on the collar, folded on a shelf near the front window. She looked at the price tag and swallowed, five dollars and fifty cents. She picked it up and touched the fabric, holding it close to her. *I would very much love to have this*, she thought, but no, the money was for supplies not frivolities. She gently placed the nightgown back on the shelf with a little frown.

She walked up to the counter and waited for Mr. Dixon, the proprietor, to finish helping a burly cowboy with his purchases.

"Will there be anything else, Mr. Cobb?" Mr. Dixon asked, with a deep southern drawl. He placed the purchases in a large crate.

"Chewing tobacco," Mr. Cobb glowered and narrowed his eyes.

Mr. Dixon nodded and made up the package of tobacco. Billy Ray Cobb turned his head and spat in a spittoon. Elizabeth looked at him from the corner of her eye and found him to be the most revolting man she had ever seen. At that moment, she wished she were elsewhere. Billy Ray's hair was greasy under a very worn brown cowboy hat. A deep, jagged scar ran down the left side of his face, and tobacco stains dripped down his scruffy, double chin. He had an air of authority and appearance of one who demanded instant obedience; it frightened her. And if that weren't enough, his odor made her eyes water. She bit her lip and stepped closer to the opened front door for a bit of fresh air.

Mr. Dixon placed the tobacco pouch in his customer's crate, took a pencil from behind his ear and calculated the total. Cobb turned and spat again. A sour taste filled Elizabeth's mouth.

"That will be seventy-five dollars, Mr. Cobb," Mr. Dixon's voice shook. He had heard rumors about Billy Ray Cobb, and none of them painted him a gentleman. It was said that he had taken the life of many a man and was fond of women with a pretty face and a fine figure. And it was rumored that when he was finished with them, they weren't attractive anymore.

"Robbery!" Cobb bared his teeth, took out his wallet and threw the money at Mr. Dixon, then grabbed the large crate and tossed it on his shoulder. He turned toward the front door and spotted Elizabeth standing near the corner of the counter and smirked, showing dark, brown stained teeth. His tongue darted out, licking his chapped lips. He looked her up and down, his fingers itching to touch her.

"Ma'am." With a wide grin, he gave her a wink and walked out of the general store.

Elizabeth wrinkled her nose and rubbed her forearms. Why anyone would want to look or smell like that, was beyond her. She had noticed that many of the supplies he was buying were for a trip, most likely on a wagon train. Her heart pounded nervously. Surely, he wouldn't be on the same one as her, she hoped. Once Mr. Cobb left, Mr. Dixon sauntered up to her with a half-hearted smile.

"Good morning, Miss Cornwall. Forget something since yesterday?" He smiled, placing his elderly hands on the counter.

"Good morning." Her British accent still sounding strange against his southern drawl. She pulled a small piece of paper out of her drawstring purse and handed it to him. "Yes, just a few more items. I'll just be over here while you complete my order."

He took the paper from her slender hand, stared at it then gathered her items. Elizabeth strolled around the store once more, looking at the beautiful dishes, china, and crystal, when she spotted a charming, little tea set. She gently picked up a cup and smiled to herself; a comfortable warmth filling her. The cup was white with tiny blue flowers, rather plain in her eyes. The one she brought with her from England, was far prettier than the one that sat before her. It was the only thing she had left from her mother, and she cherished it above anything else in the world.

A tear tried to fall, but she blinked it away. Crying wouldn't bring her parents back. It seemed a lifetime ago since she was back in England. Now here she was standing in a mercantile in Missouri buying supplies for her trip across the great frontier. For several weeks she had procured a wagon, team, and things she needed for the long trip ahead. A scout she had met earlier in the week, named Lucas, had told her it would take at least five months to get to Oregon City. He and Mr. Dixon had helped her purchase the items she required and tomorrow her new life would begin. She gently sat the cup back on the saucer.

"Miss Cornwall will there be anything else?" Mr. Dixon asked, interrupting her thoughts.

"Yes, one more thing." She walked over to the white nightgown she spotted earlier, bit her lip, and picked it up. Why not treat herself to this one delight? Her eyes danced and sparkled as she carried it over to the counter. "Now I'm finished."

"Oh, you have good taste, Miss Cornwall. This here came all the way from Paris," he said folding the gown and wrapping it in paper. Suddenly, he stopped and looked at her with a fatherly glint in his eye. He placed an aging hand over hers. "Miss Cornwall, is there nothing I can say to stop you from going tomorrow? I don't think you know what you're up against," his voice trembled a bit. He admired this girl, but he knew she wasn't ready to face what the trail would bring, only hardships and death.

"I thank you for your interest in my personal welfare, Mr. Dixon, but this is something I must do." She nodded, understanding his concern.

He sighed, finished wrapping the nightgown and placed it in the crate along with the other items. After taking her money, he handed her the small crate and wished her well. Elizabeth smiled, and with a spring in her step, walked out of the general store.

∞ ∞ ∞

John Evans moseyed down the street toward the general store. There were a few more things he needed before the long trip to Oregon. Crossing the dusty street, he stopped to allow a buckboard and a few horses to go by then continued walking to the mercantile. He noticed Sam, the barkeep, sweeping the front of the saloon and smiled to himself. He thought about Buck, his cook, trying to run after him this morning, breathing hard and reminding him not to forget the five cases of whiskey he planned to trade along the trail. Buck had a way of bargaining and could trade the last shirt off a man's back with a wooden nickel.

John was thinking about Buck and his shenanigans and didn't notice the young woman leaving the store. He collided with her, sending her parcels falling from a small crate onto the ground. With a racing heart, he reached out and grabbed her arms, preventing her from falling. She was a tiny, little thing; the top of her head only reaching the middle of his chest. But of course, he towered over everyone by a full seven inches.

"What on earth? Why don't you watch where you're going?" she snapped, her body tensing. *How dare this brut run into me and scatter my belongings about.*

"Ma'am, I am so sorry," John said with a heartfelt apology. His voice deep and smooth as a glass of brandy. He quickly released her and removed his hat.

"You should be." She waved him away and began fluffing her royal, blue dress.

She glared up at him and he had to take a step back. She was the most beautiful thing he had ever seen. She was truly captivating. Her raven, black hair was tied up with pretty ribbons and waterfall curls. The flush on her pale cheeks was like the flush of a pink rose and her lips were full and rounded over even, white teeth. But it was her eyes that took his breath away. They were beautiful, like a Nebraska violet sunset. He gently shook to relax after the initial shock of seeing her.

"Here, let me," he said, placing his hat back on.

He bent down and began collecting her belongings, placing them back in the crate. She stood with her hands on her hips and huffed at him. He picked up a parcel and got a whiff of roses; bars of soap would be his guess. When he collected the last package, he had a deep, gratifying smile while putting it away; it was a white nightgown with a pink ribbon.

"I should have watched where I was going, ma'am," he apologized, picking up the crate and handed it to her.

"Thank you." She smiled, took one last look at him, and made her way to the hotel.

"Whoa," John whispered. His body tingled with pleasure and a devilish smile crossed his lips. He put his hands in his jacket pockets and entered the general store.

∞ ∞ ∞

Elizabeth couldn't believe what had just happened. One minute, she was walking out the door of the general store and the next, she was in the arms of a total stranger; the tallest man she had ever seen. She spread her fingers out like a fan and placed them against her chest and sighed. Never had she seen a man like him before – ever.

He looked like a Greek god from a book she had read. He had short, brown hair, chiseled features and the shadow of his beard and mustache gave him an even more manly aura. His complexion was tanned in a way that made her believe he must spend a great deal of time outdoors. He had long, sturdy Viking legs, massive shoulders that filled the coat he wore, and his open shirt revealed a muscular chest covered with crisp, brown hair. Her skin tingled as she thought of him. She had to admit, he was a very handsome man, in a rugged sort of way.

Oh well. It didn't matter, she thought. *All that did matter, was getting to the west coast and open a tea shop like the one my parents had back in Seaford.* Marriage was the last thing on her mind.

While she made her way to the hotel, she didn't notice a man following her. He stepped up to the saloon and leaned against one of its pillars, curling his lip while playing with a sharp hunting knife. He watched her closely as she walked up the stairs and into the hotel.

Sauntering over to the saloon's swinging doors, he pushed them aside and entered; fiendishly walking up to the bar. He ordered a whiskey and while drinking it, several of the men around him backed away or left. The bartender's hand shook while pouring him another glass. The stranger sneered and guzzled his whiskey. One defiantly didn't want to see their name on the top of this man's shit list. If they did, he was a dead man.

The stranger threw the glass at Sam, the barkeeper, grabbed a saloon girl by the hair and pulled her up the stairs. The young girl struggled and yelled her displeasure before being thrown into an empty room. The door slammed shut and the woman began to scream. The men in the saloon looked down at their tables, talking quietly; trying to ignore what was happening in the room above them.

Sam stood there shaking his head. Poor Charlotte, she'll need a doctor tomorrow. He sent word to young Thomas and told him to go get old Doc Sanders; he'll be needed first thing in the morning. Sam wanted to help Charlotte, but he wouldn't dare go up against the famous killer known as Billy Ray Cobb.

∞ ∞ ∞

After going to the general store, the saloon and the blacksmith, John went back to the livery to make sure everything was ready for tomorrow's drive. He walked through the barn and exited from a side door. Coming around the corner of the barn, he spotted his little brother leaning against a fence post watching the mules.

"Hey Jed," John called, strolling up to his brother clapping him on the back.

He gazed at Jed and recalled that after the death of their parents back in New York, he had taken his little brother Jed, fifteen, and moved west. Soon the two became involved in the Great Expansion, moving settlers across the plains to California, the Territories of Oregon and Washington. He became so good at his job, that after five years, he became Captain of his own wagon train.

He loved his job, even with all the hardships and tribulations, but something was missing. He didn't find it as worthwhile as he once did, he lacked vigor, and he needed a change. This was his last trip----hopefully. He'd earned enough money to buy some land near Oregon City, settle down and maybe start up a business. Jed was old enough to be Captain, so he was willing to hand the job over to his brother, if he wanted it. *Which he better or so help me, I'll give him a thrashing he'll never forget.*

"John," Jed grinned, a piece of hay hung from his mouth.

Looking at Jed, one would never guess they were brothers. Though he had John's height, that's as far as it went. Jed took after their mother, with a handsome face that was kindled with a sort of beauty, dimples, palomino blonde hair and sky-blue eyes while John looked more like their father.

"Everything alright?" John asked, climbing the fence and took a seat, his feet dandling in the mule pen.

"Yep. Everything is ready and rearing to go." Jed put a booted foot on the railing and placed his chin on his folded arms. "Well, one question though." He rubbed his jaw then the back of his neck.

"Shoot." John looked at him, his body sagging and relaxed.

"Well, there's ten wagons' in our party including Buck's, right? Then why are there eleven parked out back?" Jed asked, tilting his head to one side.

"Uh, don't know. I'll check after dinner," he said, scratching his beard.

Jed nodded and turned to leave, when he saw a beautiful young woman in a royal, blue dress stroll into the livery stable. He let out a whistle and elbowed John in the thigh. A minute later, the young woman exited the stable and started walking straight toward him. A grin, that couldn't be contained no matter how hard he tried, spread across his face and he situated his gun belt and fixed his hat.

"I'll handle this," Jed said overconfidently.

The young woman stepped up to him, cocked her head and eyed him up and down. "Um, excuse me, I'm looking for the Captain of the wagon train. Are you he?"

John's back became as ridged as a two by four. Shaking out his hands, he closed his eyes and took a calming breath. It was the woman from the general store. *What the hell was she doing here?* he thought wringing his hands. His mouth went dry, and he had an empty feeling in the pit of his stomach.

The place was filthy. Why would an upstanding English lady such as her, wander into an area with the most offensive odors known to man; that even he would find a reason to leave just to escape from it?

"No, ma'am. That'd be my brother John." Jed pointed to John sitting on the fence. "I'm Jedidiah, but everyone calls me Jed."

"Nice to make your acquaintance, Jed." She took his hand and shook it. She could feel the pad of his thumb gently caress her skin.

He gave her hand a light squeeze, noticing how silky smooth her skin felt. She'd clearly never done a day of manual labor in her life. With one quick squeeze, he let her hand go.

"Is there something I can do for you?" he asked, putting his thumbs in his front pockets, holding still with cautious hope.

"Thank you, no. I need to speak with your brother, Mr…" She tilted her head and paused.

John got down from the fence and faced her. He couldn't help looking deep into those stunning eyes. *Damn, she was as beautiful now as she was earlier that morning.* He towered over her like a mighty oak gazing down upon a sapling. Utterly confused as to why she was here, he became overheated, and he felt a tightness in his chest. His eyebrows pinched together, and he narrowed his eyes.

"Evans, ma'am." He tipped his hat. His heart beat fast and sweat beaded on his forehead.

"Mr… Mr. Evans." She paled and held her breath when she caught sight of his chiseled face. "He… hello, my name is Elizabeth Cornwell," she stuttered. "I wanted to meet you before tomorrow." She held out her slender hand.

"Tomorrow?" John frowned, not taking it. *What the hell was she talking about?* He placed his hands on his hips and glared at her.

"Why yes. I will be joining you on your venture to Oregon City." She lowered her hand.

"I don't understand. I've met all the men in our party. I don't remember meeting a Mr. Cornwall.

Where's your husband, so I can talk to him about tomorrow?" He had a steely tone to his voice, his eyes narrowed, confusingly.

"Damn… a husband?" Jed whispered under his breath. He lowered his head, shifting his weight to one leg and stuck his thumbs into his gun belt.

"What makes you think I'm married?" Elizabeth asked, raising her left eyebrow, folding her arms against her chest and tightened her jaw.

"You're not married?" John frowned again, biting the inside of his check.

"No." Spots of color entered her checks.

"Yes." Jed smiled, his face beaming. John glared at him. "Um, I'll just go see what Acngus' up to. Ma'am." Jed tipped his hat and quickly made his way to the livery stable.

John was horrified when he learned that she intended to make the journey on her own; women of good breeding simply did not travel without a male escort. It just wasn't done. But here she was telling him she was going. He had never met a woman who had the nerve to stand up to him like this one.

He scowled back at her. "Ma'am… Miss Cornwall. Let me get this straight, you want to go to the Oregon Territory without a chaperone? What's in your head, girl?" His voice deepened. "No, it's too dangerous. People die out there. I'm sorry, but no." He removed his hat and ran his fingers through his hair, causing a piece to stick straight up.

"I sold nearly everything I own to buy a wagon, a team, and supplies for this trip. What am I supposed to do with my belongings?" she pleaded.

"You might be able to get some of your money back." He hit the side of his leg with his hat. "Where are your folks?"

"They're dead," she said, her voice breaking, and a tear slowly ran down her cheek.

"I'm sorry." He watched the tear fall, wanting nothing more than to wipe it away and take her into his arms and console her. Instead, he stood like a mountain, gazing down at her, a scowl upon his lips. "Miss Cornwall, I don't think you understand what you're getting yourself into."

Elizabeth put her hands on her hips. "Mr. Evans, I did not sail across the Atlantic Ocean to Boston, then make my way here to Independence Missouri just to have some cowhand tell me I can't go!" She raised her voice with every word. The tightness in her jaw and facial muscles caused her discomfort when she clenched her teeth.

"Cowhand?" John's eyebrows shot up while he stared at her.

In the corner of his eye, he saw movement and clenched his jaw. He pulled away from her hypnotic stare to see Jed and Aengus coming out of the livery. His little brother displayed a wide grin, leaned against the stable wall, and played with the piece of hay he still had stuck in his mouth.

"Miss Cornwall..." John poked his tongue lightly into his cheek and inhaled a long breath. "I just can't..."

"Look, I'm going, Mr. Evans, and that's all there is to it," she said matter-of-factly.

"Like *hell* you are," he shouted then heard chuckling over by the livery and glared at them. John was always the practical one, but Jed still had some growing up to do. He always followed John's instructions while on the trail, but when a pretty face was involved, all bets were off. There were times when John could box Jed's ears, and this was one of them. Jed was the only family he had and felt he needed to be there for him; to guide and protect him, but at this very minute he would just as soon see him mount his horse and leave. He turned his head back to her, trying to remain calm. "I know you want to go, but I can't allow it.

"Mr. Evans..." She tightened her fists, her fingernails biting into her palms.

"Look girl, I don't give a damn if you want to go or not, this is my wagon train and I'm telling you no. Don't you realize some of the people going aren't gonna make it to Oregon? One of them could be you," he snapped. Though he was angry, there was something about this woman that made his heart melt. When God made her, He broke the mold. All the other women he'd known would never have stood up to him like this spit of a girl.

"I'll take my chances." She pouted, folding her arms and planted her feet firmly to the ground.

"Aw, come on, John, let her go." Jed pushed away from the stable and ambled over to his brother, Aengus followed close behind. "We'll watch over her. She'll be fine."

"I need you to watch everyone, Jed." John barked and pointed to the wagons parked behind the livery.

"You don't think we'll do our job? Thanks for the vote of confidence. Don't worry, John, we will. Honest." Jed and Aengus nodded. "Besides, she won't be too much trouble, will you, ma'am?" She shook her head with a pleading gaze. "See? Look John, it must be something important for her to cross an entire ocean and then want to travel west to Oregon City. Come on, give her a chance."

John flared his nose, threw up his hands and brushed past her. "Damn it!" he yelled and headed toward the saloon. Jed was being too sensitive toward Miss Cornwall, and men with soft hearts and weak constitutions didn't last long on the trail.

"Mr. Evans, we're not through." Elizabeth called after him.

"Best leave him be, lass," Aengus said in a Scottish brogue.

Elizabeth was confused, she wasn't quite sure what had just happened. Turning back toward Jed

34

and Aengus, she swallowed hard. She felt a painful tightness in her throat.

"But what about…" she began.

"Don't worry, Miss Cornwall, that's just his way of saying he'll think about it," Jed snickered. Whenever John became too overwhelmed, he always left the situation to collect his thoughts over a glass of whiskey, before tackling it head on.

"Oh." She touched her bottom lip. "Please, call me Elizabeth," she said in a light voice.

"With pleasure, ma'am." Jed smiled. "Miss Elizabeth, is there anything I can do for you?" He winked at her.

"No, I don't believe so." She blushed and twiddled her fingers.

"Well then, we'll see you bright and early tomorrow morning. Boss wants to roll outta here at the first sign of light." Jed tipped his hat.

Elizabeth thanked Jed and Aengus, left the livery, and made her way down the street; Jed watching her fade into the distance.

"What a gal." Jed smirked.

Aengus punched him in the arm. "You glaikit bastard."

"Ow." Jed rubbed his arm and smiled at him. Aengus rolled his eyes and trudged back to the livery stable.

Aengus MacGregor was Jed's best friend and had known him since they were boys living in New

York City. After Jed and John got jobs helping settlers cross the plains, John wrote Aengus and told him he had work for him. His job was digging out dried stream beds, help push wagons out of the mud and repair them if needed. Aengus was a mountainous man with green eyes and long red hair pulled back with a black ribbon, legs as enormous as tree trunks and arms so monumental, he could lift a wagon wheel one handed over his head without even trying.

Jed rubbed his sore arm and followed his friend into the stable. Before entering, he turned his head, hoping to catch one more glimpse of Elizabeth. With a wide grin, he stepped into the livery.

Chapter Two

"Another one, John?" asked Sam.

Sam Dooley stood behind the bar eyeing John. He was a tall, lanky man with fine, grey hair and a bushy mustache. His brown, beady eyes, the gap between his front teeth and his nasally voice gave him the look of a villain from the latest penny dreadful. He reached behind him and grabbed a bottle of whiskey.

"Thanks." John watched Sam pour the amber liquid into his shot glass.

The saloon was filled with cowboys, drunks, and gamblers. An elderly man played a piano while three saloon girls danced on a decorative stage. Along the bar, men drank hard liquor and beer. At the front of the saloon were two swinging doors and a big window on either side of the entryway where the bar's name was painted. A staircase led to several rooms where Sam and the girls slept and overhead, were two large wagon wheel chandeliers. A bluish haze of smoke coiled like vines along the timbered ceiling, the air pungent with the scents of whiskey, smoke, and human sweat. Behind the bar was a large mirror with a big crack in the upper left corner, and the room was filled with tables and chairs, most of them occupied with men playing cards.

"Trouble?" Sam put the bottle of whiskey on the bar and began cleaning a glass with a bar towel.

"Yeah, about five feet four inches worth of trouble. Can you believe she wants to go all the way to Oregon alone, with no chaperone?" John threw back his head and swallowed his whiskey with one gulp then slammed the shot glass back on the counter.

Several men at the end of the bar were snorting and laughing. One of the drunks repeated a punch line spurring more laughter, so loud that it seemed to shake the ceiling timbers and the scarred wooden floor. One cowboy pounded his fist on the bar while another wiped tears of mirth from his eyes. John glared at them while Sam poured him another drink. He picked it up and swirled the golden liquid, making a small cyclone.

"She don't have a husband?" Sam asked, wiping down the bar.

"No. And no family either." John shook his head. "Aengus and Jed want her to go, but I don't know. She could cause a lot of trouble on the trail." He scratched his jaw.

"Pretty, is she?" Sam smiled and wiggled his eyebrows.

"You've no idea." He finished his drink and gave the glass to Sam. His anger began to subside. He smirked at the thought of Elizabeth standing up to him like a small street dog barking at a Timber Wolf. He gave her credit, she was a determined little thing.

"You take care, now." Sam took the glass.

"Thanks, Sam." Reaching into his pocket, he pulled out a few coins and placed them on the bar.

"Anytime." The bartender took the bottle and glass and placed them under the bar.

John was about to leave, when a saloon girl with blonde hair and a green, tight fitting satin dress grabbed him by the arm. "Oh Johnny, you ain't leaving yet are ya?"

"'Fraid so. Sorry Delilah, maybe next time." He peeled her hand off his arm. She smelled of cigarettes and booze with a hint of perfume. "Look. I think Tom wants you over at his table." He pointed to a cowboy in a black hat playing cards.

In his younger days, John would have accepted her offer, and gladly. But he was no longer young, or rather he didn't feel young. Even though he was thirty, he neither wanted nor needed the company of cheap women and saloon girls.

Delilah leaned in closer, stroked John's ear and whispered, "You're gonna miss me when you're gone." She stood on her tippy toes, wrapped her arms around his neck while her tongue traced the fullness of his lips.

He placed his hands on her shoulders and lightly pushed Delilah away. "I'm sure I will." *Shit. What was it about Elizabeth that made me feel as if*

I'm being unfaithful to her? He smiled, tipped his hat, and quickly left the saloon.

Later that night, John lay on his pallet, unable to sleep. He stared up at the rafters of the livery stable, watching a mouse scurry across the beams. Nearby, Buck, Jed, and Lucas slept soundly, except Aengus, who sounded like a wild boar. He took a deep breath and let it out slowly, smiling to himself. The stable smelled of hay, horses, leather, and saddle soap. He listened to the sound of the horses as they moved around their stalls, tails swishing and hooves stomping on the packed earth.

Though it was relatively cool, John was sweltering. All he had over him was a thin horse blanket. His arm over his eyes, but all he could see were those beautiful violet eyes. A sheen of sweat covered his cheeks and forehead. What was he going to do with her? What he really wanted to do was give her a swift kick in the ass.

He ran his hands through his hair and down his face but stopped when he heard a noise behind the livery. It sounded like crates sliding over wood. He sat up in bed and hesitated. He got a surge of adrenaline and could feel his heart racing. The noise happened again. He jumped off his pallet, put on his trousers and pulled his gun from its holster. He quickly checked to make sure it was loaded; the cylinder clicking into place.

"What's going on, John?" Lucas asked, rolling over.

"Nothing, just gotta visit the outhouse. Get back to sleep." said John with a nod and stepped over his friend.

"You need a gun to go to the outhouse?" Lucas asked, sitting up.

"Bears," he snickered. "I just need to check something out." As he passed a stall, a pinto stuck its head out and whinnied.

"You need any help?" Lucas threw the blanket from himself.

"Naw, I'm sure it's nothing. Go back to sleep." He patted the pinto.

John went to the side door and slowly pushed it, creaking as it opened. He slipped out and crept along the far wall to the corner of the building. He carefully peeked around and noticed a lantern lit, hanging inside one of the covered wagons.

"Dammit," he whispered. *Of all nights to be robbed.*

He crouched down and cocked his pistol. All was quiet, except for the thundering sound of his heart. He tried to see and hear everything at once as he took a deep breath. Sidestepping, but keeping his eyes on the lantern, he watched a silhouette clumsily move about the wagon. The stranger stepped out, bent over, and struggled with a small, wooden chest lying on the ground.

John circled, using the darkness, and snuck up to the stranger. With slow, cautious movements, he pointed the gun at him. "Hold it!"

The stranger nearly dropped the chest. Sitting it down, he spun around and put his hands up. Though there was lantern light, the thief stood in the shadows. The outsider shook nervously while standing in the dark, not sure what he should do. He started to lower his arms, but John glared at him and shifted the position of his gun.

"Steal from me, I don't think so. Let's just see what the sheriff has to say about this." John grabbed the stranger by the collar of his jacket and shoved him, causing him to stumble and fall.

The thief hit the ground with a loud thud. He rolled over and glared at John. "I'm not stealing, you Knobber. I'm packing my wagon."

"Dammit." John rubbed his forehead. *Was he ever going to be rid of her*? He let down the hammer of his firearm and shoved it in the front of his trousers. He grabbed Elizabeth by the arm and pulled her to her feet. "I could have killed you."

"But you didn't." She pointed out.

"It's the middle of the night, what the hell are you doing here?" he whispered loudly.

"I told you, I'm packing my wagon. I couldn't sleep, so I thought I'd do some work." Elizabeth said, brushing the dust off her hands and stepped back to the wagon. "Lucas helped me with the heavy stuff a couple days ago." She reached down and attempted to pick up the small, wooden chest.

"He did, did he? Here, let me help you." He took it from her and tossed it onto the tailgate, landing with a loud bang. He noticed the back of her wagon was filled with everything she would need for the trip, but lacked furniture, which was a good thing. He was impressed with her dedication.

"Oh, be careful!" she gasped and leapt onto the tailgate, turned the box toward her and unlatched it. "Please, be alright." She lifted the lid, moved some straw aside and looked inside. "Thank goodness." She placed a hand on her bosom and sighed. It was safe and unbroken, her face lit up like the sun shining off the water.

John leaned against the tailgate and crossed his arms. "What's so important about what's in that chest?" He watched her pick up a teacup and smiled. "A cup?" He raised his right eyebrow.

"This isn't just a cup, this is my mother's tea set. It's the only thing I have left of her. It's very precious to me," her voice was bubbly. Her mother was her best friend and now with her gone she felt so lost. There was a certain novelty to the situation, she admitted, since before the death of her parents, she had never been alone in her life.

He watched her kiss the cup and gently placed it back in the chest, covered it with straw and closed the lid. "Well, that ain't gonna make it to Oregon, I can tell you that." He shook his head and thought about all the belongings that would eventually be dumped on the side of the trail. Every time he would lead another wagon train, he couldn't believe how full the wagons would be, only to see most of the cherished possessions tossed aside. He just couldn't bear to see Elizabeth having such high hopes for the things she loved.

"It made it from England, didn't it? If I pack it good, I think it will do simply fine." She started to pick up the wooden box, but he grabbed her arm.

"Get out," he sighed and helped her out of the wagon and climbed in himself; the wagon shifting side to side.

With his height, it made movement difficult, but he was able to take the chest closer to the front of the wagon. With some rope he found, he was free to secure it. While he was there, he made sure everything was anchored down. Noticing a trunk that wasn't fastened down, he slid it to the corner of the wagon. Spotting a sleeve hanging out of the chest, he lifted the lid to put the dress back in and got a dainty whiff of rose petals. His mouth went dry as he closed the lid. He looked up, trying to calm his breathing. After securing the trunk, he climbed back out of the wagon.

"There," he said wiping his hands together, "that ought to hold it." He looked down at her and smiled. She stood with her mouth agape and a dazed look in her eyes. "What?"

"You…you helped me pack my wagon. Does this mean I can go?" she asked, covering her mouth with her hand, eyes wide and shinning.

"Yeah, I guess so." He rubbed the back of his neck.

"Oh, thank you!" She reached out and hugged him, pressing her face against his bare chest.

I never want to move again, she thought. *How blissful it would be to just stand like this forever.*

He stood there, as electrical jolts shot through his body. Her hair smelled of rose petals. Tilting his head back, he looked at the stars, trying to calm his heartbeat; he knew she could hear it beating like a stampede of horses. There was something happening between them, and it worried him. How he longed to grab her and kiss her until he took her breath away. God, her face felt warm against his skin. He placed his hands on her back, as she looked up at him and smiled. *Those eyes are going to be the death of me.* She released him and stepped back, he felt his skin burn where her face had been.

"Thank you, Mr. Evans. You don't know how much this means to me." She put up the tailgate, looked at him and smiled. "Well, goodnight." She took the lantern and walked back to her hotel.

He stood there in the dark. "What are you doing?" he asked himself as he ran his fingers through his hair. *You're too old for her. She's just a kid and closer to your brother's age.* He didn't need this, he just wanted to finish this trail ride and buy some land. And he didn't need a woman in his life. He groaned and rubbed his hands over his face. This defiantly was going to be a sleepless night. He walked back to the livery and his pallet; those eyes haunting him with every step.

∞ ∞ ∞

Elizabeth opened her hotel room door and entered. After closing it, she leaned her back against it and covered her face with her hands. What just happened? She ran into his arms like some Jezebel. What must he think of her?

Shaking her head, she went behind the screen and undressed, putting on a light-yellow nightgown and climbed into bed. She lay there staring up at the ceiling, shadows playing on the wall while the curtains blew gently in the breeze.

"John." She whispered, rolled over and pulled the covers up over her ears.

A tingling sensation swept up the back of her neck and across her face as thoughts of him haunted her. He had a solid chest, but his skin was smooth and warm against her cheek. The heat of his body made the petals of her womanhood pulsate with pleasure. He had the manly smell of soap and hay.

She knew her hug lasted longer than it should have, but she needed to feel his body pressed against hers. She had felt him tremble as she slide her hands across his wide back, and for a moment she thought he might kiss her, but she had stepped away before he had the chance. She couldn't allow him to do it. He was far too old for her, and she didn't need a man in her life right now. She had to remember why she was here, why she traveled so far from home.

"John." She closed her eyes and sighed, pulling her pillow closer to her. She drifted off, and the last thing she saw was his brown eyes staring down   at   her

Chapter Three

John sat tall in the saddle watching the eleven wagons slowly park in a long row, taking up most of the street in front of Independence Town Square. Most of the wagon trains, by now, left from Westport, but he liked Independence and the people who lived there. He'd known them a long time.

The lead covered wagon was driven by Buck. John gazed at his friend and smirked. Buck Mercer had seen a lot of winters, as displayed on his face. He had a hard life, losing his wife and children, twenty years ago, to cholera on this same trail. John had found him deep in the bottle and offered him a job as cook. At first, Buck had told him to go to hell, but after he ran out of money for his whiskey, he took the position. John shook his head and snickered. Buck must have tasted everything he fixed, his stomach rolls were evidence enough. He sat in the middle of the seat to give it balance. If he didn't, John was sure the wagon would tip over. He and John had been making this run for over five years and every year Buck would tell him it was his last. He knew Buck would be doing this until the day he died.

"Buck, those nags gonna get you all the way to Oregon?" John asked, eyeing the two horses doubtfully.

"I'll have you to know, these here are the finest mares this side of the Missouri. They'll get me there; don't you worry none. You just wait and see," he laughed, showing his two missing front teeth.

Aengus, Jed, and Lucas trotted up to John. Jed yawned and rubbed his face with his gloved hand. He hated getting up at the crack of dawn. Lucas looked up at the sky with a smile on his tan face.

"This is a good day," he said with a nod.

It was a beautiful spring day. The sun shone bright on the horizon and the sky was a crisp purple with just a few clouds. John felt the morning chill on his arms and neck while he sat looking in the direction they would soon be traveling. He hoped that by leaving in late April, they would make it to Oregon City sometime in Mid-September; at least five months on the trail.

"You know what to do, Lucas. Meet us at the ferry and make sure you get a good spot in line; a lot of wagons will be crossing today. Pay Harry well, I don't want to spend all day getting these wagons across the river." John handed Lucas a bag of coins.

Lucas took the purse and placed it in his saddle bag. "See you in a few hours." He kicked his black and white pinto and headed out of town.

Lucas 'Snow Wolf' Tanner was John's trusted Indian scout. He would ride ahead and make sure there wasn't any danger to John or the wagons. He knew the land and the rivers, doing everything he could to aid John in making it safely to Oregon City. He'd been a tracker for nearly twenty years, ever since he left home. Lucas' mother was a Shawnee, and his father was a trapper. After the rape and murder of his mother, Morning Dove, at the hands of another trapper, when Lucas was just six years old, his father took him high in the Kentucky hills and taught him everything he needed to know about being a great trapper and hunter. However, his father was also an alcoholic and beat Lucas nearly every day. When Lucas was fifteen, he left and made his way west; that was nearly twenty years ago. John and Lucas met when John was still new to the trail and needed a tracker to help him find his way to Oregon City. He stayed on ever since. Lucas was a tall man with piercing black eyes and long, dark hair that hung clear to his waist. He wore buckskins, carried a Sharp rifle, and had a Bowie knife tied to his lower leg.

John signaled Jed and Aengus to follow him. They turned their horses and made their way down the long row of covered wagons. Each one was filled to the brim with supplies and personal belongings. Except for the driver of each wagon, everyone else had to walk.

"Aengus, you're the middleman this trip. Make sure the wagons are going at a good pace. If we need you to shovel, I'll let you know." John called as he continued down the rows.

"Aye, Captain." Aengus smiled down at a little girl hugging her mother's leg. "And what'd be your name, my wee one?"

Her mother patted her daughter's head. "She's a bit shy. Her name is Rachel."

"Aye, Rachel, very pretty name. If ye get tired of walking, ye let me know and I'll bring ye up here with me, alright, lass?" The little girl smiled, and her mother agreed.

John and Jed continued their way down the line, nodding at each of the drivers and their families. *What a bunch of greenhorns*, John thought. He peered into each of their faces and knew some of them would never make it. Each member of the party had hope in their eyes and dreams in their hearts and it was up to John to keep each of them alive, so they could see their hopes and dreams come true.

As John passed the seventh wagon, a foul looking man spat tobacco in his direction, landing on his horse's front hoof. The man sneered at him.

"We're not going to have any trouble on this trip, are we Mr. Cobb?"

"No sir." Cobb's mouth curled deviously.

"Good." John kicked his horse and continued down the line.

He was all smiles with the rest of the families until he got to the last wagon. He spotted Elizabeth sitting alone, holding steadfast to the leather reins. She wore a light blue cotton dress and a cream-colored bonnet tied lightly under her chin. There was both delicacy and strength in her face. He and Jed trotted up next to her wagon.

"Good morning, Miss Elizabeth." Jed said, removing his hat and bowing in his saddle.

"Good morning." She smiled at him and gazed shyly at John.

"Where are your work gloves?" The tensing of John's jaw betrayed his frustrations.

"I…I don't have any," she stammered, shocked at his tone.

"Don't you? Your hands will wish you had. They'll be chewed to bits before we stop." John roughly pulled his off and handed them to her. "Here, take mine."

"Thank you." She slipped the large gloves over her small hands and smiled. They still held his warmth. "Won't you need them?"

He shook his head, the line of his mouth tightened a fraction more and he looked at Jed, who was still gawking at Elizabeth. John leaned over and grabbed Jed by the collar and pulled his face toward his.

"Keep your eyes on your work, or so help me, I'll box your ears." John growled.

"Sorry John. I will, I'll do my job." Jed swallowed hard, showing respect and fear in his eyes.

John pulled Jed even closer and whispered in his ear. "But keep at least one eye on her from time to time." He released his brother and sat in his saddle. Jed nodded and trotted to the back of Elizabeth's wagon.

"If you need anything, Miss Cornwall, signal Jed and he'll help you out." He tipped his hat and rode to the front of the line.

Jed walked his horse next to Elizabeth and smiled. "You got a canteen of water and some hardtack or jerky up there with you?"

"Yes, thank you. Lucas let me know I should have them." She smiled back, trying to show some bravado.

"Good. We won't be stopping for quite a while, and it gets hot out here. Don't worry, Miss Elizabeth, you'll do just fine." Jed nodded to her then kicked his horse and trotted back behind her wagon.

Her stomach was full of butterflies, and she wished she had Jed's confidence. She was starting to think she may have made a big mistake. But it was too late, she was here, and she had to see this through.

"Wagons, ho!" John shouted and waved his hand forward.

Slowly the wagons began to move. People lined the streets to wave their farewells. Elizabeth snapped the reins, and her four mules began to move down the crowded street. There was no turning back now, she was on her way.

Six miles and a few hours into their trek, they finally reached the crossing of the Missouri River. Elizabeth pulled the mules to a halt, set the brake on the wagon, and began to massage her arms. The pains in her back and arms were agonizing, she had never felt so sore in her entire life. She wasn't sure if she was going to make it to Oregon. With shaking hands, she picked up the canteen and took several swigs.

Jed rode up beside her. "You alright, Miss Elizabeth?"

"Yes, I'm fine." She took another drink from the canteen then put it next to her and took off her gloves. Her hands were tight and swollen. She began to rub them, trying to get the blood flowing again.

Jed watched her. "How are your hands holding up?"

"I'm awfully glad Mr. Evans gave me his gloves. I don't think I could have made it this far, without them." She gazed at the countryside and the river. "Will we be here long?"

"Not long. Once John gives us the okay, we'll go across." Jed heard his brother whistle and signal to him. "I'll be back in a few. You can hop down and walk if you need to." He tipped his hat and rode off toward John.

Elizabeth slowly stepped down from the wagon and stretched her back. As she walked around, she gazed out over the countryside and sighed. It was beautiful; however, she had never seen so many livestock, wagons, tents, and people. Everywhere she looked, hundreds covered the landscape. It was grassland as far as she could see except near the river, where the trees grew all the way to the water's edge. The sun beat down on her and she wiped the sweat from her forehead and face with her sleeve. She put her hands on her lower back and stretched again. She was beginning to realize how long and harrowing this trek was going to be. A wave of sadness swept over her, not for the comforts she was having to do without, but rather the people she was missing, her family and friends. Between the loss of her parents, her friend, Ellis, and her native land of England, her heart was full of guilt and sadness, knowing she would never see or touch them again. She gently wiped away the tears that dared to fall.

"Hello there." A young woman said, walking up to Elizabeth.

She jumped and turned around, placing a hand to her bosom, willing her pulse to slow. "Oh, you startled me. Hello." She knew, just by looking at her, that they were going to be good friends.

She was a lovely young woman with long blond hair pulled back in a pretty braid while her sparkling light blue eyes matched the color of the morning sky. Her face was a perfect oval, with a daintily pointed chin; the corners of her mouth turned upwards. She wore a pretty red and white gingham dress with a white apron.

"Sorry." She laughed. "My name is Abigail Pritchard." She extended her hand and Elizabeth took it.

"I'm Elizabeth Cornwall." The beginning of a smile tipped the corners of her mouth as she looked at Abigail's stomach.

Abigail rubbed her very pregnant belly and grinned. "Our first. I have a feeling this little one won't wait until we get to Oregon City. I hear we have a doctor in the party though, so that makes me feel better."

The two women started walking up the wagon train, toward the front. Elizabeth could see John talking to his men while a few children ran around playing.

"Come on, I'll introduce you to the ladies." Abigail waddled over to the other women standing in a group chatting. "Ladies, this here's Elizabeth," she said, putting an arm around her shoulders.

The women gathered around her, smiling. Elizabeth had found an abundant of friends. Though these ladies had families of their own, they had just welcomed her into their circle.

"I'm Rebecca Dickens and these here are my three children. Henry who's ten, David's seven and my baby girl, Rachel, she's three. We're from Tennessee." She stood tall and proud, but her eyes told a different story. She was worn to the bone and scared of the long journey ahead. She slumped when the two boys started chasing each other again while Rachel hid behind her mother's legs, peeking out with big, hazel eyes.

"Hello, it's nice to meet you," Elizabeth said.

"This is Bridget O'Brien. She and her husband are from Ireland," said Abigail and Bridget nodded. "And that there is Anna Sordorff. She and her husband, Oscar, are from Denmark."

"Ya, and we have four children. Frederik he's nineteen, Edna who's seventeen, Emma she's fifteen and Victor who's thirteen." Anna broke into an open, friendly smile. She was a stout, pudgy woman with grey hair wrapped in a braided bun and blue eyes.

"You're a very brave woman, Elizabeth, to be traveling all alone," Bridget said. She had beautiful green eyes and was dressed in an emerald-green plaid dress; her red hair was pulled back with a pretty, wooden comb.

"Ya, but she is not alone, she has us." Anna took Elizabeth's hands and looked at her. "If there is anything you need, just ask. We're all in this together, are we not?"

"Thank you." Elizabeth said with a smile.

"Yes, what made a young woman, like yourself, decide to travel all by herself?" Abigail asked gently rubbing her belly.

Elizabeth gazed at the women as a tear rolled down her rosy cheek. She fingered the necklace that hung around her neck, feeling suddenly cold. She knew her new friends would be there to wish her comfort. She was about to divulge her sad story, but a shadow of a man crept into their midst.

"Ladies." Billy Ray Cobb stepped up, leaned against the O'Brien wagon, and cut off a piece of tobacco, putting it in his mouth. He looked Elizabeth over seductively. "You all look lovely this morning, especially you, Elizabeth."

"Do not address me so informal, sir. It's Miss Cornwall." She gave him a hostile glare.

He saluted her with his knife and spat some tobacco, never taking his eyes off her. The women scoffed at him. The look in his eyes scared Elizabeth. The hair on the back of her nape rose as she hugged herself. *Of all the wagon trains leaving Missouri, why did he have to be in this one?* She started to shake while his eyes roamed over her, as though he were slowly undressing her.

"Elizabeth, would you like to see the cradle, my husband, Jesse, made for the baby?" Abigail asked.

"Yes, I would. Thank you." Elizabeth said, turning away from Billy Ray. Abigail put her arm around Elizabeth and the ladies all marched away.

"Stay clear of him, Elizabeth. Jesse told me that he killed a man out east somewhere and just yesterday, it's rumored he attacked a woman. He's no good," Abigail whispered.

Elizabeth nodded. She would heed Abigail's words and stay as far away from him as she could. She looked over her shoulder to see if he was following, but he was still leaning against the wagon. His smile grew across his face before she hastily rotated her head and quickened her pace to Abigail's wagon.

∞ ∞ ∞

Jed and Aengus loped up to John and Lucas. John gazed around the area full of wagons and people, then at the blue sky. "What'd Harry have to say, Lucas?" he asked.

"We're next on the ferry. We'll be able to get two wagons on at a time plus two of our horses." Lucas replied.

"Alright. You and Aengus head on over with the first two, Jed and I will go with Miss Cornwall and the Callahan brothers." John looked at the sky again, the clouds were turning dark. "Aengus, Jed, start bringing the wagons to the river," John said. Lucas nodded and rode back over to the ferry.

John trotted down the line. "Alright everyone, back to your wagons. We'll be loading them on the ferry real soon. Ladies," he pulled his horse to a halt, "best break up the hen party."

He watched Elizabeth say goodbye to the women and walk back toward her wagon. He kicked his horse and made his way down the line of wagons, letting wagoneers know they'd be leaving soon. John's nerves felt raw and his skin tingled, something told him Elizabeth needed his help, so he turned in the saddle to see Billy Ray step in front of her. John pulled his horse to a halt, so he could hear what Cobb was planning to do.

"May I walk you to your wagon, Miss Cornwall?" Billy Ray asked, touching her elbow with his finger. He was being charming and played on her emotions.

"No thank you," her voice deepened, and she pulled her arm away.

"Oh, come on, honey," he took her arm, "I don't bite."

"Let me go." She tried to pull away. Her heart pounded and her pulse quickened. She attempted to push his hand off her arm, but his grip only tightened. "No. You're hurting me," she shouted. She could smell Billy Ray's pungent odor when he stepped closer and licked his lips; his eyes narrowed, and a malicious smile creased his mouth.

John dismounted and walked back over to Elizabeth. He towered over Billy Ray. "Mr. Cobb, I believe the lady said no. Miss Cornwall, if you please?" He nodded to a place next to him and she quickly stepped to his side. "Go back to your wagon, Mr. Cobb."

Billy Ray glared at him, gave a quick, disgusted snort and stomped off. John thought he heard, "You'll regret this" as Billy Ray marched away.

"Thank you, Mr. Evans." She was trembling.

"You're welcome, Miss Cornwall." He placed his hand on the small of her back and they began to walk to her wagon. Before removing his hand, his thumb caressed her back for a moment, then he dropped it and at once, missed her warmth.

"Mr. Evans." They stopped next to her wagon. "We'll be traveling together for several months; don't you think we should address each other less formally?" Her tongue darted out to touch her lips.

"If you wish, ma'am." He touched his hat and he watched her moisten her lips and it took all his willpower not to pull her against him and kiss her. *She's too young.* He swallowed hard and rubbed the back of his neck.

She looked up at him with an inquisitive smile then began to climb up her wagon when she saw his hand extend toward her. She slowly placed her hand in his and he helped her to her seat. John frowned to himself, her hand felt so right in his, but he knew it could never be. *Why would she, so young and beautiful, want an old fart like me?* Besides, he wanted to remain a bachelor, didn't he?

"Thank you… John," she said, biting the corner of her lip. She put on her gloves and picked up the reins.

"You're welcome." He mounted his horse and looked at her. He began to wonder just what he wanted of her. "Follow me to the river, I need to help Jed get these wagons loaded."

Elizabeth snapped her reins and followed him to the other wagons. When they grew closer, John waved her to stop. He looked around and spotted Jed helping the O'Brien's and Hank Davis onto the ferry. Riding up to Elizabeth, he gazed at her and saw the fear reflected in her eyes. Her hands shook, and her teeth chattered, so he came closer to her.

"Don't worry Beth, I'll be there with you. Just do what Jed tells you and everything will be fine." He leaned over and gripped her gloved hands then rode to where Jed stood watching the ferry leave the dock. John looked back at Elizabeth and smiled to himself. *I called her Beth. Did she like being called that? Had I stepped over the line?* He smacked the heal of his palm against his forehead. "So stupid."

∞ ∞ ∞

As Elizabeth sat in her wagon, warmth radiated throughout her body. A beaming grin crossed her face as she hugged herself. "Beth. He called me Beth," she whispered to herself.

Though she was elated, she nervously watched the ferry cross the river and land on the other side. She swallowed hard, soon it would be her turn. *Will I be able to do this?* The two wagons disembarked the ferry, rode up a hill and disappeared through the trees. Soon the ferry started back to pick up the rest of the wagon train. It was relatively small compared to ferries she had seen back east. This one was operated by horsepower. A horse on either side would walk on a treadmill, powering the paddles making the ferry go forward and then back again.

Jed loped up to her and smiled. "Miss Elizabeth, you ready?" She shook her head. "You'll be alright. Follow the Callahan wagon until I tell you to stop. John and I will load them first, then you'll follow."

She nodded as she saw the ferry park at the dock. "Jed…"

"Just follow the wagon." He waved and loped back down the small hill to where John sat high on his horse. She glanced at him, and he nodded encouragingly.

Elizabeth slowly did what Jed had told her to do and followed the wagon in front of her. Once she reached the dock, Jed signaled for her to stop. She watched as the two brothers told Bill Callahan how to walk onto the ferry. Her hands tightened on the reins, and she began to tremble, and her teeth started to chatter. Tears welled in her eyes. Bill's wagon was parked --- she was next. *I can't do this.*

"Okay Miss Elizabeth, slowly have your mules go toward Harry, the ferryman, he'll help direct you. John and I will follow you in case you need us." Jed patted the side of her wagon. "Okay Harry, here she comes!"

Elizabeth cracked the reins and started forward, the mules' hooves clopped loudly on the wooden dock. Her brow wrinkled, and she took deep breaths to calm herself, her mouth went dry, and her throat constricted. Every sound she heard was deafening. She tightened her hands on the reins and the mules sensed her panicking. Their eyes grew big, and they started to toss their heads and flare their noses. The front mules began shaking and side stepping toward the edge of the dock. Their tails swished violently, and Elizabeth tried to control them, but they were pulling at the reins and jerking their heads. One of the back mules tried to kick its back legs, its hoof thudding against the front of the wagon.

Elizabeth couldn't relax, her limbs too paralyzed with fear to function. She felt faint as the mules fought against the tightening of the reins.

"Help! Somebody, help!" Elizabeth couldn't contain the horror in her voice as the edge of the dock came closer. At any moment, the wagon would tip over and she would be crushed under its weight.

John and Jed jumped off their horses and ran down the dock. Jed grabbed one of the mule's harnesses and tried to calm it, but it pulled away and started backing up.

"Damn you, mule! Come on!" Jed snatched the harness, pulling with all his might.

John climbed the wagon and pushed Elizabeth aside, nearly knocking her out. He grabbed the reins and started pulling on them. "Whoa, whoa!"

The front mule reared, knocking Jed to the dock with a loud thud. He rolled away before the mule's hooves stomped on him, smashing down on the wood.

"Jed." Elizabeth screamed, clutching her throat.

He quickly stood up and grasped the harnesses again. Elizabeth saw blood cascade down the side of his face and drip onto his shirt front. She covered her face and whimpered, cringing at every startling sound. She felt the back wheel of the wagon roll off the dock, so she grabbed the side of the wagon, willing it not to fall. *We're going to die*, she thought as the wagon began to tip. She heard the supplies rattle and shift. John's arm muscles bulged, as his hands gripped tighter on the reins.

"Harry, help Jed get these sons-of-bitches under control." John stood up and pulled the reins harder. Harry grabbed the other mule, straining to make it stop. Between the three men, the mules started calming down. Jed and Harry pulled the harnesses while John got the wagon down the dock and onto the ferry. "Jed, grab our horses before they run off."

Jed saluted John and ran back to get their horses, who were grazing near the dock. Elizabeth thought she was going to faint, she had never been so terrified, even the fire wasn't as frightening as what had just happened. Her face had turned ash white, and she felt dizzy as though she had the vapors, and her body shook uncontrollably. She tried to control her breathing while John pulled the wagon to a stop.

After setting the brake, John gazed at her. "Well, that was exciting." He laughed, resting his elbows on his knees. His grin spread across his face.

Still holding the side of the wagon, she glared up at him. She wanted to smack the smile right off his face. Her anguish peaked to shatter the last shreds of her control. "Exciting? Bloody hell, we almost died," she said in a harsh voice.

"Ah, but we didn't. Come on, let's stretched our legs." He jumped down, took her around the waist and sat her gently on her feet. For a moment, his eyes caught and held hers. She stared deep into his eyes which sent little tingled explosions firing throughout her body. She blushed and shyly glanced away.

Jed pulled the horses onto the ferry while Harry slipped the roped gate in place then unhooked the rope from the dock. Elizabeth stepped up to Jed and looked at his head then went to the back of her wagon and started searching for a small towel.

"Oh my God. Are you guys alright?" Bill and his brother, Joe, ran up to John and Jed.

"Yeah, we're fine. Just part of the job," John said with a smile. He watched Elizabeth as she walked over to his brother.

"Sit." She pointed to some barrels. Jed sat down while Elizabeth placed the towel against his head.

"Ouch." Jed gritted his teeth.

"Stop being such a baby." She dabbed at the cut on his scalp. "When we get to the other side, you should have the doctor look at it. You might need some stitches."

"Yes, ma'am." He gazed up into her beautiful eyes and sighed.

The ferry started making its way across the river. Elizabeth looked out over the scenery and took a deep breath. The sun shimmered over the smooth water while a gentle breeze blew the wisps of her raven hair away from her face. She glanced over at John and saw a gleam of interest in his eyes. Taking a deep, unsteady breath, she turned away.

Chapter Four

Later in the day and a little rain, John was able to get the wagons up the hill, out of the trees and on the Kansas side of the river. He then had them stop for lunch. Dismounting his horse, he tied her to Buck's wagon and walked around camp, helping when needed. He saw Jed go over to Elizabeth's wagon, so he followed him. He leaned against the other side with his arms crossed and listened to what he had to say. What could a little eavesdropping hurt?

"Miss Elizabeth, you okay?" He helped her down off the wagon.

"Thank you. I'm fine," she said brushing her skirt, puffs of dust blew in the breeze.

"Do you need anything?" he asked shyly, slipping his hands in his back pockets while the toe of his boot scuffed at the ground. *God, she was beautiful. What I wouldn't give to make this little gal mine.* His rapid heartbeat thumped wildly against his chest, waiting for her to say yes.

"No thank you, Jed." There was disappointment written across his face. "But if I do,

I'll let you know, I promise." She smiled and patted his arm.

He grinned and rubbed his hands up and down his thighs. "Okay, well I better see to the mules." He stepped backwards, almost tripped, and smiled. "See you later, Miss Elizabeth." He bit his lip and walked quickly away.

John stood there shaking his head. *What a goofball*. He stepped around the wagon just as Elizabeth came to the back, and almost collided into her again.

"Oh John, you startled me." She put a hand to her chest.

"I think my kid brother likes you." One corner of his mouth pulled into a slight smile, yet his chest was burning with jealousy. If only he were younger. His fingers tingled, longing to touch her soft, porcelain skin.

"A little too much I'm afraid." She frowned, an unwelcomed blush crept into her cheeks.

John leaned against the back of the wagon, crossed his legs, and looked at his boots. "Jed's a good man. He'd make a woman very happy." He lifted his eyes to watch her reaction.

"I'm sure he would." She reached in the wagon for a bit of wood she had brought with her. She started piling it into her arms.

He smirked and scratched at his chin. "Oh, here, let me." He grabbed the wood and their fingers brushed, sending little sparks shooting straight through his heart. They stood there in awkward silence, before he finally broke away and placed the wood in the shade by the wagon and started a fire. He gazed at her over by the wagon, her skirt softly blowing in the wind. What was it about this woman that pulled at his heartstrings? Yes, she was beautiful, but there was something else --- and he couldn't wait to find out what it was.

She walked over to him and placed a tea kettle on the embers then opened her collapsible stool and took a seat next to him. She sat two cups with sugar, a few biscuits, and some dried fruit on a small blanket.

"You know, you could've had Jed do this for you," he said, adding more wood.

"Yes, but I didn't want Jed's help." Her eyes had a burning, faraway look in them.

He watched her eyes shimmer in the sunlight and for a moment, he thought he noticed her lean toward him. He cleared his throat and looked at the bounty sat before him.

"What's all this?" He pointed at the food, his stomach growling.

"Tea and biscuits. I thought you might fancy a cup." She took one of the tin cups and poured tea into it.

"Tea?" He wrinkled his nose. "Never touch the stuff." He reached over and took a biscuit, taking a large bite. "Mmmm, this is really good."

"Well, what do you drink?" She finished pouring and placed the tea kettle back on the fire.

"Coffee mostly and at times, whiskey. Haven't you heard, all us cowboys drink whiskey. Keeps us warm on lonely nights." He snickered. "So, do all you Brits drink tea?"

"Not all. I, myself, love it. My parents owned a tea shop in Seaford. That's why I'm here, I'm going to open my own tea shop when I get to Oregon City." She took a sip then sat the cup on her knee.

He stood up and put his hands in his pockets. "Well, I better go. Thanks for the biscuit."

"John." She put the cup aside and rose. Stepping over to him, she placed a hand on his arm. "I never thanked you for saving my life this morning." Her thumb caressed his forearm.

He glanced at her hand on his arm, then into her eyes. "You're welcome," his voice turned husky. He wanted to kiss her, to feel those soft pink lips against his. He reached down to touch her face but recoiled. "I was just doing my job." He tipped his hat and walked away.

He stomped over to Buck's wagon and kicked the dirt, then poured himself a cup of coffee, almost burning his hand. Buck was busy making lunch when John walked up.

"John. Good to see you, boy," Buck drawled, cutting up some salted pork.

John groaned and took a seat by the campfire. He sipped his coffee with a pensive expression. His head hurt as he sat there, looking at the fire. How could he have feelings for a woman he only met yesterday? No, this had to stop. He had a job to do and besides, she was just a kid. He had no right mixing himself up with a yearling. He closed his eyes and groaned, wishing he had never seen those wonderful eyes.

"What's eating you, boy?" asked Buck, wiping the knife on his apron.

"Nothing," he snapped, taking another swig of coffee.

Jed happily sauntered to the campfire and poured himself a cup of coffee. "Hey John. Wow, this morning was crazy, wasn't it? But I think Elizabeth handled it really well."

John nodded, making a hmmm noise in his throat and gazed at Jed from the corner of his eye. Jed had a stupid grin on his face.

"Elizabeth, she's something ain't she? Pretty little thing," Jed said with a light voice.

John glared at Jed, his teeth clenching. He tried to disguise his annoyance in front of the others.

Jed sipped his coffee and grinned. "You know, I think maybe I'll invite Elizabeth to dinner when we stop tonight."

Buck grabbed a pan and placed the pork over the fire watching John while Jed talked. John's hands tightened on the cup, his cheeks flushing, and his mouth was set in annoyance.

"Buck, do you think you could fix your beef stew tonight? Elizabeth just might like that." Jed nodded and smiled at John.

John swallowed hard, trying not to reveal his anger, but it was too late. He stood up and started pacing. "Why don't you go jump in the river and cool off?" he replied in anger. He tossed the coffee out of his cup, gave it to Buck and stormed away.

"What'd I say?" Jed asked, puzzled by his brother's outburst.

"You're messing with fire, boy. If I were you, I'd back off." Buck pointed at Jed with his knife.

Jed watched John mount his horse and ride out of camp.

∞ ∞ ∞

Elizabeth packed up her lunch and placed it in the wagon. She was very confused about John's behavior. Just when she thought they were getting closer, he'd pull away. She could feel the attraction between them, and she wanted to see where it would lead. Her mind told her to ignore John, but her heart had other plans. *Maybe I can have both, John, and the tea shop.* It didn't make any sense. How could she have feelings for a man she had just met? She knew nothing about him, only that he ran a wagon train and was obviously much older than she. Elizabeth stood with her arms crossed, willing her heart to calm down.

Abigail waddled up to her. "Why Elizabeth, I thought you'd come over and have lunch with us."

"I'm sorry. Maybe tomorrow." She smiled weakly.

"Tonight, you'll join Jesse and me for dinner. Okay? We're having rabbit stew with biscuits." Abigail rubbed Elizabeth's arms.

She nodded and looked at the ground, a fluttering in her stomach. She clasped her hands and held them close to her body.

"Honey, what's the matter?" Abigail prodded, placing a finger under her chin, and lifting until Elizabeth's eyes focused on her face.

Elizabeth shook her head. "Nothing. Don't worry about it. I'm fine." She felt as hollow as her voice sounded.

Aengus walked up to the two women. "Ladies, we need to be going. Miss Elizabeth, Abigail." He nodded at them and strolled away to inform the others.

"Well, we'll talk tonight. Alright?" Abigail rubbed her cheek.

Elizabeth nodded and hugged her then watched the woman waddle away. As she started to climb the wagon wheel, Elizabeth looked back at the other wagons, but didn't spot John anywhere. *Where was he*? she asked herself as she picked up the reins.

"Wagons, ho!" shouted Lucas.

Chapter Five

After a couple of hours Jed rode alongside Elizabeth. She still was questioning John's motives when Jed started talking. She didn't want to have a conversation with him, she just wanted to be left alone. She needed to figure out what to do about John. Should she continue to pursue her feelings for him or leave well enough alone?

"Hey there, Miss Elizabeth. How you doing?" Jed greeted, trotting next to her.

"I'm sore but doing alright. Where's John? I didn't see him after lunch," she questioned, worry in her voice.

"Oh, he took Lucas' spot. He's a few miles ahead scouting out the territory." He pointed ahead of the wagon train and grinned at her. She knew he liked her and somehow, she needed to let him know she liked him, just not in a romantic way.

"But why?" She listened to the jingling of the harnesses while the mules made their slow pace across the prairie. She looked at her gloved hands and rubbed her thumbs over her fingers wishing they were John's.

"Don't know." Jed shrugged. "There we were talking and suddenly he gets up and takes off."

"That's not like him, is it?" She regarded him with curiosity.

"No, not really. I mean he's got a temper, but today he's acting real strange." He shook his head. "Um, Miss Elizabeth, would you care to join me for dinner?" He asked, dipping his chin, and shyly glanced at her.

"I'm sorry, but Abigail invited me." She saw the disappointment in his eyes.

"Well, that's okay. Maybe next time. We'll be stopping soon." He tipped his hat and rode off to talk to Aengus.

She blew out a sigh of relief and looked to the heavens wondering what was happening and why John was obviously avoiding her. She rubbed the base of her neck and tilted her head to one side, the muscles sore from sitting so long in a bouncing wagon. Elizabeth didn't know which was worse – the hot, humid day or the constant jolting and swaying as it moved over the bumpy plains. Seconds later her opinion was confirmed when the wagon hit a particularly large rut. She shifted her weight, searching for a comfortable spot. There wasn't one.

Except for a few stops so Aengus, Lucas and a few of the men could dig out stream beds and make small dirt bridges out of them, they continued a slow and steady pace until about five o'clock when Lucas and Jed told the party to circle the wagons and make a corral for the livestock. After the mules and horses were fenced in, fed and watered, it was time for the women to start dinner.

Jed told Elizabeth not to worry about her team, that he would unhitch them, so she made her way to Abigail's wagon with her tea kettle and a tin of tea. She looked around but couldn't find John anywhere. With sadness in her eyes, she walked into Abigail and Jesse's camp.

"Elizabeth." Abigail hugged her, took her tea kettle, filled it with water and placed it on the fire. "Come sit."

Elizabeth sat on a wooden chair, obviously hand carved by Jesse. "Is there anything I can do to help?"

"Oh no, stew's all made, just needs to finish cooking." She came over to sit next to Elizabeth. "Now, tell me, what has you so upset?"

"Really, it's nothing." She smiled. How was she going to tell her she had feelings for the trail boss? That the harder she tried to ignore the truth the more it persisted.

"I see you with that young man, Jed. I heard how he rescued you this morning, even got hurt. He really fancies you." Abigail sat wiggling with excitement.

"So, I've been told." Elizabeth whispered under her breath. She stared at the fire while jiggling her knee. She felt so tired and questions about Jed, only made things worse. In fact, she really wasn't hungry, she just wanted to crawl in the wagon and fall asleep. There, in her dreams, she could see John.

"What was that?" Abigail asked stirring the stew.

Elizabeth shook her head and looked around trying to spot John, while tapping her fingers together. *Am I rushing things*? She had only met him yesterday, but there was something about him that made her believe she had known him longer. Her heart felt whole when he was near.

"So?" Abigail asked. "Do you feel the same way? I mean, he is very handsome and the way he saved you." She fanned herself with her hand, dramatically acting a swoon.

Elizabeth did have feelings, but not for him. She wanted John. Jesse came into the firelight, sat down, and smiled at his wife and lit his pipe.

"Um, how's the pregnancy going?" Elizabeth asked, wanting to change the subject.

"Very well. He moves quite a bit." She took Elizabeth's hand and placed it on her stomach.

A feeling of euphoria spread over Elizabeth's body as she felt the baby move across Abigail's belly. What would it be like to be more like Abigail? To have her own little boy or girl to cradle and sooth, a child with wavy brown hair, a child who looked like his father?

Exactly like John.

A child? She and John Evans? The idea was unthinkable. Insane.

Yet she had thought it, had she not?

"John!" Jesse stood up from his chair and shook his hand. "Join us, we were just about to eat."

Elizabeth snatched her hand away and placed it in her lap. When she saw him, her only emotion was giddiness; her stomach fluttered and the heavy lashes that shadowed her cheeks flew up. She stared wordlessly across at him, her heart pounding and her whole body tingled as her eyes glistened with tears.

"I'd love to, but I just came over to talk to Elizabeth. Could we talk?" He took off his hat and stepped away.

"Yes, of course. Excuse me." She stood up from her chair and followed him into the darkness. They walked back over to her wagon where they could talk privately.

He stood with his back to her. "I took Lucas' place today."

"Yes, I know, Jed told me. But why?" she questioned. She heard him sigh deeply as though he would never take another breath and then he bowed his head.

"I needed to think, to get away." He hit his thigh with his hat and started pacing, she could tell he was uncomfortable.

"From me?" A wave of apprehension swept through her. *Maybe he doesn't feel the same way about me.*

"Yes, I mean no." He looked at her. His expressive face changed and became almost somber like a man walking to the gallows. He sat his hat on the wagon seat. "Elizabeth, I... I'm thirty years old, too old for you." He plunged his hands deep in his jacket pockets and gazed at the stars. "I think it's best you take up with Jed."

At first, she couldn't believe what she was hearing. Did he seriously think she could be happy with his brother, when her heart belonged to him? The feelings she had for him was the most powerful thing she had ever felt. She never dreamed she would ever get involved with any man; even in England every suitor who came to the door, she would turn away. She was happy helping her parents in the tea shop and had no desire to marry. Now at twenty, many people would call her an old maid, and at the time she was fine with the name. But at this very moment, she no longer wanted to be a spinster. Her pulse raced, and she longed to touch him... to be in his space, to be loved by him.

Elizabeth stepped up to him and placed her hand on his chest. "I don't want Jed. And I don't care how old you are, you foolish man."

Maybe he shouldn't touch her. It would be for the best. No matter what he might feel for her, or think he might feel for her, nothing could come of their time together. Better to behave as if they were no more than ordinary traveling companions who had no emotions for each other at all. But that would be a lie.

The moon shone in her tear-filled eyes. With one hand, he untied her bonnet, pulling it off and tossing it onto his hat then he gently tugged at the pins holding her bun in place; her raven hair spilled over her shoulders and down her back. He slowly ran his fingers through it. She felt her flesh color and burn.

"So beautiful," he whispered, fingering the strands, and watching them fall to her shoulders.

She closed her eyes and turned her face, softly brushing her cheek across his calloused hand. "John, please." She looked up at him with wanting. His closeness was so male, so bracing, it sent shivers of delight through her.

He licked his lips, bent over and gently brushed his lips against hers, cupping her head. "Beth." He breathed, pulling her closer to him.

"Elizabeth, where are you? Your stew's getting cold." Abigail called near the wagon.

He stood up, shuffled back a step, grabbed his hat, and marched into the darkness.

"Elizabeth? Oh, there you are." Abigail walked up to her. "Come on, dinner's ready." She wrapped her arm around her shoulders, and they walked away.

Pensively, Elizabeth looked back in the darkness and saw John standing in the shadows.

Chapter Six

After weeks of traveling, John and the wagon train finally entered the Nebraska Territory. He couldn't wait to get to Fort Kearny and maybe have some time alone with Elizabeth. Since their almost kiss, he hadn't been able to see her or even talk to her without the women smothering her, but by smothering her they also kept Billy Ray far away from her. He saw how Cobb eyed her as she went about doing her daily chores and it put him on edge. So lately, he'd been sleeping closer to Elizabeth's wagon.

He brought his horse to a halt and signaled the train to stop. Lucas came running up to John, dirt scattered when his pinto seemed to stop on a dime.

"The fort is just over that ridge. There's Indians there, you may want to tell the emigrants it's safe, before one gets it in their head to start a war," Lucas said, wiping the sweat from his brow.

"Notify Jed and Aengus. Have them help you spread the word." John looked over his shoulder at the wagons. Lucas nodded, kicked his pinto, and cantered toward Aengus.

Since these last few weeks, John became very aware of every person on his train. There was Hank Davis, the oldest member on the train, Robert Mulligan who wanted to be a logger in Oregon after working in Maine, and Dr. Arthur Grant looking to open an office in Oregon City. They all wanted something, he just prayed to God they all made it safely.

"Wagons, ho," he shouted and began to move forward.

∞ ∞ ∞

Elizabeth wondered what was happening. Everyone looked alarmed as Jed, Lucas and Aengus rode around the wagons talking to the families. They had been a great help over these past weeks, with the river crossings, building sand bridges over stream beds and pushing wagons through the mud after huge thunderstorms. But now they seemed panicked. *Oh God, were we under attack?* She chewed on her gloved knuckle, her mouth growing dry.

Jed rode up to her, breathless. "Miss Elizabeth, there are peaceful Indians at the fort, so don't be alarmed when you see 'em." He trotted beside her, his face red and sweaty.

All the tension went out of her body and her hand pressed to her heart. "Thank goodness."

"You okay, Miss Elizabeth?" He reached out to steady her.

"Yes, yes." She closed her eyes and nodded compulsively. "The way you three were acting, I thought something horrible was happening." She gave him a wide grin.

"Naw, we just needed to spread the word, is all." He saluted to her and took off to tell another wagon.

Elizabeth couldn't wait to get to the fort, her rump was as sore as if she had been beat with a leather strap. She also needed to stock up on a few things and have someone look at her wagon, the back axle was making her uncomfortable. It would be nice to take a few days to rest up and take some time to get the chores done, especially the laundry.

"Lass, did ye hear the news?" Aengus rode up beside her.

"Yes, thank you." She smiled and nodded.

He bobbed his head and rode on ahead. She was starting to be less a stranger when around John's men. She loved listening to the stories they would tell about all the adventures they'd had crossing the country. She smiled at all the little facial expressions John would give her when their tales were a bit farfetched.

She looked around as they approached the fort. Jed was right, there were several Indians wandering in and out of the fort's entrance. The men looked fierce with their buckskin outfits, head dresses, jewelry, and half shaved heads, while the women were more delicate with their lovely dresses, and braided hair. Though Jed said they were peaceful, Elizabeth felt intimidated as she drove past them. She was told back east that the Indians were thieves and murderers, scalping many settlers and were nothing more than savages. But while she passed by, she couldn't believe those stories told to her. Yes, they were different, but every culture seemed to be. Was she not different to these Yanks?

When she had to stop for a moment, an Indian with a head dress gazed up at her and smiled then stepped up to her wagon and handed her a beaded necklace. "Thank you," she said and placed it around her neck, but when she glanced at him again, he had already left.

The fort was too small, it wouldn't fit the wagons inside, so John had them park in a circle near Little Piney Creek. Elizabeth slowly climbed down from her wagon and watched Jed take the team to be fed and watered. She gazed around at the fort, stretching, and cracking her back. It wasn't much to look at and found herself disappointed at its structure. The forts in England were much larger and heavily fortified. The walls of Fort Kearny were made up of long wooden posts about ten feet high surrounding the exterior, a guard tower at every other corner, stables on one side, the buildings where the army stayed on the other and one large flagpole that waved the American flag. She walked around to stretch her legs and get her bearings. Except for a few trees, there was nothing but prairie as far as the eye could see.

"Isn't this exciting, Elizabeth? We've made it to Fort Kearny," Abigail said. The other women all gathered around her.

"John Evans sure is a wonderful guide," said Rebecca, wrapping a shawl around her shoulders.

"Yes, he is." Elizabeth agreed, looking around for him. Her heart beat faster when he approached. Her face flushed as his eyes locked onto hers. The wind was blowing, and she caught a whiff of his manly scent of horse, sweat, trail dust and a touch of soap.

"Ladies, I've just been informed that there will be a dance tonight, so put on your dancing shoes." He took off his hat and held it in front of him, rolling the brim. "Elizabeth, would you do me the honor of allowing me to escort you to the dance?"

"Yes, you may." She smiled with excitement. *Finally, a chance to spend some time with John.* She felt a lightness in her chest and swallowed a shout of glee. John had asked her to a dance, a chance to feel his arms around her --- all night.

"Good, I'll come for you around seven. Ladies." He placed his hat back on and walked away.

"Why Elizabeth, I believe he fancies you," said Abigail, rocking back and forth on her heels and grinned.

Elizabeth shook her head, "He's just being kind. He knows I don't have a partner, that's all." She didn't want it spread around the camp that she and John had feelings for each other.

She loved her new friends, but since that night, they never gave her a moments peace. She was never alone except when she went to the necessary or the wagon to sleep. And sometimes, one of them would even sit next to her while she drove, so they could talk. She hoped the party would distract them long enough, that she and John could slip away. She was still waiting for her first kiss, and if the brushing of their lips was any indication, it was going to be wonderful.

Chapter Seven

She was out of breath while John twirled her in the center of the wagons where the party was taking place. Around her, people drank, clapped, shouted, and danced. It was a lightheartedness that the train hadn't had in quiet awhile. When the music stopped, Elizabeth fanned herself with her hand. Her face was beaming, and she broke into a wide, open smile. She hadn't been this happy in a long time. For hours, she was in his arms, and she wished the night would never end. It was perfect, nothing could take away this feeling of elation.

"Want to sit the next one out?" John asked.

"Yes, please." Tonight, there were no shadows across her heart.

He took her hand and walked her over to her wagon. She took a seat on her collapsible stool and continued to fan herself.

"I'm parched. Want some punch?" He touched the back of her head.

"I'd love some, thank you." She looked up at him and her heart sang with delight. Though he hadn't really kissed her yet, she was starting to fall for this tall, handsome cowboy. When he finally did kiss her, she knew it would be like nothing she had ever experienced before.

"I won't be a moment." He kissed the top of her head and walked away.

She sat there watching everyone having a good time while cooling down. She tapped her foot to the rhythm of the music and gazed over at the musicians. Aengus played his bagpipes, while Jesse played the guitar, Bill on the harmonica and Joe fiddled. It was a wonderful party, even several of the soldiers had attended. A small bonfire blazed in the middle of the circle, casting shadows of the dancers across the bonnets of the wagons. She sat there swaying to the music when she suddenly felt two hands on her shoulders.

"John, I thought you were getting us drinks." She placed her hand on his, brushed her cheek against his hand and turned her head; smiling, she looked up. Elizabeth jumped out of her seat and stared into the eyes of Billy Ray Cobb. Her legs turned weak and for a moment she thought she was going to faint. She covered her mouth to stifle a scream. *Dear Lord, I touched him.* At that moment she thought she might retch.

"Hello there, missy." He stepped toward her as she backed away. "Could I have this dance?" He asked with a sneer.

She shook her head. "No... no thank you." Fear gripped her insides and she wanted to run.

"Oh, come on now, just one dance." He seized her by the waist, took her hand and pulled her close to him.

His smell made Elizabeth gag. He reeked of sweat, liquor and chewing tobacco. She pushed at his shoulder, trying to get away, but he held steadfast. Panic rioted within her. *John, where are you*? She knew if this continued, she would be in big trouble; with everyone enjoying the party, they wouldn't notice she was gone.

"Please, let me go!"

"Not a chance. Evans had you all night, now I want a piece. You sure are pretty and you smell good, too." He leaned in and sniffed her hair. "You know gal, you and me, we could have a right good time." He pulled her closer, crushing her bosom against his chest. He placed his chapped lips against her slender neck while sliding a hand down her back and cupped her buttock.

"Let me go," she gasped, panting in terror, and pushed at his shoulder. He was holding her hand so tightly, she lost all feeling in it.

Suddenly John was next to them, and the music stopped. Everything went quiet. Not a sound came forth except for the crickets in the darkness and a coyote howling in the distance. All eyes were fixed on John and Billy Ray. The look in John's eyes reflected that of a wild animal, flaring his nose and balling his hands into fists.

"The lady told you to let her go," John said through clenched teeth.

Billy Ray held her tight. "Music, I want music!"

John lifted Billy Ray by the scruff of the neck and pulled him away from Elizabeth. She fell to the ground in a heap at the men's feet. "The lady said no." He shoved Cobb away.

Billy Ray stumbled back and glared at him. "She hasn't been spoken for. She's free range. Why not let us all have a taste?" He swung his arms around, inviting all the men to sample Elizabeth. "Or maybe you already have. Was she good?"

John swung his fist back and hit him hard in the face, sending Billy Ray sprawling to the ground with a loud thud. Cobb started to stand up, blood dripping from the corner of his mouth. As he stood and pulled out a large knife.

John drew his gun and aimed it at Billy Ray. "If I see you anywhere near her again, Cobb, I'll shoot you down like a dog. You got that?" His face was full of rage.

Billy Ray looked at John and the gun, then standing, he straightened his shoulders and strolled over to him. John cocked his gun as Billy Ray came closer. When they were eye to eye, Cobb spat at John's boot then turned on his heel and strode from the party.

John released the hammer and holstered his gun. Elizabeth stood there shaking, the fearful images building in her mind. He pulled her against him in a warm hug and walked her back to her wagon. He sat her down and squatted in front of her, taking her hands. The women ran up to her, their faces clouded with uneasiness.

"You, okay?" he asked, rubbing her cold hands and placed his forehead against hers.

She looked at John, tears glistened on her pale, heart-shaped face. *Just an hour ago, I was so happy.* Abigail placed a blanket around her shoulder.

"No," she whispered.

"You ladies take care of her." He stood and looked at everyone standing around waiting for the party to start after the interruption. "I'm sorry, but I believe the dance is over. Get some sleep, we'll leave first thing in the morning."

Elizabeth looked up at him, deep sobs racked her insides. They were so happy tonight and she knew that he would have kissed her if it weren't for Billy Ray. John touched the top of her head, smiled weakly and walked away.

Later that night, she lay in her wagon staring up at the bonnet that covered it. A tear ran down the corner of her eye and onto her pillow. She longed to feel John near her, to touch her; she needed him. Every time they would get close, something would drive them apart. She heard a quiet knock on the back of her wagon.

"It's me." John whispered.

She scrambled to the back of the wagon and peeked out. He was there, in all his grandeur. His firm mouth curled as if always on the edge of laughter.

"What are you doing here?" she asked, bringing the blanket up to her neck.

"I wanted to see if you were alright." He bit his bottom lip. His eyes sparkled in the moonlight.

"I'm fine, now that you're here." She smiled, touching his cheek.

He kissed the palm of her hand and smiled. "I need to go. Don't want to ruin your reputation now do we?" He smirked. "Good night, Beth."

"Night," she said and watched him leave.

Billy Ray stood in the darkness watching them, his knife glinting in the moonlight.

She ran through the bushes scraping her skin while tree branches tangled in her ebony hair and snatched her plum-colored dress like hundreds of boney fingers. Her breath burned like hot flames in her lungs, her throat constricted, and her feet ached as she ran.

The forest echoed with footfalls of him giving chase, and she knew just how the fox felt as the poor animal darted for freedom from the dogs and hunters.

She stopped and leaned against a tree. She was so tired, her legs were giving out, but she had to run; she had to get away.

Suddenly Billy Ray's hot breath whispered in her ear, his arms wrapped around her waist, and she screamed.

Elizabeth sat bolt upright in her bedroll, a silent scream lodged in her throat. Shaking, disoriented, she gazed around in the dark, not sure where she was.

The wagon, she realized suddenly. *I'm in my wagon*.

She peered through the low light toward the back of the wagon, relieved to find the flap still closed.

A nightmare, she assured herself. *It was nothing more than a nightmare*.

Her gaze went again to the flap, her pulse racing fast, her mouth dry. Before she gave herself a chance to lose what sliver of nerve she had left, she cast aside the tangled blankets and crawled over to the flap to make sure it was secure.

She rushed back to her bedroll and climbed in, pulling the blankets over her ears. Gazing at the bonnet above her, she knew she wouldn't be getting anymore sleep tonight. *Oh, if John were only here.*

Chapter Eight

After getting her wagon repaired and picked up some more supplies, Elizabeth and the rest of the wagon train headed Northwest along the Platte River toward Chimney Rock. John put her forth in line, just after Hank Davis. John wanted her close, so he could keep an eye on her and talk to her when the urge came over him. Elizabeth found Hank to be a sweet old man who just wanted to see the ocean and spend his last remaining years watching the waves crash onto the beach.

They were a few days into their trip when they could see the top of Chimney Rock in the distance.

"Won't be long now. Maybe another day or so. Just wait till you see it, Beth. It's amazing." John rode beside her.

"John, how long have you been doing this?" She cocked her head to one side.

"About ten years. Why?" he questioned, squinting in the hot sun.

"Have you ever thought of giving it up?" she asked, wanting to put all the pieces together.

"Maybe. Oh, I don't know. Now that I'm thirty, I guess I've sown my wild oats and it's time to settle down. I'd have to find the right woman, though." He winked at her and grinned.

Elizabeth bit her lower lip and smiled. They looked in the distance and spied Lucas standing on a ridge signaling to John. She could barely make out what he was saying.

"I gotta go. See you later." He kicked his horse and rode away.

∞ ∞ ∞

John rode up to Lucas. "What's up?"

"Buffalo. A big herd. We'll catch up to them tomorrow." Lucas said excitedly.

"Good." John said, "We need fuel and…."

They heard screaming. John quickly turned in the saddle and saw a wagon and four large animals racing like a bolt of lightning across the prairie. Lucas and John headed down the ridge, their horses running across the land, leaping over stream beds, and kicking up dirt. They passed the wagon train; Jed and Aengus rode up beside them. John, using his reins, whipped his horse and urged it to go faster. All four of them ran like the wind after the wagon. It bounced and jolted as it raced over the grassland.

God don't let it be Elizabeth! he thought, chasing after the wagon. Terror mounted in his heart while his horse raced across the prairie. Never had he been more frightened than at this very moment. He searched his heart and soul and realized he would do anything for her, even give up his life for her. He loved her ---- unconditionally.

When they started to get close to the wagon, the front wheels hit a small stream bed and went air born. It flipped high in the air and rolled end over end, coming to a crashing halt on two wheels. It teetered there for a moment before falling over and pinning the driver under the wagon.

John pulled his horse to a stop and jumped off as the others followed suit. He scrambled toward the wagon, trying to find the driver. One of the wheels still spinning as John scurried around to see Hank Davis lying in the dirt, his body pinned under the wagon. The three others ran up to John.

"Is he dead?" Jed asked, seeing all the blood.

"No, not yet." John looked at them. "Aengus let's get this off him. Jed, go back to the train and tell them to make camp, then tell the doc to make sure his wagon is ready for Hank."

"I will." Jed ran to his horse and took off toward the wagon train.

Aengus and Lucas went to the front of the wagon and started lifting. John could hear them grunting as the wagon was pushed upward. John grabbed under Hank's arms and pulled him from beneath the wagon and laid him down. The two dropped the wagon with a crash.

"John, three of his horse are dead and one's pretty banged up," said Lucas, standing with his hands on his hips. They could hear the horse's pathetic whinny.

"You know what needs to be done." He became more uncomfortable by the minute as his dismay grew.

Lucas went over to his pinto and grabbed his rifle then sadly went to Hank's horse.

"Hank? Hank, you're in good hands. Don't worry," John said as he heard Lucas' gun go off with a loud bang, echoing though out the valley.

Thirty minutes later, a wagon pulled up next to John and he looked up to see Dr. Grant and Jed jump off the wagon and run over to him.

Dr. Arthur Grant was a short man with thinning grey hair, a bushy mustache and wore silver rimmed glasses. Though his face was wrinkled with age, it still reflected that of a young man.

"How in Sam's Hill did this happen?" said Dr. Grant kneeling next to Hank. He looked down at the old man, taking his pulse near his neck. Hank groaned when the doctor examined his wounds. He had a compound fracture in his right thigh, his pelvis was crushed, and his face was badly cut and bruised. Both of his arms were broken, his head was cracked, and a five-inch splinter of wood pierced his side; he laid in a pool of blood. It didn't look good.

"Don't know. Lucas and I looked over and there he went, like a bat outta hell." John gazed down at Hank, sadness reflecting in his eyes. He felt completely mortified that this would happen under his watch. Once they returned to camp, he would need to find out exactly what had happened to him. Though he felt bad for the old man, he couldn't help but feel grateful that it wasn't Elizabeth lying there.

"Well, let's get him in the wagon," said Dr. Grant. He stood up and shook his head. "He's beat up pretty bad, John."

The two of them gently picked up Hank and put him in the back of the wagon. Doc climbed in and pulled the old man onto the bedroll and placed a pillow under his head.

"Where's your supplies?" asked John, watching Hank's eyes glaze over.

"When Jed told me what happened, he helped me make room." Doc rolled up his sleeves and began to unbutton Hank's shirt.

After the men loaded Hank, Jed climbed the wagon and they all headed back to camp. As they rolled across the prairie, Hank moaned with every jolt of the wagon.

The wagons were already circled, and suppers were being prepared. When the party saw John and Jed approach, they left their fires and surrounded Doc's wagon.

"Is he dead?" asked Joe Callahan.

"No. Now all of you get back to your wagons and let Doc work," John said. He glanced around and spotted Elizabeth. His heart suddenly lightened, she was alive. John sprinted over to her, took her hand, and quickly walked her back to her wagon. Once there, he pulled her into his arms and held her. "I thought it was you. Dear God, I thought it was you. You just took ten years off my life, girl." His voice lowered to a whisper as he smoothed her hair.

He felt Elizabeth shaking and knew she was crying. He gazed heavenward and let out a huge breath. The moment he thought it was her wagon, his life changed forever, and realized he never wanted to be alone again.

"What happened, Beth?" He lifted her chin and stared into her tear-filled eyes.

When she lifted her eyes, the pain flickered in them. "A rattlesnake. It spooked the horses, and the wagon took off. Hank couldn't stop them." She wiped away her tears. "Is he going to die?"

"I don't know. Doc and Lucas are working on him now." He took a deep breath through his nose.

"Oh John, I was so frightened." She hugged him, wrapping her arms around his waist.

"You come on over to Buck's wagon. Grab your tea kettle and he'll make you some tea. You look like you could use it."

They walked toward Buck's wagon, when a shrill scream echoed throughout the camp site.

Elizabeth dropped the tea kettle and put her hands over her ears as Hank continued to whimper and scream.

John picked up the kettle, placed his hand on the small of her back, and led her to the wagon. "Come on." John peered back at Doc's wagon with a heavy heart. He knew Doc was doing all he could for Hank, he just hoped it was enough.

Chapter Nine

The next morning, John strolled over to Doc's wagon. He brought over a pot of coffee and a cup as he watched Doc climb out of the wagon, rubbing his bloody hands on a towel. He took the cup, had a few swallows then poured the rest out, watching the liquid drain from the cup and onto the ground.

"How is he, Doc?" asked John, offing him another.

"Just lost him a few minutes ago," said Dr. Grant sadly.

The doc yawned and ran his fingers through his grey hair, trying to shake off his exhaustion.

"I'm sorry, Doc. I know you did your best." John gripped Arthur's shoulder.

"Best wasn't good enough and I'm too tired to be cynical." He leaned against the wagon wheel, took off his glasses, closed his eyes and pinched the bridge of his nose.

"You get some rest Doc, I'll have Aengus drive your wagon today." John took off his hat and hit his thigh with it. "Well, we better bury poor Hank."

Doc nodded, put his glasses back on and rubbed the back of his sore neck. The two men stepped to the back of the wagon. First death on the trail. Even though John had been a trail boss for ten years, losing a member of the wagon party was still hard to overcome. He was responsible for these people and when one died, he felt he'd let them down.

∞ ∞ ∞

Elizabeth stood next to Abigail and Jesse. Everyone remained motionless around the grave, bowing their heads in prayer, except Billy Ray who leaned against his wagon chewing his tobacco.

John opened the bible and read Psalm twenty-three, "The Lord is my shepherd…"

Elizabeth couldn't concentrate on the words, she could only watch Lucas and Jed throw dirt over Hank's wrapped body. She shivered, remembering John telling them that after the funeral, all the wagons were to roll over Hank's body to pack it further in the ground. This helped prevent wild animals and Indians from finding the grave.

After John was through reading, everyone went back to their wagons and started preparing for another long day. John sauntered up to Elizabeth.

"Thank you for letting me borrow your father's bible," he said, handing it back to her.

"You're welcome." She sadly took it and held it against her chest. "Oh John, must we ride over the grave?" she spoke in a broken whisper.

"Yes." He rubbed her shoulders. "Come on." He walked her to her wagon, but stopped; noticing a wagon missing, and it wasn't Hank's. "Dammit, where's Billy Ray?" He glanced around, spotting his wagon over by Hank's. "Stay here."

"No, I want to come with you." Elizabeth went with John to his horse. He helped her up then mounted behind her; Jed and Aengus rode over.

"What's up, lad?" asked Aengus, Rachel sitting in front of him. The last few weeks Rachel rode with him nearly every day. The two were inseparable. She held tight to the horn of the saddle.

"Giddy up horsey," she bounced up and down, trying to make the horse move.

"Hush Rachel," Aengus scolded, putting a finger to his lips. "I canna hear what John's talkin' aboot."

"Trouble. Follow me," said John, kicking his horse. "Seems Mr. Cobb wants a five-finger discount."

Aengus put Rachel down. "Go see Mummy." He watched the little girl toddled off in search of her mother. Once she was safe, he turned his horse and followed Jed.

John wrapped an arm around Elizabeth's waist and loped over to Billy Ray's wagon. The bouncing of the animal jarred her body and rattled her teeth.

He dismounted along with Jed, Lucas, and Aengus. "Beth, you stay here." He handed her the reins, patted his horse, and walked away. She ran her fingers through the horse's mane and watched as the men searched for Billy Ray.

"Hey, what the hell are you doing?" John found him coming around from behind the wagon with his arms full of Hank's supplies.

"That old coot don't need 'em anymore," said Billy Ray, placing the goods in the back of his wagon and headed back to Hank's for more provisions.

"He's dead. How could you?" Elizabeth asked, narrowing her eyes as the horse shifted its feet and swished its tail.

"You watch yourself, girly or you'll be next," said Billy Ray, the angry retort hardened his features.

Aengus marched up to Cobb, snatched his collar and shoved him toward the front of his wagon. "Get your arse up on that wagon before I cowp you into next week!"

Billy Ray shook with anger but climbed aboard his wagon. Elizabeth noticed from the expression on his face that Cobb was afraid of Aengus, he just wasn't going to admit it. John took the reins from Elizabeth and mounted up then kicked his horse and clopped over to Billy Ray.

"I see you stealing from anyone, dead or alive, I'll hang you from the nearest tree. You got that Mr. Cobb?" John asked through clenched teeth. Billy Ray nodded. "I didn't hear you!"

"Yeah, okay. I got it," he snarled.

"Good, now get back in line." He stared at him with an expression that sent his temper soaring.

Billy Ray reacted angrily to the challenge in John's voice. He whipped the mules harshly and rode across the prairie to the line of wagons. Bulling himself between two wagons, he sat glaring at John, the devil in his eyes.

"He frightens me, John." Elizabeth swallowed hard. Her eyes reflected the fear she had for Billy Ray.

John squeezed her and kissed the back of her head. "I won't let him hurt you, Beth. I promise." He kicked his horse and they trotted back to the wagon train. Elizabeth leaned against his chest, and she felt John's arm tighten around her abdomen. Her heart fluttered being so close to him and nuzzled under his chin, enjoying the ride back to camp.

Once they arrived at the encampment, he jumped off his horse then helped her down. After she was loaded on her wagon, John rode to the front of the line, made sure everyone was in place then gave the signal to move forward.

Elizabeth looked over at Hank's crushed wagon and his four dead horses and a chill went down her spine. John was right, this was a dangerous trek and people were going to die. That could have easily been her. She covered her face and thought *who would be next*?

Chapter Ten

They caught up with the buffalo herd near Chimney Rock. The sunset shone brilliantly against the rock, bringing out the colors of red, brown, and orange. The rock stood hundreds of feet high, giving it the look of a tall chimney stack.

John told the train they were going to stay there for a few days to hunt, repair and get some well needed rest. They circled the wagons and made camp. Elizabeth started setting up camp when John walked up to her. *Good Lord he's handsome*, she thought.

"Come with me, I want to show you something." He took her hand and led her to his horse. He helped her up then sat behind her.

"Where are we going?" she asked holding onto the horn of the saddle.

"Wait and see," he whispered in her ear. His voice was a velvet murmur. He gently wrapped his arm around her abdomen, gave his horse a little kick and loped away from the camp toward the herd of buffalo.

John took Elizabeth for a ride within the herd. Though she was elated, she had a nervous feeling in the pit of her stomach. Her body quivered while watching the animals trample the ground around her.

John felt her quiver. "Relax, I've got you. I won't let you fall."

"I've never seen anything like this in my entire life." She touched one as it walked alongside John's horse. Its body shook as her fingers touched its hump. Its fur was soft and warm from the sun. She understood why the Indians used it to keep them warm in the winter. There were thousands of buffalo, as far as the eye could see. She couldn't believe how massive these animals were or how beautiful as they roamed over the grassy plains. It was a river of brown moving as one.

John guided his horse out of the herd and loped to the base of Chimney Rock, he dismounted and helped Elizabeth down. She walked slowly away while he wrapped the reins in a bush. He followed her as she gathered wildflowers. Her raven hair blew in the gentle breeze and her eyes shone in the prairie sun. *Lord Almighty, she was heaven sent. Beautiful couldn't even come close to describing her*, he thought while watching her slender body sway to the rhythm of the flowers blowing in the wind.

"What's your horse's name?" she asked frolicking through the tall grass.

"She doesn't have one. I just call her Horse." He strolled up beside her itching to touch her.

"She needs a name. Give her one." Elizabeth picked some chicory and added it to her bundle.

"By all means." He waved his hand toward the animal grazing on the tall grass.

"Joy." There was a spark of emotion in her eyes. She turned away, and picked some beautiful Golden Alexander, a bold yellow flower, and added it to her bouquet.

"Why Joy?" He stepped toward her and took a chicory flower, placing it behind her ear.

"Because that's how you make me feel when I'm with you." Tears of pleasure found their way to her eyes. A tear trickled down her cheek and he gently wiped it away with his thumb, caressing the side of her face.

"You are so beautiful." He gently placed his large hands on either side of her face.

A sensuous light passed between them. Slowly leaning over, he licked his lips, and the prolonged anticipation was almost unbearable as he gently brushed his lips against hers. She felt his lips touch her like a whisper. The kiss sent the pit of her stomach into a wild swirl, and she closed her eyes, leaning into his waiting arms. He felt her quiver at the sweet tenderness of his kiss.

She dropped the flowers she was holding and gripped his shirt, pulling him even closer.

He'd known she would be delectable, but not this delectable. He shook with longing that went far beyond any he'd ever known. *God but she tasted sweet.*

Her blood pounded in her brain and made her knees weak. He swept her into his arms and held her tight against him.

Kissing her was by far better than he imagined --- and he'd never been the kind to suffer from a shortage of imagination. He gently raised his mouth from hers and gazed at her.

She slowly opened her eyes and looked at him, her mouth swollen from his assault on her lips. There was a dreamy intimacy between them as she rested her head against his shoulder.

"It's getting late, we better go." He put her down, took her hand and walked back to the horse.

∞ ∞ ∞

They approached Buck's wagon in time for dinner. Aengus, Jed, and Lucas were already digging in. Jed had been more forlorn lately, ever since John had told him that Elizabeth was off limits. John recalled how hurt his brother looked when he said he was in love with her. They sat near the fire while Buck plated up their grub.

"What's for dinner tonight, Buck?" John asked handing a plate to Elizabeth.

"Beans, biscuits and salt pork," he said, scooping a spoonful and slopped it on John's plate and then gently placed some onto Elizabeth's plate.

"Beans, again?" John wrinkled his nose.

"Once you boys go hunting tomorrow, I'll fix ya'll some buffalo steaks."

As they sat around eating, John heard a commotion by the Dickens wagon. He sat his plate down when he heard Rebecca yelling. They all observed the woman frantically going from wagon to wagon.

"Rachel! Rachel, where are you?" She spun around, searching. She ran over to the Callahan wagon. "Have you seen my daughter?"

"No ma'am, I'm sorry," Joe said, taking a bite of his dinner.

John and the others raced over to Rebecca. Panic had taken over her senses. She looked crazed as she grabbed Joe's shirt and shook him, causing him to drop his plate to the ground.

"What's the matter, Mrs. Dickens?" John asked, pulling her off Joe.

"Rachel, I can't find her. Have you seen her?" She wrung her hands in her white apron, tears streaming down her cheeks.

"No, but we'll round up a search party and start first thing in the morning," John said.

"Morning?" Rebecca bit her knuckle. She looked over toward Aengus. "Mr. MacGregor, you were with her today, where is she?"

"Aye, I was with the bairn, but when Lucas and I went scouting for buffalo, I took her over to the Sordorff wagon, so Edna and Emma could look after her."

Rebecca and her husband, Tobias, frantically ran over to the Sordorff wagon. "Emma. Edna. Where's Rachel?" She grabbed Emma's shoulders and shook her. "Where's my daughter?"

John pulled Rebecca away from the crying girl. "Now girls, tell us what happened."

"We played for quite a while, but she got tired, so we laid her down under the wagon and started helping mama with dinner. When I went back to check on her, she was gone. I thought she went back to your wagon, Mrs. Dickens. I'm sorry," said Emma.

"We have to find her." Rebecca wailed in shock.

"And we will, but we must wait until morning," John said, trying to calm the woman down.

"No. She's just a little girl and she's out there all by herself. We have to find her now." Rebecca began to cry.

"It's too dangerous to go out there tonight. Elizabeth, take her back to her wagon." John pulled her free, tearing his shirt.

Elizabeth put an arm around Rebecca and led her away, Tobias and the other women followed her.

"Alright. Jed, Lucas start looking around the wagons, maybe she's hiding or sleeping somewhere. Aengus, you and I will start rounding up men to help search tomorrow."

"You got it," Jed said and took off with Lucas.

John and Aengus made the rounds asking for help and all the men agreed. John went regrettably to the last wagon. Billy Ray sat playing with his knife. He leaned back and smirked.

"Well, good evening, gentlemen."

"We need you to help us in locating the little girl." John folded his arms across his chest and curled his lip. How he loathed having to deal with this man. If he'd known more about Billy Ray in the beginning, he would never have allowed him on the wagon train. Now it was too late, he was stuck with him, and it worried him when it came to the safety of Elizabeth. He knew Cobb wouldn't bother the other women because of their husbands, but Beth was all alone and if she wasn't careful.... the thought was too horrific to think about. He shook his head, trying to wipe the image from his mind.

Billy Ray cut off a hunk of tobacco and slipped it in his mouth. "Ain't my kid. Serves her right, wandering away." He chewed and spat in their direction. John took a step back in disgust.

"Ye a clarty bastard," Aengus said sneering and pointing at him.

Billy Ray laughed as the two men stormed away. John realized that time was of the essence, not only for the little girl, but for the party as well.

∞ ∞ ∞

Elizabeth sat holding Rebecca as she wept. Her child was gone and there was no sign of her. Elizabeth tried to comfort her, but she would have none of it.

"We need to find her. She's out there all alone. Why won't John find her?" Rebecca cried, pulling away from her.

"Rebecca, it's dark out. It's too dangerous for anyone to go out and look for her. John's doing everything he can. We'll find her." She patted the young woman's back.

Rebecca thanked her and the other women, then climbed into the bed of the wagon and checked on the boys. Elizabeth rubbed her eyes and walked over to her wagon, John was there waiting for her.

"How's Rebecca?" he asked taking her hand and leading her to the back of the wagon. He put the tailgate down and helped Elizabeth up. He knew she was exhausted and needed some rest.

"Not good. Bridget's going to stay with her. So, what did you find out?" She leaned against his chest.

"Most of the men are going to help us tomorrow. I want you to say here," he said, rubbing her back.

"When you say most…let me guess, Mr. Cobb." John nodded. She looked deep into his eyes. "Well, if he's here then I won't be." She crossed her arms and pouted.

He smirked, proud to have such a woman by his side. "Alright, you and me." He put his arm around her and pulled her close. "I better go. See you tomorrow morning." He leaned over and kissed her cheek and walked into the darkness.

Chapter Eleven

Elizabeth finished dressing and ran a brush through her hair and climbed out of the wagon bed. She looked around and saw all the men, except Billy Ray, standing by the Dickens wagon; many of them had rifles. John was talking to them when she walked up.

"Alright, does everyone have their instructions?" All the men mumbled and nodded. "Good, let's get moving." John waved at them.

Buck brought over a plate of pork and biscuits and a cup of tea. "The men already ate and if you're going out too, then you better eat as well." He handed them to Elizabeth. "John, you make sure she eats."

"I will." He walked her over to her wagon, grabbed her stool and pointed to it.

"John, why all the guns," Elizabeth asked sitting down and taking a bite of biscuit.

"Oh, in case someone spots her, they fire in the air." He pointed out, leaning against the wagon and watched the men leave the circle. Lucas and Aengus saddled their horses, cinching them good and tight.

Once she finished her breakfast, John led her to Joy and helped her up then mounted himself. Aengus and Lucas trotted up to them.

"Where should we start?" Aengus asked, his horse anxious to get going. It pranced in place and whinnied.

Lucas gazed at John with a somber look. "I found a few tracks going east of Chimney Rock. John, there's a lot of rugged territory…If we do find her, I'm afraid it doesn't look good."

"We'll do what we can. You and Aengus head toward that rock formation, Elizabeth and I'll head east." John kicked Joy and followed the tracks Lucas had found.

Elizabeth was frantic as she held onto the saddle. She shuddered inwardly at the thought of finding Rachel hurt or worse, dead. How could she tell Rebecca her daughter died?

John pulled Joy to a halt and slide off then grabbed Elizabeth and helped her down. They headed toward an embankment and started to climb.

"We have to find her John, we just have to," she exclaimed, her foot sliding on the rocky ledge. Her hands were cut and scraped from climbing, but she was determined to find the little girl.

∞ ∞ ∞

Hours past with no gun shots. Elizabeth knew time was running out. She and John had left the horse at the base of Chimney Rock and started to climb. Lucas and Aengus had split up and were searching, the rock formation nearby. Elizabeth slipped, but John caught her hand and pulled her up next to him.

"You alright?" he asked, putting his arm around her waist.

"Yes, thank you." She wiped her brow and took a seat. "Well, at least if we don't find her today, we can stay until we do. That poor little girl, she must be so frightened." She shook the dust from her dark blue skirt.

"Beth, we can't stay." He took her hands in his and squeezed them. Sadness growing in his eyes when he gazed at her.

"What do you mean, John? We have to stay."

"If we don't find her in the next two days, Beth, we have to go." He touched the side of her check. Her face paled as she gazed into his eyes.

"John…" She heard his voice and bit her lips in dismay.

"Beth, if we don't leave, we stand a good chance of getting stuck in the mountains. I don't want to leave, but I have to think of the whole wagon train as well as Rachel." He put his forehead against hers. "I'm sorry."

"But she's just a baby."

"I know. Come on, let's keep looking." He pulled her up and they began searching around the ravines at the base.

∞ ∞ ∞

She could be anywhere, Elizabeth thought. Some areas the grass was as tall as John and there were stream beds, deep gullies, and ravines. If she fell into one of them, how would she ever let anyone know where she was. The sun was getting close to setting, they only had about two hours of daylight left and then they would have to go back to camp. It was getting harder and harder to see. Elizabeth gazed at the sunset. It was beautiful with its oranges and reds, and it brought out the magnificent colors of the rocks they were combing.

While searching an area near the base of Chimney Rock, John heard his name being called. He looked around and spotted Lucas standing on a rock formation, waving his rifle.

"Beth, look." John pointed at Lucas. "Come on." They slid down the rock, their boots scrapping against the pebbles and ran to Joy, mounted up, and galloping toward the rock formation. Lucas hopped off a boulder and sprinted up to John and Elizabeth.

"I found her. She's fallen down a ravine." Lucas was breathless as he took the canteen Elizabeth offered.

"She alive?" John questioned, dismounting then helped Elizabeth down.

"I don't know. We called down to her, but she won't answer. We're going to need your rope." Lucas wrapped the canteen around the horn of the saddle. "Aengus is up there with her."

John grabbed the rope and they followed Lucas up the hill. It took at least fifteen minutes of climbing to get to the ravine. Lucas led them around a ledge causing Elizabeth to panic. She looked down and nearly fainted. The bottom was so far that it made her dizzy; clinging to the rough wall, she slowly followed John. Suddenly she slipped and fell backward, but Lucas caught her arm just as she began to fall. Her heart beat erratically while trying to calm her breathing.

"Thank you, Lucas," she gulped, hugging the canyon wall.

"You're welcome. Mind your footing from now on." He demanded with a snort.

They came around a corner and as they approached the ravine, they saw Aengus laying on his stomach, calling to the girl.

"Dinna fash, Rachel, ye be alright. I'm here ye ken?" He looked up to see John, Lucas, and Elizabeth. "She's down there." He pointed to the deep ravine.

Lucas grabbed the rope and tossed it to Aengus. "You be anchor and lower me down." He wrapped it around his waist, walked to the ledge and climbed down without another thought; Aengus and John held fast to the rope.

Elizabeth laid down and watched Lucas slowly make his way to the bottom of the ravine. His moccasins slid against the wall, causing rocks to dislodge and tumble to the ground near Rachel. Elizabeth stared unblinking, her heart racing and she was so afraid the little girl was dead. Rachel was lying on her side; her leg crooked, and it seemed she wasn't breathing. The ravine was about thirty feet deep with rocks, bushes, and tall grass. It was a miracle Lucas had found her. Rachel must have slipped and slid all the way to the bottom.

John and Aengus stepped to the ledge and looked down. It was getting dark and hard to see Lucas. He squatted next to the little girl, his hand on her head.

"Lucas how is she," John called down, his voice echoing.

He looked up and shook his head. Elizabeth's world seemed to spin out of control. She sat up, crossed her arms, and rocked back and forth. Tears ran down her smudged face and her mind lost hope. How was she going to tell her friend, that her little girl was dead?

Chapter Twelve

"She's hurt badly, but she's not dead," Lucas called up. He gently rolled Rachel over and picked her limp body up in his arms. He grabbed the rope and looked up at the men. "Aengus pull us up!"

John rushed over to Elizabeth and pulled her into his arms. "We found her, Beth. She's alright," he exclaimed with intense pleasure. He gently kissed her forehead.

Elizabeth opened her eyes and was caught off guard by the sudden vibrancy of his voice. "She's alive? Oh, John." She threw her arms around his neck and held him close. Tears stung her eyes, but she blinked them away. They watched as Lucas reached the ledge.

Aengus grabbed Rachel and gave her to Elizabeth and John then took Lucas' hand and pulled him out of the ravine.

"Why won't she wake up?" Pondered Aengus, clasping the little girl's hand in his huge palm.

"We have to get her back to camp." Elizabeth said, smoothing down Rachel's auburn hair. Her mood seemed suddenly buoyant.

Aengus gently picked up the little girl and they all carefully made their way down the rocky formation to the horses. John held her while Aengus mounted then took Rachel and cradled her in his massive arms. When they got closer to camp, Lucas pulled out his rifle and fired a shot in the air.

It was dark by the time the group rode into camp, the campfires were the only light that could be seen. In the distance they could hear a lone coyote howling, echoing through the night sky. Rebecca came running up to them, arms open. Her eyes were red and blood shot from crying and she looked aged and worn out from worry.

"Where is she? Rachel?" She stretched her hands up to her daughter.

"Lucas, go get Doc." John took the child in his arms and dashed quickly toward the Dickens wagon, her parents followed close behind.

Dr. Grant ran up as John laid her down in the wagon. Rebecca quickly climbed in after the doctor. Tobias took Henry and David and began to finish the chores Rebecca had started.

"Henry, start a fire, your sister will be hungry." Tobias said then went to the back of the wagon to collect the food needed for their supper.

"Alright everyone, let's let the doc do his job." John said, a weight lifted off his shoulders. He leaned his hands against the wagon wheel and bowed his head. *Shit. I have never been so scared, knowing a tiny child was lost and could have died.*

Elizabeth took his arm and led him over to her wagon. After starting a fire, she put the tea kettle on and sat next to him. Fatigue settled in pockets under his eyes. Buck came over with some supper and a bottle of whiskey.

"I figured you'd need this more than I do right about now." He handed him the bottle and started to walk away but stopped. "You did good, boy." He nodded and waddled back to the wagon.

Elizabeth gave John a cup and watched him pour the amber liquid. He took a sip, closed his eyes, and leaned back against the wagon wheel. He put his hand over his face and sighed.

"I honestly didn't think we were gonna find her." He took another sip.

She made her tea and sat with him. Her exhausted eyes smiled up at him. "I never gave up hope. I knew you and your men would find her." She rested her head against his shoulder.

He gazed down at her and smirked. He put an arm around her and pulled her close. Taking another sip, he watched as his party bustled around getting supper ready, tending to chores, or getting ready for bed. A crisis diverted and hopefully the last for quite a while. He hoped that the rest of this trip would run as smooth as a mountain stream. *Only time would tell.*

A couple of hours later Doc emerged from the Dickens' wagon, a quirky smile across his face. John and Elizabeth ambled up to him as he poured a cup of coffee.

"What's wrong with her, Doc?" asked Tobias.

"She broke her leg, mild cuts and bruises and she's dehydrated, but she'll be fine. I splinted her leg. Tobias, I want her to stay in the wagon for a few weeks until that leg heals." He took a sip of coffee and snickered.

"What's so funny?" John said.

"What she told me. Seems little Rachel woke up and spotted a bunny and decided that she wanted to play with it. She told her ma that she wanted a pet rabbit. She followed it until it got too dark to see so she tried to come home, but fell down the ravine," he stated and finished his coffee. "It's late, I'm going to turn in."

John and Elizabeth watched Doc slowly make his way to his wagon. He pulled the canvas aside and climbed in. A few minutes later, the lantern was blown out and darkness filled the wagon.

"Thank God, Doc is a part of this wagon train," Elizabeth said, wrapping her arms around John's waist.

"I'll walk you to your wagon," he said, wrapping his arm around her shoulder.

She nodded, and they strolled over to the wagon, and she climbed in. Before dropping the blanket in place, John leaned over and kissed her.

"You were great today. You never gave up."

She blushed. "I couldn't. I needed to find her for Rebecca's sake. Goodnight, John," she whispered, caressing his cheek.

"Goodnight." He kissed her forehead and dropped the blanket. He was so proud of her. Even with all this life and death, she was handling it better than he thought she would. She was turning out to be a true pioneer.

∞ ∞ ∞

The next morning John and Lucas lay in the tall grass watching the buffalo slowly make their way passed them. The herd was gigantic, roaming over the prairie and leaving a trail at least a mile wide.

"We only need two. Try to take down males, as the females most likely have calves." John said, cocking his rifle.

Lucas nodded and they both aimed their weapons at the herd. John hated to kill these magnificent animals, but they needed the meat and the hides. He watched the beasts migrating passed them, and waited for the right moment, both having to pull the trigger at the same time.

"At the count of three. One…two…", John closed his left eye and peered down the barrel of his rifle, setting his sight on a large male, grazing fifty feet from him. It was huge. At least six feet tall and weighing in at about fifteen hundred pounds. John took a deep breath and blew it out slowly. "Three."

John and Lucas pulled the trigger and the bullets exploded from the barrel of the rifles and the two buffalo hit the ground with a loud thump. As soon as the guns discharged, the herd stampeded away from John and Lucas, their hooves thundering over the prairie.

Lucas and John stood up and made their way down the hill and over to the dead buffalo.

"Well, let's get to work." John took off his jacket and rolled up his sleeves.

Lucas quickly braided his hair, pulled off his shirt and took out his Bowie knife. "The camp will have buffalo steak tonight and then we'll make jerky out of the rest. You want the hides?"

"Yeah, I can trade 'em or maybe give one to Beth for her bedroll," John said making the first cut into the thick hide.

"You love this woman?" asked Lucas as he started to pull the hide from the carcass, exposing the meat to be butchered.

"I think I do." He nodded with a smile. His friend gave him a wide grin. "Shut up." John snickered.

"I didn't say a thing." Lucas said, raising his blood-stained hands.

"Yeah, but you were thinking it. We have a long day, let's get back to work." John said, digging into the carcass. Though he had to kill this animal, it made him proud that he could provide food for the wagon train. Some of the families had run out of meat and were living on beans, rice, dried fruit, and hardtack. Tonight, the camp would eat well.

Chapter Thirteen

A few weeks later, the party crossed the South Platte River, and followed the North Platte out of Nebraska and into Wyoming. Here, the party headed Northwest to Fort Laramie. The fort was a former outpost used by fur traders and was purchased in 1848 by the army to help protect settlers on the trails. This was the last army post until they reached Oregon City. Fort Laramie was also the end of the cholera outbreaks. John tried to make sure they stayed away from other wagon trains and had the women boil the water before drinking. This seemed to work, for not one person on his train died of the deadly illness. In some cases, a person might look healthy in the morning and by nightfall, be dead. It was believed that Fort Laramie was the stopping point for cholera because of the swift, moving waters in Wyoming, where before, the water moved slower, causing bacteria to build up.

John was glad they had made it to the fort, he needed a breather before tackling the Rocky Mountains. From here on out, the journey would only get harder. He had the wagon train park near the fort by the Laramie River. He spotted Elizabeth climbing off her wagon and walk to the back. He trotted over, dismounted, and tied Joy to the wagon then ambled over to her.

"Beth, how are you doing?" he asked shoving his hands in his jacket pockets.

She wrapped a shawl around her shoulders. "Quite well. John, would you escort me around the fort. Jed told me this is the last civilized place before Oregon City?"

"It would be my pleasure." He offered his arm, and she took it.

He walked her to the fort's entrance and looked around at the scenery and the fort itself. The area was still flat, but looming in the distance was Laramie Peak, the Gateway to the Mountains. It told John that the mountains were ahead and soon they would have to cross them to get to Fort Bridger. The climb was dangerous, and he hoped everyone would make it.

The fort was an impressive structure. Its walls were wooden posts at least twenty feet high covered in adobe. It was always an open fort that depended on its location and its garrison of troops for its security. It had three large guard posts, the one over the entrance, made it intimating to anyone coming in or out of the fort. Inside, were the barracks, the guard house, stables, black smith, Sutler's store, bakery, the powder magazine house, and Old Bedlam where the officers worked and slept.

They entered, and John witnessed a multitude of soldiers, Indians, trappers, and emigrants all walking around, making it crowded and difficult to move throughout the fort.

"Where would you like to go first?" he asked, patting her hand.

"The store. I need to pick up some supplies." She smiled at him.

As they were walking to Sutler's store, two soldiers marched up to John and stood in front of him. Their uniforms of royal blue and yellow with a gold G, told him they were from the Company G, 6th infantry regiment.

"Mr. Evans, sir?" asked a young soldier who was no more than nineteen in John's eyes.

"Yes, I'm John Evans," he said, sticking his thumbs in his gun belt.

"Captain Garnett heard you had arrived, sir, and requests the pleasure of your person to dine with him tonight, sir." The young sergeant commanded.

"You can tell your Captain, the pleasure is all mine, if I may bring along a friend," said John squeezing Elizabeth's hand.

"Yes, sir. That shouldn't be a problem, sir." They turned abruptly and marched away.

John smiled down at Elizabeth. "Would you do me the honor of accompanying me to dinner tonight." He studied her, a thoughtful expression on his rough-hewn features. He touched her face, caressing her cheek with his fingers.

"I would love to," she said sweetly, batting her eyelashes.

John walked her to the store and entered, but not before remembering the last time he did, he collided with the most beautiful woman he had ever seen, who was now on his arm. They walked in, and Elizabeth saw things she hadn't seen since Boston and Independence. Clothing, furniture, dishes, books, food, guns, trinkets, jewelry, and candy. She was so elated, she clapped her hands against her chest and hurried over to the books, John followed, curious that she would choose books over trinkets or jewelry.

"John, look *Pride and Prejudice* by Jane Austen. Oh, how I love this book. I lost my copy in the fire. I read it so many times, the pages were faded, and the spine broken." She held it to her chest.

"Well, why don't you get it?" John asked.

"No," Elizabeth placed it back on the shelf, "It's too expensive. Besides, my money needs to go to supplies and tolls, not frivolous things such as books." She smiled weakly and walked to the counter.

John looked at the book then back at Elizabeth and smiled. *I'll return later and purchase it for her.* He couldn't wait to see her face when she saw it. Warmth spread over his body. She was truly his heart's desire.

Elizabeth put on the nicest dress and petticoat she had and brushed her hair, pinning it up with pins and ribbons, letting only one curl drape across her shoulder. John would be at her wagon at any moment, and she needed to be ready. She sat on a chest and put on her patent leather lace-up boots. As she did this, Abigail poked her head in.

"Oh Elizabeth, you look lovely. I heard that John was taking you to dine at the captain's quarters. You'll have to tell us ladies all about it." Abigail pulled the blanket aside.

"I will. I'm so nervous." Elizabeth climbed out of the wagon.

"Don't be." Abigail started fluffing Elizabeth's pink dress. It had lace on the sleeves and around the collar at her throat. Pearl buttons ran down from her neck to her abdomen and a big pink bow tied in the back. "Remember the Captain puts his pants on like every other man, this one just happens to have a title."

Elizabeth smiled and took both of Abigail's hands and squeezed them. "Thank you."

John walked up and immediately stopped in his tracks. Elizabeth glanced up to see the look of shock on his face. He stepped over to her and gaped at her exquisite beauty. As she stood there, he couldn't help but notice that her features were dainty,

138

her wrists small with long sensitive fingers. Her soft cheeks were rose, and pearl and her mouth was a smiling rosy flower. He looked into her eyes and his heart melted.

"You… you look absolutely beautiful," he stammered and rubbed the back of his neck.

"Thank you, John." She smiled shyly and batted her eyelashes as she wrapped a cream-colored shawl, purchased that afternoon, around her delicate shoulders.

She looked him up and down and liked what she saw. He had groomed himself, trimming his beard, mustache, and hair. He wore a black three-piece suit, a silver and turquoise bolo tie, black spit-shined cowboy boots and a black cowboy hat. He was the most devilishly handsome man she had ever seen, and he was all hers.

His powerful well-muscled body moved with easy grace as he offered his arm and she willingly accepted it. He tipped his hat to Abigail, and they began walking to the fort.

∞ ∞ ∞

"Dinner was magnificent, Captain Garnett," Elizabeth said gently touching her lips with her napkin.

"I'm glad you enjoyed it, Miss Cornwall. Shall we retire to the parlor for some brandy and cigars?" said the captain.

John stood and pulled Elizabeth's chair out and escorted her to another room where the captain and several lieutenants entered. The room was well furnished with tables, chairs, and a long leather sofa. A picture of the captain hung over the fireplace. The room had the robust touch of true masculinity. Elizabeth entered and the men would not sit until she was seated and quite comfortable.

"Brandy, Miss Cornwall?" The captain offered and poured the amber liquid in a large glass.

"Yes, please," she responded, taking the glass and took a small sip. The liquid warmed her insides. She smiled and slowly licked her lips.

The captain poured a glass for himself and John, the lieutenants had to fend for themselves.

"The proprietor of the general store told me a few tales about the fort. Is it true you have a ghost who lives here at Fort Laramie, Captain Garnett?" Elizabeth teased, taking another sip. John looked across the room and gazed upon her beautiful face.

"Actually, we have two. One of a woman rider and the other is believed to be William Guerrier. Would you like to hear the tale?" He tempted her with a smirk.

"Oh, yes, please. In England, we are known to have many apparitions." Elizabeth pointed out and took another sip, looking at him over the rim of her glass.

"Richard, that story may not be suitable for her, it might give her the vapors," John argued, swirling the brandy in his glass.

"Nonsense. Please Captain, do tell," she beseeched with a smile.

"Alright. As the story goes," Captain Garnett began to pace, "Mr. William Guerrier, on an otherwise not so noteworthy afternoon, seated himself upon a small barrel near Sutler's store. Then negligently knocked out his live embers from his pipe against the small barrel. Unfortunately, the said barrel was a keg of gunpowder, which in combination with the live embers, fatally disbursed William over a considerably large area of the fort. It's said he still sits near the store, still trying to light his pipe."

"Good Lord." Elizabeth placed her hand against her bosom and paled.

"Richard." John, who was leaning against the fireplace, quickly sat next to Elizabeth and took her free hand in his.

"I'm okay, John. The poor man." She shook her head, her eyes wide with shock.

"Well, it's getting late." John helped Elizabeth to her feet. "Thank you, Richard for a wonderful dinner. It was good to see you again." He shook the captain's hand.

"It was good to see you, too, John. Have a safe trip to Oregon City." He then took Elizabeth's hand, leaned over, and kissed her knuckles. "Miss Cornwall, it has been a true delight."

John nodded, put his hand on Elizabeth's back and strolled out into the darkness of the fort. She gazed back at Old Bedlam and the officers standing there. It was a beautiful building, with its two stories, painted white with a porch on the top and bottom and six beautiful pillars all along the front.

She had the most wonderful time. Never had she experienced such a night like that before in her life. Her eyes were wide and glowing, and she had a skip to her step.

"John, thank you for inviting me, it was lovely." She looked up at the stars shining so bright in the night sky.

"Well, I thought you'd be better company than Jed." He smiled down at her.

They strolled out of the fort and toward the wagons. She sashayed over to her wagon, but he took her elbow and guided her to his saddle and saddle bags.

"I have something for you," he divulged, taking a wrapped parcel out of the bag. He took her hand, walked away from the wagons and over to the river, wanting a little privacy.

"John, you didn't have to get me anything," Elizabeth murmured, rubbing her arms.

John sat the gift on the ground and took off his jacket, wrapping it around her shoulders then picked up the gift and handed it to her. She looked at it for a moment then took hold of the twine and pulled it, slipped the paper away and saw the title of her favorite book. She looked up at him, her eyes were bordered with tears.

"Oh John. You shouldn't have." She stroked the leather-bound cover.

"It's not much, I mean it's just a book, but I remembered you told me you lost yours, so I thought I'd get it for you." He nervously shrugged.

"This means the world to me. I shall cherish it always. Thank you." She held it against her chest.

"You're welcome." He smiled. The look on her face was pleasure enough.

She leaned into him, wrapping her arms around his body, resting her cheek against his chest. She listened to his heartbeat as he held her. She stared with longing at him, a faint twinkle in her eyes. Noticing he was watching her intently, his large hand took her face and held it gently as his lips pressed against hers. His kisses were intoxicating, stronger than liquor, his touch like nothing she had ever known. He softly pulled away, leaving her mouth burning with wanting more. His lips nibbled her earlobe while popping the first two buttons at her neck, kissing the pulsing hollow at the base of her throat.

"John," she whispered, "we could be seen."

He stood and looked down at her, his eyes glowed with a savage inner fire, that was slowly going out. He nodded and buttoned her dress then took her hand and walked her back to the wagon.

As they approached, Abigail ran up to Elizabeth, pulled her to her fire and sat her down in a chair. "So, do tell."

Elizabeth smiled. She would tell the women, who were gathered together, all about dinner, the story of William Guerrier, and about the book John gave her, but the kiss and him unbuttoning her dress she would forever keep secret.

Chapter Fourteen

It was July the third when they finally arrive at Independence Rock. It was named after Thomas "Broken hand" Fitzpatrick during his Fourth of July celebration in 1830. The giant piece of granite was close to 2,000 feet long and 128 feet high and became a popular resting spot to emigrants along the Oregon Trail.

Elizabeth pulled her wagon to a stop in the circle. Like always, Jed would jump off his horse, tie it to her wagon and take care of the mules.

"Jed, thank you," she said.

"No problem, Miss Elizabeth." He chatted, gathering the harnesses, unhitched them, and walked them away to be grained and watered.

She made her way along the wagons waving and smiling to everyone she met until she reached Buck's wagon. He was stoking up the fire and getting supper ready.

"Well Elizabeth, how you doing, girl?" he asked, adding another log.

"Very well, thank you." She sat down near the fire and smiled, warming her calloused hands. Her fingers and hands were no longer soft and demure as they were at the beginning of the trek, now they were rough and tan; as well as her face which was no longer porcelain white.

She was content with where she was in her life. She thought her life would begin in Oregon, but it had really started the day she snapped those reins in Independence Missouri. Her mother always said good things would happen when you least expect it. She never really thought about it until recently and Alice Cornwall was right. If it weren't for the fire, she would have never come to America and never have met John.

"Thank you, mother," she whispered, looking up at the heavens.

John walked up with Joy and tied her to the wagon. He rummaged through the wagon, but Buck pushed him aside. "What's gotten into you, boy?"

"I need a hammer and chisel. Where'd you put 'em?" John asked.

"I'll get them, just stand back. I don't need you messing up my wagon." Buck started moving a few things around until he found what he was looking for. "Here." He handed them to him.

John took Elizabeth's hand and escorted her to Joy and helped her up. Joy stomped her hoof impatiently while Elizabeth settled in the saddle. She took up the reins and gazed at John questionably while he placed his foot in the stirrup.

"What about supper?" she asked, holding onto the horn.

"This won't take long." He mounted his horse, handed the tools to Elizabeth, and led Joy toward Independence Rock. It was a beautiful evening, just perfect for their little adventure. It was so quiet except for the rustle of Joy's hooves through the tall grass. The sun began to set in the west, creating one of the most picturesque sunsets she had ever seen; the brilliant purples and blues stretched across the open sky.

"As beautiful as your eyes," he whispered in her ear. She could light up the dark with those eyes.

This time she couldn't control her blush, warmth spreading through her cheeks as if they'd caught fire. She bowed her head, using her hair to cover up her smile and the twinkle in her eyes.

∞ ∞ ∞

Once at the rock, he helped Elizabeth down and walked her to the gigantic dome of granite. She looked closely at the rock and noticed that people had carved their names and dates into the surface along with Indian paintings. John took the tools and walked around until he found an area not yet marked.

"I already carved my name several years ago, so let's add yours to the register," he said, squatting down and began to chisel her name in the granite.

While he carved, she wandered around looking at all the names and couldn't believe she was there or that John was making her mark in history. She stepped up behind him and placed her hands on his shoulders, the muscles working hard hammering. She watched as her name became a permanent mark that would stay there for all time.

"There." He stood and wiped his brow. "Elizabeth Cornwall July 3rd, 1850. What do you think?" He put his arm around her.

"I love it. Thank you." She hugged him.

Never did she think someone would be so generous as to carve their love for her in stone. She stared at her name, feelings of adoration filled her heart. She couldn't keep from trembling, a delicious tingle radiating from her head down through her body and curled her toes. The sensations turned her weak and she knew she couldn't move, not even if her life depended on it.

John gazed down at her, leaned over, and kissed her. It started as a caress, but with every passing moment, the kiss grew stronger. He helped her to the ground while his lips devoured hers. He laid over her, his arm propping him up, so his large size wouldn't crush her. She grabbed his shirt with her long, slender fingers and slowly unbuttoned it, pulling his shirt out of his jeans. She peeled it over his massive shoulders. He unbuttoned her blouse and pulled the ribbons of her corset until he found what he desired. She moaned with sweet surrender when his hand caressed her throbbing bosom. She raked her fingers over the bulging muscles of his back. He pulled away and stared down at her. Her eyes were sultry with wanting.

"Do you want me, John?" she asked rubbing her hands seductively down his chest to the button of his jeans.

"God, yes." He took her lips violently while his hand slipped under her dress. Here he lay, his shaft stiff and aching, each throbbing pulse a primitive reminder of just how long he'd gone without a woman.

She started to unbutton his jeans when they suddenly heard a commotion and a gun shot from camp. John immediately pulled away from Elizabeth and sat back staring toward camp.

"Right yourself." He commanded. Standing, he tucked in his shirt. He glanced at her while she fixed her corset and blouse and shook out her dress then took his hand and stood up.

They ran to the horse and took off like lightning toward the sound of another gun shot. A few minutes later, they entered the circle of wagons to witness Lucas wrestling a gun from Billy Ray. John jumped off Joy and hastened over to Lucas, who pulled the gun from Cobb's grip.

"What the hell is going on?" John snapped, flaring his nose.

"Them Indians are gonna massacre us. I was just protecting the women folk," said Billy Ray.

John glanced around, noticing a band of Indians setting up a small camp between the river and the wagon train.

"I tried to tell him they were peaceful, but he wouldn't listen. Damn near took my head off when he fired." Lucas seethed, checking his scalp to see if there was any blood.

"They're here to trade, you jackass. What are you trying to do, start a war?" John questioned, taking his hat off, and throwing it on the ground.

Jed helped Elizabeth off the horse. She stood watching the altercation, hoping Billy Ray wouldn't start another fight.

"Mr. Cobb, you're trying my patience. I'm this close to asking you to leave the party," John said.

"You can't kick me out, I paid good money and signed a contract," Billy Ray yelled.

John sighed, rolled his eyes, and stepped over to Elizabeth. "Let's get some supper." He snatched his hat and put his arm around her waist, leading her to Buck's wagon. Lucas followed behind with Jed.

"Hey, what about my gun?" Billy Ray called after them.

"You'll get it back tomorrow," John snapped.

'Maybe.'

Chapter Fifteen

The next morning, Elizabeth sat by her fire sipping tea. She watched the sunrise and knew it was going to be a beautiful day. John told her that later, he was going to take her to the Indian encampment along with Lucas. She was excited and uneasy, having read a dime novel about Indians and it painted them as blood lustful savages, yet from where she sat, they seemed peaceful and friendly.

She finished her breakfast, put her things away and went to see what Abigail was up to.

"Jesse, how are you?" she asked, stepping up to the wagon.

"Doing great. I'm sorry, Elizabeth, but Abigail's a little under the weather today. She's in the wagon sleeping." Jesse informed her while sipping his coffee.

"Oh. Not serious I hope." She frowned.

"No, baby's just giving her trouble. Kept her up most of the night," he said, taking a bite of his breakfast.

"Well, if there's anything you need, let me know," she offered, walking toward Buck's wagon.

"I'll do that. Thank you." Jessie waved at her.

Elizabeth walked up to the fire and sat down, Buck smiled at her. He handed her a cup of tea with some sugar. She had given him a tin of tea, so he could fix her some if she happened to mosey over.

"How you doing, girl?" He went back to cooking.

"Scared." Elizabeth looked into his eyes. He was such a kind man and so full of life.

"Why, cause John and Lucas are taking you to the Indian encampment? Girl, there's nothing to fear. They're peaceful." He smiled a toothless grin.

John had finished his rounds with Lucas and Aengus as they walked up to Elizabeth smiling, their saddle bags draped over their shoulders.

"You look lovely today." John took a seat next to her, Buck handing him a cup of coffee.

"Morning Elizabeth," Lucas said, pouring himself a cup and leaned against the wagon.

"So, you ready?" John asked finishing his coffee and took her hand.

She gave him a hesitant smile. She felt daunted when he helped her to her feet. He laughed and brought her to him. "Beth, what do you think's gonna happen?" She shrugged shyly. "Come on." He took her hand and they walked toward the encampment. Lucas chugged his coffee and ran to catch up with them.

"What are they called?" she asked as they drew near, her heart palpating with anxiety.

"They are Cheyenne, a very proud people." Lucas responded.

Their camp was relatively small with only about seven teepees. They were made of animal hides and painted with beautiful artwork. Some of the women were cleaning fish while others cooked and kept the fires burning. The men groomed their horses, tanned hides, or sat and talked among themselves.

They approached, and Elizabeth noticed not how proud the people were, but their beauty. The women wore deer skin dresses and moccasins detailed with fringes and beads and they wore braids in their hair. The men wore buffalo leggings and deer skin vests. Their facial features were delicately carved as their jet-black hair flowed from a center part.

She was no longer frightened, but curious as they walked into the camp. Lucas marched ahead and greeted the Cheyenne in their native language, then pointed to John and herself. A tall Indian walked over to John and embraced him, clapping him on the back.

"Good to see you, John Evans," he said, taking his hand and shook it.

"Ahtunowhiho, your English is getting better each time I see you." John smiled at him.

Ahtunowhiho was almost as tall as John. He had a round face, with a pointed nose and high cheek bones. His hair was parted, and two braids hung over his shoulders. He wore buckskin shirt and britches with a huge feather head dress. He was a very impressive man.

"Thank you, John Evans. Who is this?" He nodded at Elizabeth.

"This is Elizabeth." He placed his hand on the small of her back and gave her a little push toward Ahtunowhiho, who took her hand and showed her how they greet one another.

Other Cheyenne began to surround the couple. A woman walked up to Ahtunowhiho and spoke to him in her native tongue then looked at Elizabeth.

"My woman wants you and Elizabeth to eat with us. Come." He turned and walked toward a teepee.

John took Elizabeth's hand and followed, Lucas right behind. They entered the teepee and sat around a fire, Elizabeth sitting on her knees and tucking her legs under her. Three boys sat on a buffalo hide in a corner waiting for their food. Elizabeth noticed that every family member slept in one teepee. *How was there any privacy*? she thought. She looked around the dwelling at the children and the couple across from them. *They seemed so happy and peaceful with their life, no blood lust at all. Maybe the books were wrong*, she thought to herself.

The woman laid down baskets and platters of food. There was meat, corn, berries, fruit, and vegetables. While eating, John and Ahtunowhiho talked about the tribe and the wagon train. Elizabeth started to feel uncomfortable while she ate her lunch; the woman would not take her eyes off of her.

"John, what's her name?" Elizabeth asked, nodding toward the maiden.

"Lomasi. She's Ahtunowhiho's wife," John said, taking a bite of buffalo.

"Why is she staring at me?" Elizabeth whispered, looking at Lomasi from the corner of her eye.

She was by far the loveliest Indian she had ever seen. Her skin was deep brown, with a wealth of long black hair. She had high, exotic cheekbones in a delicate face, a slender body, and fiery eyes.

John looked at Lomasi then back at her. "Don't know. It's alright, maybe she thinks your beautiful. I know I do."

Elizabeth blushed, looked at her lap, and smiled shyly while playing with her fingers.

"John Evans, what is wrong?" Ahtunowhiho asked, putting down his plate.

"Elizabeth was just wondering why Lomasi was looking at her," John said taking a bite of jerky.

Ahtunowhiho spoke to his wife in their language. They carried on a lengthy conversation before he got up and came over to Elizabeth. She was confused and frightened. He placed his finger under her chin and lifted until the light caught her violet eyes. His deep brown eyes were so intense, it sent a chill down her spine; she could feel his breath on her face. Suddenly, his lower lip began to tremble then he looked at his wife and nodded.

"John Evans, your woman has made Lomasi very happy. She has our daughter's eyes. We lost Leotie two moons past before she marries. Lomasi has been very sad, but now we mourn no more. Thank you, John Evans, for bringing her to us. Come, let us trade." Ahtunowhiho left the tent, Lucas, John, and Elizabeth followed. They went over to several large blankets with food, clothing, jewelry, pipes, beads, and blankets.

Elizabeth couldn't believe what she was seeing. Everything was so beautiful.

"Oh John, such treasures. I never imagined such beauty." She touched a colorful blanket then picked up some beads and rolled them between her fingers.

John looked at her and grinned. He took several items from his bag that included a knife and two bottles of whiskey. Elizabeth had nothing to trade so she walked around the camp smiling. Two teen girls came up to her and touched her hair, pointed to their braids and back to her hair. She nodded and sat down in the prairie grass. The girls took out her bun and ran combs made of bone through her hair, which went past her waist. Once they were done brushing it, they began to braid it. She was in heaven while they gently styled her hair. When they were done, she looked at one of the braids and a tear ran down her cheek. She hugged the girls and smiled.

∞ ∞ ∞

John showed his offerings in exchange for many of the things he saw in front of him. He spotted a buckskin pouch among the food. "What is that?" he asked.

An elderly woman picked it up and spoke in Cheyenne.

"You would call it tea," said Lucas.

"Tea?" John asked, gazing at it. "Just plain tea?"

"It's for healing," Lucas replied.

John smiled and picked up a bottle of whiskey. "This for the tea." He listened to Lucas speak then watched the woman hold up two fingers. "Two bottles? Oh...alright." John nodded and handed her the whiskey.

Lucas snickered. "She got one over on you, Boss." He rubbed his nose.

"Ha-ha, very funny. The knife for two blankets and that necklace," he said.

The Cheyenne woman nodded and handed the items over to him. John stuffed what he could in his saddle bags and held onto the rest.

"Do you love this woman?" Ahtunowhiho demanded.

John watched Elizabeth getting her hair braided. "I want to, but I'm not sure," he said rubbing the back of his neck.

"She is a good woman. You should make her your wife." His friend suggested, placing his hand on John's shoulder.

"I'm too old for her. Besides, what kind of life can I give her?" John asked him.

"A happy one." Ahtunowhiho patted John's arm, walked over to Lomasi and kissed her.

Lomasi talked to her husband then went into their teepee. A moment later she came back holding something wrapped in buckskin.

"Call your woman, Lomasi has a gift for her." Ahtunowhiho commanded.

"Beth, come here." John held out his hand. She walked over to him and took it.

Lomasi began to speak and Lucas interpreted what she said. "This was their daughter's. You have her eyes, so you have given Lomasi peace. She wants you to have this."

Elizabeth took it and thanked her. She unwrapped the buckskin and stared down at a beautiful deer skin dress with bead work patterns, shells and carved bone cascading down the front and the sleeves. Under the dress were a pair of matching moccasins.

"This was to be her marriage gown. Now it is yours," Lucas said.

Elizabeth found it difficult to find the right words to say, she was in shock. "Thank you. I shall cherish it always," Elizabeth muttered, her throat tightening.

Lomasi nodded and went back into the teepee.

"I'll stay here. Some of the party want to trade and they'll need an interpreter," Lucas said.

"Alright, I'll see you later." John walked over to Ahtunowhiho and embraced him. "Thank you, my friend. I'm so sorry for the loss of your only daughter."

Ahtunowhiho nodded. "Thank you, John Evans. You are a good man." He patted John's arm.

Elizabeth walked up to Ahtunowhiho and kissed him on the cheek. "Thank you for everything."

"You are welcome," he remarked and nodded.

John and Elizabeth left the encampment and headed back to the wagon train. As they wandered away, she glanced back at the camp, happy to have experienced something new and different. She held the dress close to her and smiled.

"John, I had a wonderful time. Thank you for taking me." She squeezed his hand.

"My pleasure." They walked over to her wagon. "I have something for you." He laid down the blankets and searched his saddle bag until he found what he was looking for. "Here." He handed her a buckskin pouch.

"What is it?" she asked.

"Tea, for healing. At least, that's what Lucas said it was for. I traded two bottles of whiskey for it," he snickered.

"John…" She took the tea and smelled it.

"I thought you might want it for your new shop," he said.

She stood on her tippy toes and kissed him. "Thank you," she whispered against his lips.

After dinner, she put everything away then climbed into the wagon and got ready for bed. She laid there staring at the bonnet of the wagon thinking about the day's events. John was introducing her to a whole new world, and she was enjoying every minute of it.

Chapter Sixteen

John led the party over the Continental Divide at South Pass. From there, the trail continued southwest crossing the Big Sandy Creek, which was only ten feet wide and one foot deep, then headed toward the Green River and from there, Fort Bridger.

Elizabeth's mules plodded on, the wagon creaking around each curve and winding trail that led through the mountainous terrain. The sun rose high overhead as morning set around the wagon train, warming the air. A gentle chorus of insects added their own brand of music to the symphony of birdsongs already underway.

All day, wagon followed wagon in a monotonous line of future Oregonians; except for lunch, never stopping. John rode next to Elizabeth, a smile crossing his face. Whatever it was about this slip of a girl drew him in, in ways he did not understand, evoking one conflicting emotion after another. One minute he wanted to protect her, the next provoke her, and then kiss her until neither of them could think straight. And at that very moment, that's exactly what he wanted to do. His shaft stiffened, thinking about that night near Independence

Rock when she allowed him to touch her in ways that were boldly sinful. How he longed to hold her again.

That evening, John had the wagons park near the river they would cross in the morning. He loved this part of the trek. Now they were in the mountains, foothills, and mesas. Gone were the Great Plains, lightning storms, and the use of buffalo chips, now they could use wood as their main source of fuel.

He made his rounds then meandered over to Elizabeth's wagon, but found she wasn't there. He walked around, until he found her with Abigail. She was enjoying a hearty meal with good friends. He walked over to her and sat in the grass beside her.

"John, you're just in time." Abigail served him some stew and a cup of coffee.

"Looks good, thanks." John took the plate and cup. He looked as Elizabeth took a sip from her own cup. "Since when did you start drinking coffee?"

"I'm not." She pointed to her tea kettle and smiled. He laughed.

John watched Elizabeth tuck into the hearty rabbit strew Abigail provided for supper. Although he had to confess that *tuck* might not be the right word for the delicate way Elizabeth wielded her fork and knife. Her precision was almost mesmerizing, as she cut each piece of food into neat, easily consumable portions before bringing each bite to her lips. She ate, drank, and patted her mouth with her napkin with equal measures of refinement.

When dinner was finished, and the dishes done, several members of the wagon train came over to enjoy an evening of music and friends. Rebecca, Abigail, Bridget, and Anna sat around Elizabeth and talked while John conversed with the men. It was a wonderful night to spend with friends. Everyone attended except for Billy Ray. John knew the man was sitting near his wagon staring at him. He could feel Cobb's eyes boring into his skull, but he wasn't going to let it bother him. He was with Elizabeth and that's all that mattered.

Rachel hobbled over to Aengus as he played the bagpipes, sat, and snuggled close to him. John smiled as he watched the little girl yawn and start to fall asleep. Aengus looked like a fierce warrior, but John knew he was a kitten at heart.

Elizabeth leaned against John's broad shoulder as she talked to the women.

"I can't believe we're halfway there," Rebecca exclaimed with a smile.

"It seems like forever since we left Denmark," Anna uttered.

"Aye, Ireland and now here. I can't wait to get to Oregon City, so I can rest," said Bridget. The women laughed.

"Well, it's getting late. We have a big day tomorrow. Elizabeth, may I escort you to your wagon?" John asked. She nodded and pushed herself up. After saying their goodnights, they walked away, toward Elizabeth's wagon.

"Hey John, don't do anything I wouldn't do." Bill Callahan yelled after them, then started laughing and smacking his leg.

John took Elizabeth's hand and sauntered past the wagon and into the woods near the river. They strolled along the bank, listening to the rush of the water.

"Beth…" He let go of her hand and stepped away from her, his back to her. "I … I really like you." He turned around to face her. "I think I may even love you." He rubbed the back of his neck.

"You think?" She shook her head and smiled. "I guess I'll have to take that much… for now." She walked into his open arms and rested her face against his chest. She could hear his heart beating fast.

She felt so good in his arms. He needed her, wanted her, but not like this. When he took her, if he took her, she'd be his wife first. He needed to feel her lips on his, so he looked around and found a fallen tree. Taking her hand, he led her to it. He picked her up and placed her on the log. She stood on it and gave him the funniest look, he couldn't help but laugh.

"Look, we're the same height now." He took her arms and lifted them to his shoulders. She wrapped them around his neck, his hands locked against her spine.

Her gaze was as soft as a caress, it was a definite turn-on. Her invitation was a passionate challenge, hard to resist. First, she kissed the tip of his nose, then his eyes and finally, she kissed his mouth. Their tongues danced as each of their bodies melted together. He kissed her back, lingering, savoring every moment. A small breathless whisper escaped her lips while trailing his fingertips down her back and found her round buttocks. He pulled back a little and watched her. She took one of his hands and gently kissed each fingertip, her tongue licking, teasing. His heart responded, thumping hard and steady in his chest.

"Touch me," she whispered as she unbuttoned her dress and placed his hand on her breast.

He stared down at her ample cleavage. As he cupped her breast, he felt her arch her back as a sensual moan escaped her lips. He wanted to taste her, love her, but not tonight; he pulled away gazing into her eyes. *God, he wanted her*.

"Beth, we better get back," he said breathlessly.

"John." She whispered against his lips, holding onto his collar. "I need you."

"Not tonight." He leaned in and kissed her forehead.

He helped her button up her gingham dress. Her eyes glistened when he helped her off the fallen log. They walked back to her wagon and he kissed her goodnight, watching her until she was safe in her wagon then disappeared into the darkness. He went to the river and splashed cold water on his face. *I have to be careful or I may not make it to my wedding night.*

∞ ∞ ∞

The next morning Elizabeth paid the sixteen dollars to ride and sat behind her mules, waiting until it was her turn on the Lombard ferry. John, Lucas, and Aengus along with Rachel were on the other side of the river. Two wagons were left along with Jed.

"Miss Elizabeth, the ferry here is rather small, so be really careful when loading," Jed informed her.

"Thank you, Jed" Elizabeth replied, and she snapped the reins, slowly making her way onto the ferry.

It carried Elizabeth and Jed across, leaving the Dickens wagon to wait their turn. The water was high and fast running as the ferry made its way across. Elizabeth watched the ferry rock and tip a bit, sending her heart to sink to the pit of her stomach. John had told her that this was the most dangerous river they had to cross and to be extra careful. When they reached the other side, Elizabeth sighed a breath of relief as her mules left the ferry and walked on dry land. She pulled her wagon up the bank and parked it, setting the brake. Hopping off, she made her way down the bank and stood next to John.

She took his hand and he raised it, kissing her knuckles. "Good job, Beth." She smiled at him.

Aengus rode over to John, Rachel seated in front of him. "Well, Boss, one wagon left then oaf to Fort Bridger. Ye ready to watch yer Mummy and Da?" he asked Rachel. She squirmed in the saddle with excitement. Her beautiful brown eyes smiling, and she waved at her mother.

The ferry made it to the other side and the Dickens wagon loaded up. Everyone cheered as the ferry started to cross the river. The brown water moved quickly, and they knew the Dickens wagon would be there in no time. John placed his hands' on Elizabeth's shoulders and watched the pulley as it pulled the small raft across the swift river. Suddenly his smile slowly faded, his eyes grew big, and his grip tightened as the rope began to fray.

"Oh God," he whispered just as the rope snapped, sounding like a gun shot.

The cheering died down and they all watched in horror; the ferry began to tip. Tobias held the reins tight as the wagon and mules slid toward the edge.

"John!" Elizabeth screamed, and he pulled her to him. She gripped his shirt and peeked over her hand.

She heard Rebecca and the boys cry out as the wagon slipped into the river and Tobias was thrown into the moving water. The river rushed over the wagon while the mules struggled to stay afloat. Elizabeth's legs gave way and she collapsed to the ground, her eyes wide with terror.

"Mama!" Rachel reached out to the floundering wagon, as if she could pull them to safety.

The mules and wagon slipped under the water and the rushing rapids took them down river. Aengus gave Rachel to Anna and raced off down the bank, Jed and Lucas followed him. John mounted his horse and chased after Aengus. The women ran over to Elizabeth as she put her hands over her face and wept.

∞ ∞ ∞

John's heart was beating out of his chest as he raced after Aengus. He caught up with him, reached out and grabbed the reins, pulling his horse to a stop. He gazed at the young man, his face wet with tears.

"They're gone, Aengus. They're gone," John shouted.

Aengus dismounted, gave a Highlander yell, and started punching the nearest tree. Lucas and Jed rode up next to John and watched the burly Scottish cowboy take his rage out on a giant pine. John heard Aengus' right-hand break and his fingers snap, but it didn't seem to effect Aengus as he swung his fist into the tree. Jed dismounted and ran over to his friend, grabbing his shoulders.

"Stop. Aengus stop it. This won't bring them back. Think of Rachel," Jed consoled.

Aengus stopped his beating and hung his head. His shoulders began to shake, and he fell to his knees. John looked at the tree and saw a large bloody area where Aengus had been punching. Jed helped his friend up and they mounted their horses.

"Let's get you back and have Doc look at that hand," John remarked turning his horse and followed them back to the wagons.

When they approached, he saw the wagons had been moved away from the river and circled about fifty yards away. The party was setting up for lunch. He knew Elizabeth was the one who had suggested this, and it brought a weary smile to his face. They rode into the encampment and over to Buck's wagon. Aengus and Jed dismounted and headed over to Doc's. Lucas and John hopped off, tied their horses to the wagon and went over to the fire. Buck handed them a cup of coffee.

"I think I need something stronger, Buck," John suggested as he slumped to the ground.

"Thought as much." He handed John a bottle of whiskey.

John threw out the coffee and poured himself a stiff drink, giving the bottle to Lucas. He got up and walked over to Elizabeth's wagon. She had started a fire and was heating up her tea kettle. She came around the corner, her arms held a basket of food, a blanket, and a cup. Her eyes were puffy from crying.

"Where's Rachel?" John asked, sitting by the fire.

"Anna's taking care of her. Please, eat." She spread the blanket and placed the basket down. She put the food on the blanket and poured herself a cup of tea. "John, what's to become of Rachel? That poor child," Elizabeth questioned, a tear ran down her cheek while she made a plate for him.

He took the plate and ate. "Don't know. Tonight, after supper, we'll all have a talk."

She nodded. His heart broke for her and he could only imagine how she must feel. She had just witnessed Rebecca, one of her good friends and her family, being swept away to their deaths.

"Beth, I'm so sorry." He reached out and touched her face.

She looked down at her lap and nodded again, her shoulders shuddering as she cried. He put down his plate and pulled her to him. She cried on his shoulder.

"Here." He gently pushed her away and grabbed her teacup, pouring some whiskey into it. "Drink this." He handed it to her.

She took the cup and sipped it, coughing as it went down.

"Thanks... I think." She wiped away her tears.

"You're welcome." He smiled, brushing his fingers along her cheek. "I'm gonna check on Aengus, you finish eating." He grabbed a biscuit and stood up.

He went over to Doc's wagon to check on Aengus' hand. Doc was leaning against the wheel, puffing on his pipe when he noticed John.

"How's he doing, Doc?" John asked.

"Busted his hand up pretty bad. I splinted and wrapped it. Only time will tell if it will ever be right again." Doc said.

John shook his head. "Thanks, Doc."

He walked around the circle, checking everyone to make sure they were alright then going over to Buck and his men, he sat next to the fire and poured a cup of coffee. He rested his elbows on his thighs and hung his head.

"What ya thinking?" Jed asked, taking a bite of his lunch.

"We're going to stay here tonight. Between Aengus and Rachel...I just think it's best for everyone."

"Whatever you say." Lucas nodded.

"Son-of-a-bitch! Why did it have to be them, an entire family gone." He threw his cup against the wagon and grabbed his hair, gazing at the ground.

"John, you can't blame yourself, it was an accident." Lucas gripped his friend's shoulder. "You gotta think of Rachel and do what's best for her."

∞ ∞ ∞

Elizabeth couldn't believe what had happened earlier that morning. One of her best friends was dead and there was nothing she could do about it. Not only that, but poor, little Rachel was now an orphan. After supper and the chores were done, Elizabeth stood next to Abigail in the crowd, listening to John talk.

"As you know, a horrible accident happened this morning. We lost a few members of our party and it left little Rachel without a family. She needs some looking after, so I need some volunteers who would be willing to step up and help. So, any takers?" John paced back and forth in front of the crowd.

Everyone looked at one another but remained silent.

"Ah canna believe ye! Ye all make me sick! She's jist a wee bairn!" Aengus stomped angrily up to the crowd and waved his broken hand. "Shite!" He grabbed his hand in pain.

"Aengus come on." Jed put a hand on his back and led him away.

"Pish oaf, Jed!" He stomped over to Buck's wagon, grabbed a bottle of whiskey, and stomped away into the darkness. Jed stood there shaking his head.

Elizabeth walked up to him and took his arm. "He'll be fine, Jed. It's going to take some time." Jed looked at her and nodded.

"Mr. Evans… John." Bridget stepped up to John, Jed and Elizabeth, her husband in tow. "Shamus and I have been talking and seeing as we can't um…" She folded her hands against her stomach.

"What my wife is trying to say is, we can't have children of our own, so we would love to take lil' Rachel and raise her as ours." Shamus stated.

John smiled and shook Shamus' hand. "Thank you, kindly. Yes, yes."

Elizabeth smiled and gazed at Jed. "Maybe you should go tell Aengus."

"No way, not when he's been drinking. He'd kill me." Jed shook his head and strolled over to Buck's fire.

Elizabeth hugged herself, trying to keep warm. Since they started climbing the mountains, the evenings became quite cool. John came over and wrapped an Indian blanket around her shoulders and took her over to her fire.

"Thank you," she said sitting and wrapping herself up. She snuggled deep into the blanket that John had traded his knife for.

"You're welcome. I'm so glad Shamus and Bridget are taking Rachel. They're good people." He sat against the wagon wheel and stretched out his long legs.

"John, is the trek going to get any better? I mean, is anyone else going to die?" she asked, her sorrow was a huge, painful knot inside.

"I can't answer that, Beth. I hope not." He shook his head. His misery was so acute, it was branded on his features.

"It's getting late. I think I'm going to bed," she said sadly.

He nodded, leaned over, and kissed her quickly. "Better get some sleep. See you tomorrow morning." He stood up and walked over to Buck's wagon.

She looked around the encampment and spotted Billy Ray staring at her, a smirk across his face. He licked his lips and winked at her. She stood up, put out the fire and climbed into the back of her wagon. She laid on her buffalo bed roll and tucked the blanket around her, not bothering to undress. The thought of him watching her sent chills up her spine. She closed her eyes and tried not to think of Billy Ray.

Chapter Seventeen

Before they left, everyone went to the river and stood together while John read the twenty-third Psalm.

"The Lord is my shepherd, I shall not want..." He began.

Elizabeth stood watching the rushing water, the same water that had taken Rebecca, her husband and their two boys. It looked so peaceful. How could something that beautiful be so deceiving? After John finished the reading, Aengus, though he was in pain, played Amazing Grace on his bagpipes. The sound was chilling, reverberating with the wind and across the river. Elizabeth could feel Aengus' sorrow with every breath he played into the pipes while tears slowly found their way down his cheeks. After the funeral, everyone went back to their wagons.

Elizabeth finished her chores and packed her wagon for another long, monotonous day on the trail. She was growing tired of the same thing every day. She wished there were more mountains and passes, instead of grasslands with foothills. She climbed up and sat, waiting for John to give the signal to snap the reins and follow the wagon in front of her.

Lately Jed had been spending more and more time over at the Sordorff wagon. Elizabeth smiled to herself. She thought she saw a twinkle in his eyes whenever Edna would walk by. She was so glad that he no longer fancied her, and that John and his brother were no longer fighting.

Days past and they finally made it to Fort Bridger. Elizabeth sat in her wagon with her mouth wide open. It was nothing more than a few log houses with sod for roofs and a wood fence about nine feet tall. John had them circle the wagons near a grove of trees outside the fort.

Elizabeth hopped down and stood there with her arms crossed over her chest. "This is Fort Bridger?" She started to make her way toward the fort, but hesitated, blinking with bafflement.

Abigail waddled over to her and stared at the fence. "Disappointing isn't it?" she stated.

"That's an understatement." Elizabeth followed Abigail to her wagon and helped with dinner. Her friend was so pregnant, she found it hard to do the simplest tasks.

John, Jessie, Lucas, and Jed played cards while Abigail and Elizabeth talked about babies, life and what it will be like when they got to Oregon City. Every once in a while, Elizabeth would catch a glimpse of John looking at her. She turned from him and smiled, so he couldn't see the flush that crept across her cheeks. She dipped her chin down, using her hair to hide her face.

When it was time to retire, John walked her to her wagon. Time stood still when he pulled her to him, taking her lips in a demanding kiss. He held her close and danced to the rhythm of the crickets.

"You are so beautiful," he said, slowly swaying with her in the shadows.

She gazed up at him and smiled, then snuggled close to his rock-hard chest and sighed. She was so happy, she didn't think anything could wipe the smile off her face. While dancing, there was a sudden clap of thunder. John looked at the sky and saw lightning cross the heavens. And then it opened; rain came down in buckets. John grabbed Elizabeth and they climbed into her wagon. She grabbed a blanket and wrapped it around her while John peaked out to see everyone scatter and jump into their wagons, then he secured the bonnet to protect them from the rain and wind.

"Well, I guess I'll have to stay here till the rain stops." He squeezed sideways, so his knees were touching his chest.

"I guess so." She laughed watching him all scrunched up. "John, there's room over here so you can stretch out. You don't look very comfortable. Come here, I won't bite." She scooted over, so he had room.

He crawled over to her and sat with his back against the wagon bed and crossed his legs and arms. "I hope it doesn't last too long. I'd hate to have everyone see me climb out of your wagon tomorrow morning. Your reputation would be ruined."

"We wouldn't want that, now would we?" She smiled up at him, teasing him with her eyes.

Thunder and lightning crashed around them while the rain beat down on the bonnet. A lightning bolt struck close, followed by a crack of thunder. Elizabeth jumped and grabbed John's arm, burying her face against him.

"Come here," he said, lifting her up and gently setting her on his lap.

She held him close as it got louder outside. "I'm sorry, it's just that we don't have storms like this in England," she said as the wagon lit up from another bolt of lightning.

She felt safe in his arms. She never wanted to feel scared or lonely ever again. He smelled so good as she laid against his chest. Her heart jolted, and her pulse pounded. She reached up and planted a tantalizing kiss in the hollow of his neck. He gently gripped her raven hair and pulled her head back, gazing into her smoldering eyes. Every time his gaze met hers, her heart turned over in response. He began to kiss her hungrily as she wrapped her arms around his neck and buried her hands in his thick, brown hair. Lifting her, he laid her on the bed of the wagon while she trailed tickling fingers up and down his back. When he pulled his lips away, she had a burning desire, an aching need, for another kiss.

"Tell me to stop and I will." His eyes sought an answer.

"John, touch me... please." She pleaded taking his hand and placing it on her breast.

His mouth covered hers with wanting while he ever so slowly unbuttoned her blouse with trembling fingers. She arched her back, lifting off the bedroll as if to fit herself more deeply into his hold. He abandoned his kisses on her mouth to roam lower, gliding across her cheek and chin, then down the length of her neck. He pulled open her blouse and undid her chemise and corset and found what he sought.

"Oh John." She whimpered, racking her fingers through his hair.

"Shh." His words were smothered on her lips.

Oh, my heavens, it felt so good. Sinful. Nothing should feel this good.

She made no grievances when his hand moved low and inched her yellow calico dress up over her calf and up her thigh. She bit her lower lip to hold back a groan. He looked up and into her smoldering eyes. He wanted her so bad he could hardly stand it.

"John, where the hell are you?" Jed yelled.

John quickly put her clothes to right and sat up. She laid there panting, her body still burning from his touch. Her heart was beating so fast she thought she might faint. While she fixed her chemise, corset and buttoned her blouse, she noticed the rain had stopped. She sat up and looked at him, her mind still reeling of what might have happened, if Jed hadn't come along.

He leaned over and kissed her forehead. "I'm sorry. I went too far," he whispered, bowing his head, and looked away.

"John, I wanted you to. I'm not ashamed, are you?" she asked, turning his face toward hers.

"I should be," he kissed her, gently running his tongue over her bottom lip, "but I'm not." He smiled at her, his large hand caressing her soft cheek.

"John!" Jed shouted near Elizabeth's wagon.

"Shit how am I gonna get outta here?" he whispered gazing around the wagon.

"I'll distract Jed while you climb out the front." She leaned over and kissed him. "Please, don't go." She put her hands on his chest.

"I have to. I'm sorry." He held her hand and kissed her knuckles.

She nodded, took one more look at his seductive eyes and climbed out of the wagon.

"Jed, what's wrong?" she asked, wanting to punch him in the nose.

"I can't find John, have you seen him?" he asked, shoving his hands in his coat pockets, and kicked at the dirt.

"No, I'm sorry. Maybe he's at the fort, waiting out the storm. Now that it's stopped…Oh, there he his." She pointed at John, walking up to them.

"John, where've you been?" said Jed letting out a long, audible breath.

"Waiting out the storm. What's up?" John asked, giving Elizabeth a wink.

"Buck wants to play some poker and I thought you might want to join in. Come on." Jed started walking toward Buck's wagon.

"Thanks a lot." He called after his brother. He gazed at Elizabeth sadly. "I better go. Goodnight, Beth."

"Goodnight, John." She turned and climbed back into her wagon. She got dressed into her nightgown and smiled. *Is this what love feels like?* she asked herself as she laid down and pulled the blanket over her. She quivered, remembering the way he touched her, and it only made her want more.

Chapter Eighteen

From Fort Bridger, the party headed due north to Little Muddy Creek where it passed over the Bear River Mountains to the Bear River Valley. Here the emigrants encountered Big Hill. It had a tough ascent requiring doubling the teams and then a very steep and dangerous descent.

Elizabeth watched while several mules were added to Buck's wagon.

"Folks, gather around," John shouted, waving the people in.

Everyone gathered in front of him. Billy Ray walked up behind Elizabeth and leaned toward her, smelling her hair.

"Did you sleep well, Miss Cornwall? Were you warm enough?" he whispered in her ear.

Elizabeth flinched, rubbed her arms, and recoiled away from him and stood next to Abigail. When she stood next to her shivering, Abigail placed her arm around her and rubbed her shoulder.

"We're at Big Hill, and this is where I have to be the barer of bad news. Because of the ascent and descent, you must only keep the supplies needed to survive. All personal items must be left behind. I'm sorry."

Everyone started arguing and shouting. John raised his hands to the crowd while Lucas and Jed stepped forward incase things got out of control. John hated this part of his job. No matter how many times he told them before they started on the trek not to bring so many personal belongings, they always did. Now he would have to endure everyone's objections to his decision on the matter. *Shit!*

"People, please. I know it's upsetting, but this can't be helped. Now, let's get to work," John said with a heavy heart. He shook his head and stalked off toward Elizabeth's wagon.

She watched the crowd dissipate and began unloading their wagons. They grabbed furniture, barrels of china, crates of books and other precious items. She couldn't believe her friends had to part with all their things. Poor Abigail, she hoped John would allow the cradle Jesse carved for the baby.

"Beth, I'll help you." John climbed in her wagon, Jed stepping up to lend a hand.

"John, what are you doing?" she questioned in a wavering voice and rushed to the back of the wagon.

"Elizabeth, go through your clothes, take only what you need," John said, handing Jed the trunk, who sat it near her.

She grabbed some dresses, the wedding dress from Lomasi, and personal items and left the rest. Jed moved the trunk off the road. John continued moving things around and handing Jed items from the wagon. Elizabeth sat on the trunk watching the two men rearrange her things. John suddenly stepped out and grabbed a wooden chest and walked over to her.

"Beth, this has to go, I'm sorry," he said, putting the chest next to her feet.

She sat there, her mouth falling open. "No, no." She shook her head, covering her mouth with her hands. She looked down at the chest then back at John. "Please John, not my mother's tea set." She gulped hard tears slipping down her cheeks.

"I'm sorry, Beth." John squatted in front of her and took her hands.

"This is all I have left of her. I can't just… just throw her away," she cried, crumpling off the trunk to the ground. She reached out and touched the chest holding the tea set, stroking it with a loving hand. She felt sick and found it difficult to swallow. *How could he do this to me*? He knew how much the tea set meant to her.

He went to pull her to him, but she resisted his advances.

"No, this is my tea set and I'm taking it," she ground out. She sent him several cool, pointed looks.

"Beth, everyone has to get rid of some things. I can't show favoritism to you or anyone." He stood up and looked down at her. "The tea set goes."

He picked up the chest and placed it under a bush, away from the wagons. Elizabeth followed, sitting on her knees, and cried. The only things left were the raw sores of an aching heart. There was a sourness in the pit of her stomach. John picked her up and grabbed her by the shoulders, shaking her.

"Beth, your mother doesn't live in a tea set, she lives here." He put his hand over her heart.

"Don't you think I know that you Blighter!" She shoved him away. "You don't understand what my mother and I had, what she meant to me. Every night she would brew her tea and we would sit in the parlor with this tea set. When I was sick, she would fix tea and serve it with that cup. Ever since I was a little girl, that tea set was a part of my mother's life… my life. And now you want me to just throw it away like it was rubbish?" she spat out the words contemptuously.

John stepped toward her, but she backed away. She shook her head and ran, crying, to her wagon. The group nearby was listening to the argument, but when John turned around, they returned to their chores.

"Alright, let's get to work. Aengus, Lucas, let's get these wagons up the hill." His anger could be read on his face.

∞ ∞ ∞

For hours Elizabeth watched sadly as the wagons made their way up and then down Big Hill. John and his crew were covered in sweat and dirt as they worked, hitching teams of eight to the wagons one at a time. John insisted that Jed drive her wagon and she was to walk. She marched alongside it, listening to the eight mules and their harnesses noisily climb the hillside. She looked back only once, seething with rage then walked with her head held high with no tears.

After all the wagons made it to the bottom of Big Hill, they were circled, and dinner started. Elizabeth sat by her fire, sipping a cup of tea. She peeked over the rim of her mug, looking for John. Abigail walked up to her, a plaid shawl wrapped around her.

"You alright, honey?" she asked rubbing her friend's shoulder.

"Yes, I'm fine," Elizabeth said, still angry.

"Why don't you come over for dinner." Abigail smoothed Elizabeth's hair.

"I'm not hungry." She looked up at her and bit her lip until it throbbed like her pulse. "Have you seen John?"

Abigail pointed over at Buck's wagon. He leaned against it, his legs crossed. With his back to her, he looked over his shoulder.

"I need to talk to him, but I'm scared. I was so cruel to him this afternoon." She took another sip of tea. A stab of guilt lay buried in her breast.

"All you can do is try. I'll see you later." Abigail hustled back to her wagon.

Elizabeth sat her cup down and stood up, fluffing her dress, she strolled over to Buck's wagon. John ignored her when she approached him. He was so tall, he towered over her petite figure. Jed, Lucas, Aengus, and Buck stopped eating and gazed at her as she stepped in front of him. Taking a bite of his dinner, he swallowed hard causing him to cough when he saw her eyes tear up.

"John," she stammered, "may I have a moment?"

"Sure." An annoyed expression briefly crossed his face. He pushed himself away from the wagon, handed Buck his plate and disappeared into the darkness. She sadly followed behind him. When they were far enough away, he spun around, shoved his hands into his jeans pockets and stood staring down at her.

"Beth, I'm sorry about today. I understand your anger toward me, but I have a job to do and that's to get the train safely to Oregon City. I can't say I know how you're feeling, but believe me, I didn't do it to hurt you." A glazed look of despair began to spread over his face.

She positioned herself in front of him, her eyes never leaving his. "I know. I'm sorry about my behavior and I'm not mad… not anymore," she sighed, clasped her slender hands together, and stared at them. An inner torment began to gnaw at her as she took deep breaths until she was strong enough to raise her head.

"Beth." Taking a hand out of his pocket, he reached for her.

Her lower lip quivered as she took his hand. He caressed it with his thumb. Little by little, warmth crept back into her body.

"Forgive me?" he pleaded, trying to swallow the lump that lingered in his throat.

She nodded as he pulled her into his warm, protective embrace. He kissed the top of her head. When she looked up at him, her only emotion was relief.

"Come on, you need some sleep." He put his hand in hers and walked her back to her wagon.

While they walked hand in hand, Billy Ray leered at Elizabeth and spat some tobacco juice on the ground next to him. He was using a rock to sharpen his large knife, his eyes appeared cold, dead, and flat.

"Thank you, John." She hopped up on the tail gate of her wagon, her eyes were soft and filled with an inner glow. "I'll see you tomorrow morning." She leaned in and brushed her lips over his as she gently caressed his bearded jaw.

"Good night, Beth." He held back the blanket while she climbed into the wagon bed. He kissed her hand as it disappeared behind the fabric.

She heard his footsteps grow quieter as he walked away. Smiling, she put on her nightgown and climbed onto her bed roll. The last thing she saw before succumbing to sleep were his beautiful, forgiving eyes.

Chapter Nineteen

Several days later they reached Soda Springs. John said it was a great stopping off point. Here, the women could do their laundry, everyone could take a hot bath and there was plenty of grass and fresh water.

After dinner was over, the chores were done, and the sun had finally set, Elizabeth and the other women brought their personals and went to the springs to bathe. She undressed behind a tree, wrapped a towel around herself and followed her friends to the water. She stepped in and placed the towel on a rock. The water was heavenly. It bubbled and soothed her aching muscles as she stretched out. *This was worth all the miles they had traveled*, she thought closing her eyes and leaning her head back.

The women talked and laughed, for the first time in quite a while. Elizabeth loved being with her friends and having time without the stress of the wagon train. She let the women borrow her soap and soon the whole area smelled like fresh cut roses. She lathered her hair, scrubbing it until it squeaked then, arched her back to rinse it, her breasts bobbed in the warm water.

An hour later Bridget, Anna, and Abigail stepped out of the water and grabbed their towels. Wrapping themselves up, they got dressed and started to leave.

"Elizabeth aren't you coming?" asked Abigail.

"I'll be along in a while. It's just so nice." Elizabeth sunk farther in the water.

"Alright, but not too long." Abigail said, and the women headed back to the encampment.

Elizabeth sat listening to the crickets as the water bubbled around her. Her nipples hardened at the thought of John. Imagining what devilish things he could be doing to her while sitting in the water. She stood and stretched like a cat. Slowly, she climbed out of the water and grabbed her towel to dry off, wishing John were there watching her. She walked over to the tree and finished drying then put on her white nightgown with the pink ribbon. She hoped John would see her wearing it. She blushed at the thought of his calloused hands untying the bow and dropping the gown to the ground. She closed her eyes and leaned her head back.

She tiredly rubbed the towel over her long, black hair. Hearing the voice of her mother inside her head, she knew it wouldn't do to go to bed with wet hair and risk waking up ill tomorrow. While drying her hair, she heard a twig snap behind her and looked around but didn't see anything. She threw the towel on a tree limb and began braiding her hair when she heard heavy breathing directly behind her. She whirled around to see Billy Ray standing holding his knife. She started to scream, but he was too fast. He put his hand over her mouth and placed the knife at her neck.

"You do that again, girly and I'll slit your throat. You hear me?" he whispered in her ear.

She nodded, and he forced her to the ground. He removed his hand, but still held the knife. Her eyes were wide with fright as she tried to gasp for air. She could feel the cold steel of the blade pushing against the flesh of her neck, blood slowly ran down her throat from the small wound.

With one hand, he unbuttoned his trousers and rubbed his member until it grew stiff.

"I know you gave it to Evans, you English whore. I'm gonna take me a piece of it, too." He bent over and kissed her, running his tongue over her lips. She squeezed her eyes shut and tried to shake her head. Her pulse raced, and she felt dizzy while seeing black spots. She placed her hands on his chest, trying to push him off.

He smelled of chewing tobacco and rot. The smell made her gag as he continued to assault her. He untied the pink ribbon and pulled the fabric aside, causing her breasts to spill forward. He grabbed one and roughly massaged it. She wept aloud, tears slowly finding their way down her cheeks as he continued to suckle her nipple and run his tongue over her breast and up her neck.

"I'll have you moaning for more before I'm through with you," he said tasting her flesh once more.

She felt the knife dig farther into her throat as his manhood move up the soft skin of her inner thigh. He breathed in her ear as his cock found the opening to her womanhood. Suddenly she heard herself screaming.

"You bitch!" He back handed her. "I warned you. If I can't have you neither will Evans." He said through clenched teeth. He hit her face over and over, causing her eyes to swell. Before they closed, she saw the glint of the knife's blade. As she pushed against his chest, he raised the blade above his head and plunged it deep into her shoulder.

∞ ∞ ∞

John sat at the campfire drinking a cup of coffee with his crew, when he saw the women enter the encampment. *Glad to see Elizabeth was enjoying herself*, he thought as he stretched out his legs and took another sip. It had been a long, rough trip for her, but with each new day she became better at handling the stress of the trek, the mules, and the wagon. He gazed over at the women and noticed

Elizabeth wasn't with them. He rose to his feet and moseyed over to them.

"Abigail." He tipped his hat. "Where's Elizabeth?"

"She wanted to stay a little longer," said Bridget, walking over to her wagon to check on Rachel.

He nodded and strolled over to her wagon, hoping she had snuck back unseen. He pulled the flap back and peered in. "Elizabeth?"

Frowning, he put one hand on his hip and rubbed the back of his neck with the other. He walked around the camp until he came to Billy Ray's wagon; he was nowhere to be found.

"Shit!" he exclaimed and ran over to Buck's wagon. He seized his gun belt and secured it around his waist. While checking to see that his handgun was loaded, he suddenly heard a scream so loud it would wake the dead. *Dear God, what was he doing to her*?

"Jed, grab your gun!" he yelled running out of camp, Jed, and Lucas at his heals. "Elizabeth! Beth, where are you?" A sudden thin chill hung on the edge of his words. He pulled out his gun, fear of what he might find at the springs, coursed through his body.

When they ran up an embankment, John slipped, but Lucas snatched him by the arm and pulled him up. They raced like bats out of hell past several pools until they came upon the horrific site.

Billy Ray straddled Elizabeth and was in the process of stabbing her. He held a blood-stained knife over his head, his other hand around her throat. She had ahold of his arms and was thrashing, trying desperately to take a breath.

Shock yielded quickly to fury. "Billy Ray!" he yelled with reckless anger.

Cobb looked up and smiled. "You'll never have her, Evans," he chuckled nastily. He dropped the knife and wrapped his hands around Elizabeth's throat, squeezing even tighter.

"Billy Ray stop." Jed bellowed, reaching for his gun.

Lucas snatched his Bowie knife and threw it. It whipped through the air, hitting Billy Ray in the chest. Cobb fell back, rolled over and grabbed his side arm. He pushed himself up and staggered, took aim and pulled the trigger. John saw the white of the pistol and felt a deep burning pain in his side; falling to his knees, he grabbed his side. Though blood pooled through his shirt, John had no feeling, nor did he notice his injury, instead, Jed and John drew their guns and squeezed the triggers, unloading on Billy Ray. The explosions from the pistols thundered around them as twelve bullets struck his body, John's final shot hit Cobb between the eyes. Billy Ray Cobb would never terrorize another woman. He collapsed to his knees, dropping the gun, then fell face down to the ground; his lifeless eyes glazing over.

John holstered his gun, rose, and sprinted to Elizabeth's side. She was covered in blood and her beautiful face was puffy and swollen. Blood trickled down her chin from a split lip, her right eye was black and blue, and she had fingerprints around her throat. He ripped off his shirt, gathered it up and placed it over the wound on her shoulder. She cried out as he pushed down, trying to stop the bleeding. Lucas ran up and knelt beside him.

"John, you've been shot. Let me take her," Lucas demanded.

"He just nicked me. We have to get her to Doc. Jed, go tell him what happened and that we're on our way!" John dabbed at the hole in her left shoulder.

"I'm going." Jed raced back to the encampment as though his boots were on fire.

John gently picked her up in his arms and quickly carried her to the camp. Elizabeth moaned and then her body went limp. *Please don't die, Beth. I love you.* He cautiously stepped down the embankment, taking care not to jar her too badly. He entered the camp to find a crowed had formed, demanding to know what happened.

"My God." Several of the wagoneers cried when they saw her lying limp in his arms.

"Is she dead?" Robert Mulligan asked.

Lucas and Jed pushed the party aside while John hastened past them and up to Dr. Grant's wagon.

His crew followed close behind trying to keep the crowd from coming closer. Abigail, Bridget, and Anna raced over to Doc's wagon while John climbed into the wagon and laid Elizabeth down on a bed roll. He gazed down at her, pinning his arms against his stomach. He yielded to the compulsive sobs that shook him.

A guilty heaviness centered in his chest. "I'm so sorry, Beth. I promised he would never hurt you." A tear ran down his chiseled cheekbone.

"John, come on out. Let me do my job," Doc said pulling the canvas aside.

He stepped out and grabbed Doc's collar. "She better live." His eyes gave the doctor a threatening glare.

"God willing. I'll do my best, John." Doc climbed into the wagon and lit a lantern then asked Anna to help him. The older woman followed the doctor and drew the canvas closed.

John paced back and forth in front of Doc's fire, clenching his fists, and blowing out a series of short breaths, trying to gain control. He couldn't help thinking about the worst-case scenarios. He thought about the what ifs, what he could have done to prevent this from happening. Jed came up to him and leaned against the wagon, crossing his arms.

■■

"John, come on, let's get a cup of coffee," Jed offered, placing his hand on his brother's shoulder.

"Don't touch me, Jed. I don't want to hurt you." His tone deep as he glared at his brother.

Jed held up his hands and backed away. "Whatever you say."

Abigail walked over to him. "John, she'll be alright. She's a strong lady." She pulled her shawl tighter around her.

"Why did you leave her there?" he snarled, stomping away and into the darkness. He'd known something like this might happen, had dreaded each day and mile of the journey that had brought him closer to this point. He couldn't get the image of Elizabeth lying there in a pool of blood. He wished Billy Ray were still alive, so he could kill him again. Walking back up the slope to the soda pools, he saw Cobb's body lying near a tree. He went up to him and with his boot, kicked him over. He stared at his lifeless eyes with pure hatred and before he knew it, he was punching Billy Ray's face to a pulp, hearing the dead man's bones crack and break.

When John was drained of energy, he stood sweating. "The buzzards can have you. You'll get no burial from me." He spat, pulling Lucas' knife out of Billy Ray's chest.

■■■■■■■■■■■■■■■■■■■■■■■■■■■■■■■■■■■■■■

He walked back down the hill to the encampment, his anger subsided to a degree. He went over to Buck's wagon and poured himself a cup of coffee. Lucas handed him a clean shirt.

"I'm so sorry, John," Lucas said, taking the knife, he offered.

John slipped on his shirt and took a sip. He sat on an old log, Aengus had brought over, and stared at the ground. It was as though someone had torn open his chest and ripped out his heart. Jed sat next to him and put a hand on his shoulder.

"John…" he began, "I can't tell you how sorry I am."

"She's not dead. Stop telling me you're sorry." He glared at his brother.

"I'm just saying…," Jed said, gazing at Lucas and pleading for help.

"Don't. Just shut your mouth." John stared Jed down, looking like a fierce, wounded animal.

John drank his coffee, but found it wasn't strong enough. He stood up and snatched a bottle of whiskey. He popped the cork and took a long swig. When John took another swig, Doc walked into the firelight. He was wiping his bloody hands with a towel. His face was pale and grim.

■■

"John, I did all I could. It's up to her and the big man upstairs. She lost a lot of blood. I gave her some laudanum to help her sleep."

"Can I see her?" he pleaded.

"Sure," Doc said, patting John on the arm. He saw a mighty man beaten down by stress and worry; definitely not the man that left Independence a few months ago.

John gave him the bottle and quickly made his way to the wagon. He climbed inside and squeezed in next to her. Her face was bruised, and her beautiful violet eyes were swollen shut. He smoothed her hair as he gently kissed her swollen lips. She lay naked under a blanket, which came just above her breasts. Her left shoulder was bandaged and propped with a pillow.

"John. Mother, mother help me. John… John," she said in her delirium.

"I'm here, sweetheart. I'm right here," John cooed, taking her hand, and brushing his lips across her knuckles.

He felt so guilty that he wasn't there when she needed him. She must have been so scared while he was back at camp enjoying the evening and drinking coffee. He hit the side the wagon bed and scrunched his face in anger. If only he could turn back time…if only he were there…if... He grabbed his hair and started to cry. He could wish and if until Hell froze over and it still wouldn't change anything---Elizabeth still laid there fighting for her life.

"Mother, I'd love a cup of tea. John, John help me! No Billy Ray!" She tossed her head and kicked off the blanket. "Mother, where are you? Help me, I need you."

"Beth, shh." He covered her up as she continued to call for her mother. He kissed her forehead. "Sleep Beth. I'll be back, I promise."

He pushed the canvas aside and jumped out of the wagon, stomping over to Jed. The sorrow he felt was like nothing he had ever experienced. He needed to help her and there was only one way he knew, he had
to leave.

"Get the train going in the morning, I'll catch up. Lucas, I need you to come with me." John marched
over to Joy.

"Where the hell are you going?" Jed asked, following him. "I can't lead the train..."

John threw his saddle on the back of his horse and cinched it up. "You have to. If you stay, you'll run into snow in the Cascades. Go, I'll catch up."

■■■

"I can't believe you're leaving." Jed grabbed his arm and whirled him around to face him. "Elizabeth needs you!" he shouted.

"She needs her mother more." John mounted his horse and turned toward his scout.

"What?" Jed questioned.

"Lucas, let's go." John kicked his horse and the two men raced out of the encampment.

■■■

Chapter Twenty

Days past as John and Lucas rode hard across the Thomas Fork Valley to Big Hill. John pulled Joy to a halt when he spotted it in the distance. What a beautiful sight. He knew he was close, just a few more hours.

"There." He pointed and gave Joy a kick. They continued to ride hard over the valley. An hour later, they came upon a stream and stopped to rest and water their horses. John didn't want to stop, but he knew Joy would collapse from exertion and maybe even die if he didn't give her a breather. He needed her to finish their mission and bring him back to the wagon train when the goal was completed.

John mounted his horse and waited until Lucas got on his pinto, then gave Joy a kick and they splashed across the stream; the water spraying in all directions.

"John," Lucas called, "why are we here?"

He didn't answer, he had to get over Big Hill as fast as possible. He knew Joy was exhausted, but he needed her to hold on, he had to retrieved what he needed and get back to Elizabeth before something terrible happened. The horse was covered in a foam of sweat, but he pushed her onward, praying he wasn't running Joy into the ground.

The valley was gorgeous with its tall grass, flowers, wild animals, and trees. The wind blew over the grassland like the rolling waves of the ocean. Elizabeth had loved it here as she walked barefoot collecting flowers. He recalled that day when he strolled with her, laid in the grass, and watched the clouds roll by. She was so giddy, like a schoolgirl as she ran through the tall grass, her raven hair blowing behind her. Now that day seemed like a lifetime ago.

Once John and Lucas reached Big Hill, they took the dangerous ascent as quickly as they could. The horses stumbled on the loose rocks and Lucas almost went down. John urged Joy forward though he knew she was near collapse.

"I hope whatever we're after is worth it," Lucas yelled as he kicked his pinto on.

At the top, John looked at the beautiful scenery and wished Elizabeth were there to enjoy it. He and Lucas started down the hill, the horses were careful as they made the descent; hooves clicking against the rocks.

"Lucas, I need you to help me find a wooded chest somewhere along the trail. I placed it under a bush close to the bottom. It's made of chestnut with engravings on the lid."

Lucas nodded, hopped off his pinto and started hunting. John dismounted his horse and looked as well. He tied Joy to a bush and started down the hill. He had to find it for Elizabeth's sake. Everywhere he looked, he noticed people's personal belongings that had been left behind. Furniture, crates, barrels, books, anything that was too heavy was dumped on the side of the trail. Some were brand new while others had been there for several years. At that moment, John wished he'd allowed Elizabeth to keep the damn tea set. He grabbed a faded book and threw it as hard as he could then fell to his knees and covered his dust covered face. *God, please, don't take her... I can't lose her.*

∞ ∞ ∞

After hours of searching, Lucas finally found it. "John is this it?" he yelled.

John ran over to his side when Lucas pulled the chest out from under the bush. It was beautifully carved with a monogram of a C on the lid.

"Yeah, that's it." He smiled at his friend and patted him on the back. *This just might work.*

John fell to his knees and gently lifted the lid. Moving the straw, he gazed at the beautiful tea set that belonged to Elizabeth's mother. He picked up a cup and grinned. It was white with pink roses and ivy, the handle swirled with intricate detail. Tears welled in his eyes as he held the delicate cup in his big hands. He usually wasn't this sentimental, but there was something about her that brought all his emotions to the surface. He gently placed the cup back in the chest; everything perfectly preserved.

"I've got to get this back to Elizabeth, but how?" he questioned, more to himself than Lucas.

"You can't, the chest is too big." Lucas said, squatting next to John.

John rubbed his chin in thought then snapped his fingers, stood, and went to Joy. He grabbed his saddle bag and walked back over to the chest. He took off his jacket then his shirt. Kneeling in front of the chest, he picked up a cup, a saucer, and a plate.

"Wait." Lucas pulled his buckskin shirt from his saddle bag and handed it to his friend. "It will be softer than your jacket."

John nodded and carefully wrapped the porcelain teacup, plate, and saucer in both shirts. They clinked together when he gently placed them in his saddle bag. He took the straw and stuffed it all around the bundle. Putting his jacket back on, he secured the bag on the back of his saddle then closed the lid of the chest and shoved it back under the bush. *Maybe someday I'll come back and get the rest.*

"Can I do anything?" Lucas asked as he stood watching his friend.

"No, you've done enough." He mounted his horse and waited for Lucas to get on his pinto. John kicked Joy and they rode back up Big Hill.

∞ ∞ ∞

Lucas spotted the wagon train near Fort Hall, an old trading post near the Snake River. They rode hard, getting to the circle of wagons just after sunset. As they approached, John prayed Elizabeth was still alive. The trip had taken over a week. He was so tired, his nerves throbbed. Besides Elizabeth, all he wanted to see was his bedroll.

"Hey, everybody, John's back!" Jed called as John hopped off his horse and tied it to Buck's wagon. Jed embrace his brother. "Good to see you."

"Elizabeth, is she alive?" John grabbed him by the shoulders, shaking him gently.

"Yeah, but she's bad off. Doc says she has a bad fever and she's still delusional. I'm sorry, John, Doc doesn't give her much hope." Jed frowned, shaking his head.

The thought froze in John's brain. He went to his saddle bag and took it off Joy, carrying it to Doc's wagon. Dr. Grant was sitting on a stool smoking a pipe when John walked up to him.

"John, where the hell have you been?" Doc put his pipe down and looked sadly into John's eyes. "You need to be with her... she doesn't have much time left. I'm sorry, son, I did all I could." He patted John's arm.

Chapter Twenty-One

John climbed quietly into the wagon and sat next to Elizabeth. She was so pale and covered in sweat. He smoothed back her ebony hair and kissed her hot forehead.

"Beth? Can you hear me?" he asked in a flat, monotone voice. Taking her hand, he gently brushed his lips against her knuckles.

She tossed her head. "Mother... Mother, help me. John, where are you?" she called.

John grabbed his saddle bag and pulled out the bundle. He unwrapped it, picked up the teacup and placed it in her hand. "Your mother's here, Beth. She's here." He covered her hand and the cup with his.

She looked so battered and broken. His heart fell as he looked at her. He leaned over and put his forehead against hers. "Please let her be alright. I need her... I love her," he whispered, kissing her swollen lips. Slouching, he covered his face with his big hands, deep sobs racked his body, his eyes were bordered with tears. He rubbed a fist over his chest and the ache that seemed permanently lodged there.

Idly, he wondered if it would ever go away or if this pain in his heart would hurt for the rest of his life.

He felt achy and exhausted; his heart longing for a reason to beat. Not sleeping in nearly a week, he laid down next to her, placed his arm over her abdomen and fell asleep.

∞ ∞ ∞

John awoke to the sound of talking, laughter and cooking. He slowly opened his eyes and stretched, his back cracking in several places. He gazed up at the bonnet, the sun shining through a small tear. Sitting up, he gazed at Elizabeth laying there, the cup had fallen in the crook of her arm; she was still black and blue. He felt her forehead and smiled, he was blissfully happy, fully alive as he leaped out of the wagon.

"Doc. Doc, come quick," John shouted, his mood was suddenly buoyant.

Dr. Grant sat near his fire, sipping a cup of coffee. He jumped, spilling his cup when John leaped from the wagon shouting. Doc stood up and stepped over to John.

"What's wrong?" he asked worriedly, grabbing John's arm.

The members of the wagon train gathered around Doc's wagon. Abigail pushed her way through the crowd, hand over her mouth. She shook her head and started to cry.

"No. No, it can't be. Please, God no." Abigail hugged herself. Jesse stood behind her, rubbing her shoulders.

John stepped aside as Doc climbed into the wagon. He pulled back the canvas and looked in and watched as Doc examined Elizabeth. Jed, Lucas, and Aengus came over, standing next to John. Everyone talked among themselves, not wanting to hear the answer to John's panic.

"John, what's going on?" Jed asked, leaning on one leg, thumbs in his gun belt.

Doc stepped out of the wagon and looked up at John. "I don't understand it, there's no fever. There must be some logical explanation for this." He walked over to the fire and picked up his pipe, cleaning out the embers.

"What are you saying?" John asked, grabbing the doctor by the shoulders. He stood there, blank, amazed, and very shaken.

"She's going to be fine, she's just sleeping." He smiled, patting John's arms. "She'll have to take it easy for a while, but she's gonna live."

John couldn't contain himself, he picked up Dr. Grant and hugged him. Putting him down, he laughed then hugged his brother, slapping him on the back.

"Thank God," John said, walking toward Buck's wagon.

"Where you going?" Jed asked, following him.

"Gonna get cleaned up. Can't have Beth seeing me like this." He rummaged through the wagon, finding some soap, a towel, and a clean shirt. Jed heard him whistling all the way to the river.

∞ ∞ ∞

Elizabeth heard talking, sounding far away, like a dream. Her shoulder was in excruciating pain and her face felt swollen and tight. She couldn't move for fear it would make the pain worse. Laying there, she kept her eyes closed and just listened to the voices all around her.

"Beth," she heard, whispered in her ear. "Beth, open those beautiful eyes."

She felt something hard and cold in her hand. Moving her fingers over it, she slowly opened her eyes, one almost swollen shut, and saw John smiling down at her.

"John." She tried to speak, but her throat was swollen and dry.

She watched him grab a canteen and put it to her chapped lips. The cool water ran down her throat and brought life back to her ailing, battered body.

"Hi." He smiled at her, setting the canteen aside. "How do you feel?"

"I hurt, John," she whispered, a tear ran down her cheek.

He smoothed her hair and gazed at her sadly. "I know, Sweetheart."

"John, what happened? Where's Billy Ray?" her voice choked. Startled at her own voice, she glanced up at him. Her lips were so swollen, she couldn't help, but slur her words.

"He's dead," he divulged. "He attacked you, so I shot him." He gently stroked the side of her face, his thumb brushed lightly over her eyebrow.

"John, what's in my hand?" she asked, feeling the object.

"You were delirious and kept calling for your mother, so I brought her to you." He smiled down at her, while smoothing her hair.

She looked at him inquisitively as he took the object from her hand and held it up for her to see. There, sitting in the palm of his large hand was her mother's teacup.

"Oh, John." She reached out and touched the cup. Tears slowly found their way down her cheeks. She looked in his brown eyes and smiled. "You went back for my mother's tea set?"

"Well not all, I'm afraid. I'm sorry, the chest was too big. I could only bring back a cup, a saucer and a plate."

"John," she reached out and touched his jaw, "I can't believe you did this for me." She began but winced as pain shot through her shoulder.

"Beth?" He put the cup down and took her hands in his. "I'll get Dr. Grant." He turned to leave.

"Please, don't leave me." She squeezed his hands. "Stay."

He sat back down and gently ran his fingers through her hair, knowing that was the only area that didn't hurt. She looked at him, his presence brought her joy. His eyes were blood shot and dark circles had formed under them. He looked exhausted, to near collapsing. He kissed her knuckles and each fingertip.

"You scared me, you know that?" John testified. "When I thought I had lost you... Don't ever do that to me again." He demanded, a silken thread of warning in his voice.

"Why did you go back for the tea set?" She grit her teeth as more pain attacked her shoulder. She closed her eyes tightly until the pain faded.

"I just felt you needed it." He watched her shake her head. "You were calling for your..."

"John, why... why did you do it?" Her heart beat faster and there was fluttering in her stomach as she gazed at him.

He leaned close to her and brushed his lips against hers, taking care not to hurt her. "I'm in love with you, that's why." He put his forehead against hers.

She felt transported on a soft and wispy cloud. She sighed and closed her eyes. A smile crossed her lips as warmth flooded her body.

Chapter Twenty-Two

Elizabeth awoke to the rocking of the wagon. She opened her eyes and watched the bonnet moving to and fro. She was in Doc's wagon, but where was hers and who was driving it? When she tried to sit up, the pain in her shoulder shot through her causing her to shutter and lay back down. The movement made her sick, she wasn't sure she could keep from retching. She didn't know how long they had been traveling or how late it was. She prayed they would be stopping soon, the motion was upsetting her stomach and causing pain to shudder through her shoulder. While she closed her eyes, she thought of her parents and their tea shop.

Her breath grew shallow as the echo of her mother's cries, both their cries, repeated in her memory.

But it did no good to dwell on such things at present.

What she wouldn't give to turn back time and to the safe, sheltered confines of her world before the fire and the death of her parents.

The last thing she saw before sleep claimed her was the fire whooshing in the doorframe, her mother on the other side.

∞ ∞ ∞

When she awoke again, the wagon had stopped, and the sun was setting. She looked around but saw no one around. She heard talking and laughter just outside the wagon.

"Hello?" She called, her throat dry and raspy. She reached up and touched her neck, it was so sore.

Doc peeked in and smiled. "You're awake. Good. Are you hungry?" he asked.

She nodded, watching him speak to someone on the other side of the canvas. He faced her again.

"Abigail is fetching you some dinner." He climbed in the wagon. "Now, let's see how we're doing." He felt her forehead and pulled back part of her nightgown, lifted the padding and glanced at the wound. "Looks good. After you eat, we'll take you over to your wagon, so you can get cleaned up and change into another nightgown."

He put an arm around her and helped her to sit up. Her head started spinning and she thought she might fall over. After a few moments, she could sit without tipping.

"Where's John?" she asked pulling the blanket over her legs.

"Around. When I see him, I'll let him know you're awake. For now, just rest," he said, lighting a lantern and hopped out of the wagon.

Abigail brought her dinner. She sat the plate and cup next to her, tears welling in her eyes. "Oh Elizabeth, I'm so glad you'll be alright. For a while there, we thought we had lost you."

Elizabeth took her hand and squeezed it. She smiled at her friend as she stepped out of the wagon. She picked up the plate and started eating but stopped when she heard an argument near her wagon. She recognized their voices.

"John, you can't seriously be thinking of still being with her," Jed said, a touch of distaste in his voice.

"Jed, you're stepping over the line." John fumed.

"She's damaged goods, John. How can you be with her after what happened?" Jed's voice rose.

Suddenly, she heard fighting and scuffling, punches being thrown and bodies hitting the ground. Someone was smashed against the wagon, causing it to rock back and forth. She could hear grunting and cursing. After a few moments, more voices arrived as John and Jed were separated.

"Break it up, you two." She heard Lucas say.

"If you ever say anything like that again, Jed, I'll kill you," John growled, his voice was cold and exact.

"Hey, none o' that, you two dunderheids!" Aengus shouted.

"Yeah, well at least I'm not in love with a whore!" Jed yelled. "She asked for what happened to her. Why do you think she stayed behind?"

There was more scuffling as the two men attempted to resume their fight.

"Aengus take Jed to the river and cool him down. John come with me," Lucas said.

"Take him and while you're at it, drown him!" John called. She heard footsteps coming to the back of the wagon.

"What is wrong with you? Jed's your brother." Lucas asked.

"Not anymore!" He fumed.

"John, no matter how angry you are right now, he's still your brother. He's the only family you've got," Lucas said.

All was quiet as Elizabeth listen to the two. She quietly finished her dinner, not giving any inclination, she was awake. She knew John needed Lucas' advice.

"I know, but what he said about Beth…," his voice trailed away.

Doc came over to his wagon, puffing his pipe. "John, Elizabeth's awake. She's eating dinner and later we can move her to her own wagon."

"Shit. How long has she been awake?" John spoke in a suffocated whisper.

"Um, about an hour. She's looking much better," Doc's voice sounded cheerful.

John's, on the other hand, sounded nervous and guilt ridden. "She heard everything. She heard what Jed called her. Damn it." She listened to him take a deep breath and pulled the canvas aside, peeked in and gave her a weak smile. "May I come in?"

She nodded, setting the plate aside and pulled the blanket farther up her chest. The wagon shifted from side to side as his big frame entered the wagon and sat down.

"I guess you heard." He looked down at his boots, his elbows resting on his bent knees.

"It was hard not to," she said sadly. She looked at her hands laying on her lap. "Does he really think that?" She tried not to cry. How could Jed say those things about her? He was so nice to her in the beginning of the trip. She was totally bewildered at his behavior.

He nodded his head. "Yeah, afraid so." He placed his hand over hers. "He may be twenty-five, but he's not as mature as he thinks, he's still just a boy."

"I feel so ashamed. Like I'm a different person." A war of emotions raged within her. "I don't remember much of what happened, only that I hurt all over." She sniffed.

"Beth, it'll be okay. It's just going to take some time." He reached out to touch her face, but she pulled away, a flicker of apprehension coursed through her.

Her eyes widened. "I'm sorry." She started to cry. She wanted John to touch her, but was so ashamed, her body was no longer her own. "Oh, John." She put her hands over her face.

"Beth, it's alright. Shh." He took her hands and held them. "You'll be alright."

"I don't know if I'll ever be right again." She looked at her lap. "You don't deserve me, John. You deserve better. Your brother's right."

"No, he's not and neither are you. This will pass, and you and I are going to be together. I promise," he said, gripping her hands.

She swallowed with difficulty and found her voice. "I'm rather tired."

"I'll leave you, then." He went to touch her but withdrew. Instead, he left the wagon.

When she had stripped off her nightgown to put another on, she'd been appalled to see the results of what Billy Ray had done to her, her skin had nearly as many shades as a rainbow. But there was nothing for it except to let time heal her wounds. Elizabeth gently laid down in her wagon and watched the lantern flicker, the nagging in the back of her mind refused to be still. She closed her eyes and fell into a dreamless sleep.

Chapter Twenty-Three

Four weeks of rough lava terrain and extremely dry climate, they arrived at Salmon Falls. John loved it here. The falls were surrounded by miles of lush pines, ferns, and moss. He knew he was getting close to home and it made him happy. Lucas found an area near the falls for the wagons to circle. For the past few weeks, Elizabeth lay in the back of her wagon while Aengus drove. Her physical wounds were healing, but the mental scar Billy Ray gave her still flared. John shared pleasantries with her and seemed to be getting closer, but she still felt ashamed and not worthy of his love. Jed wasn't helping either. Whenever John would help her over to Buck's wagon, Jed would leave without so much as a word.

After the wagons parked, John made his way around the camp. Everyone was doing well, even Rachel. She loved her new family and was fitting right in. He walked over to Elizabeth's wagon and spotted Doc stepping away.

"Doc, how's she doing?" John asked, leaning on one leg and crossed his arms.

"Physically, she's fine. The stab wound has scabbed over, and she can remove the bandages by tomorrow." Doc smiled half-heartedly. "But her mental state hasn't changed."

John nodded and thanked the doctor, walked over to the wagon, and knocked on the wood. "Beth, it's me." He pulled the canvas aside and looked in.

Since the attack, he was yet to see her truly smile or laugh. And even a more terrifying realization washed over him, she may never be the same again. The damage Billy Ray had done to her, might be permanent.

"Hello." She gave him a little smile. He helped her out of the wagon, took her hand and walked to the falls.

They strolled through the forest to the river. Once there, he took her to a big, fallen tree and they sat quietly listening to the sounds of the woods.

"It's so beautiful, John. Is this what Oregon looks like?" she asked looking around at all the trees.

"Yes. Beth, why don't you talk about your dream anymore, the tea shop you want to have some day. You were so happy talking about opening it. The shop might do you some good." He held her hand, stroking it with his thumb.

Tears welled in her eyes. "It was just a dream, John, nothing more." She looked away and gazed at the falls.

"Beth, dreams do come true. You can still have your tea shop. Do you hear me?" he asked, placing his finger under her chin, and forcing her to look at him.

"I hear you. I just don't believe you. Why would anyone buy tea from me after what happened? The only thing I'm good for these days is being a saloon girl. Maybe the Callahan brothers would hire me for their saloon in Oregon City." She closed her eyes, her misery was so acute that it was a physical pain.

"Stop!" He grabbed her hands and squeezed them. "You're better than this, Beth. Yes, you were attacked by a horrible person, but he's dead and in time you will get over this. So, for now, let's just get to Oregon then we'll see what happens next." He leaned in close to her.

She nodded, fright gleaming in her eyes. He slowly ran his fingers along her jaw. The bruises were starting to turn a yellowish brown. She tried not to pull away. He could see her shaking and wanting to bolt, but she remained still.

"I'm afraid." she whispered, gazing down at her lap.

"Of me? You weren't afraid before," he said, continuing to caress her jaw. He picked up her hand and kissed it.

"I know," she replied, her lower lip quivered as his lips touched her.

"Do you think I'll hurt you?" he asked.

"No," she responded, slowly shaking her head.

"Then trust me." He leaned close and kissed her forehead, her cheek then her lips. It was a kiss as tender and light as a summer breeze. While kissing her, her thoughts went to the attack and suddenly she saw Billy Ray instead of John.

She pulled away from him. "I'm sorry, I can't do this." She rose, covered her mouth, and ran back to the encampment.

"Elizabeth, wait." He stood up and watched her leave. "Dammit." He took his hat off and hit his thigh.

∞ ∞ ∞

Elizabeth ran into the encampment crying, making her way to her wagon. Abigail and Anna noticed her and hurried over to her.

"Honey, what's wrong?" Abigail grabbed her by the arm and spun her around.

Elizabeth hugged her, burying her face in her shoulder. She cried even harder while Abigail rubbed her back. Anna smoothed Elizabeth's hair and cooed to her until she calmed down.

"Tell us, Elizabeth. What's the matter?" Abigail asked.

"Ya, do tell," Anna said, giving her a handkerchief.

Elizabeth dabbed her eyes and wiped her nose. "I can't love John. Every time he tries to get close, I see Billy Ray and I push John away. I feel so ashamed." She put her hands over her face and cried, a sensation of intense sickness and desolation swept over her.

"Elizabeth, my child, you will learn to love again. I know you will," said Anna with a smile. "Do you know how I know? Because I was assaulted when I was your age. I thought I could never love another man and then my Oscar came along. With a little time and patience, we were married and have four children. It will happen, child, and if he loves you, he'll wait."

Elizabeth sniffed and wiped away her tears. "You were attacked?" she asked.

Anna nodded as they stared at her, their expression was like someone who had been struck in the face. "Does your husband know?" Abigail asked.

"Of course," she said. "We have no secrets."

"Elizabeth, let me fix you a cup of tea." Abigail said. She nodded and told her where her tea supplies were.

The women ambled over to Abigail's fire and took seats. A few minutes later, Elizabeth was enjoying a hot cup of tea. She took a sip, spotting John entering the camp. He started to walk toward her but stopped and retreated to Buck's wagon. Her lower lip trembled, watching him take a plate of food and sat with his back to her.

Elizabeth finished her tea and with a heavy sigh thanked the ladies and went back to her wagon. She climbed in, undressed, and slipped on a nightgown, crawled into her bedroll, and pulled the blanket up to her chin.

"John," she whispered, "I'm so sorry." She curled her body and cried herself to sleep.

∞ ∞ ∞

The next morning John, Lucas and several of the men went to the falls to fish. Huge Chinook salmon and Steelhead trout were being pulled from the river. While the men fished, Anna, Abigail, Elizabeth, and Bridget with Rachel in tow, went down stream to do the laundry.

John watched Elizabeth carefully walk down to the shore. She sat on a large rock and slowly washed her clothes. He knew her shoulder was still painful. He wanted to march over there, grab her, and kiss her until she melted into his arms, but he had to give her space. He couldn't deny the evidence any longer, after last night, he knew he would have to take it slow with her.

"John, pay attention. You got a bite," said Lucas, smacking him on the arm.

He set the hook and pulled in a large salmon. It jumped around on the bank until John took his knife and stabbed its head. He tossed the dead fish with the others on the bank and sat on a large rock, his elbows on his thighs. He stared at the river, his mind wasn't on fishing, it was on the women laughing and talking, even Elizabeth seemed to be enjoying herself.

"John, what's got into you?" Lucas asked, hitting him again.

"Nothing. It's just Elizabeth. Ever since the attack, she won't let me get close to her," John said, scratching his beard.

"Do you blame her? Billy Ray almost killed her," Lucas said. "Give it some time, she'll come around."

"Maybe." He looked back at her, playing with Rachel. The little girl splashed Elizabeth, who blocked it with her hands then reached out and grabbed the child, tickling her while she squealed.

"I love her, Lucas. Damn me, I do." John shook his head, looking up at his friend.

Lucas patted him on his shoulder. "If she feels the same way about you, then things will work out."

John watched Elizabeth gather her laundry and walked back to the encampment. He stood up and followed her. She was struggling with the basket, nearly dropping her clean clothes.

"Beth, wait," he called after her. She stopped and turned her head toward him. He marched up to her. "Here, let me help you." He took the basket of damp clothes and strolled alongside her.

"Thank you," she said looking up at him. "John, I'm sorry about last night." She gazed down at the ground.

"It's alright, Beth. I understand." He placed the bundle on the tailgate of her wagon. "Maybe it's for the best." He tucked a piece of hair behind her ear, smiled and stepped away.

John gritted his teeth and walked over to Buck's wagon. He needed her in his arms and keeping away from her was killing him. From the very start, something about Elizabeth had called to him, reawakening a host of emotions and impulses he'd thought were dead. In the virtual blink of an eye, this one young woman had caused him to change not only his mind, but all his carefully laid plans in order to see to her needs, her safety. He poured himself a cup of coffee and sat on a log. Jed stepped up to John and took a seat next to him.

"Jed, I'm not in the mood," John said, drinking his coffee. His temper when crossed could be almost uncontrollable.

"John, she's not right for you. She may have been before…" Jed began.

"Before the attack. Say it, Jed. Before she was raped." He shook his head. "I never thought my little brother would turn out to be a real asshole. She didn't ask to be attacked, Jed. It wasn't her fault."

"Maybe not, but what man would want her now?" Jed stood with his arms crossed.

"This man." He sneered and pointed to himself. He finished his coffee, stood up and sat the cup on the tailgate. He glared at his brother and walked back to the river.

Chapter Twenty-Four

That evening everyone was enjoying salmon and trout for dinner. Elizabeth sat with Abigail and Jessie. Sipping her tea, she wrapped her blanket tighter around her shoulders. Bridget was playing with Rachel while Shamus and Jesse puffed on their pipes.

"Did you get enough to eat, Elizabeth?" Abigail asked, clearing away the plates.

"Yes, thank you. It was wonderful. Do you need any help?" she asked, starting to rise.

"No, I'll do them later. Right now, I thought we'd talk awhile. Tell me about John. How's he holding up?" she said, sitting next to her, wrapping her plaid shawl around her shoulders. The nights were growing cooler.

"He's trying to be so supportive, but I know deep down, this is killing him." Elizabeth shook her head as tears welled in her eyes. "Oh Abigail, I love him, but I can't. Every time he holds me or kisses me, I see Billy Ray Cobb. I don't know how to get him out of my head." She covered her face with her hands.

"Elizabeth that Cobb fellow is dead. John killed him. He'll never hurt you again and John won't let anyone hurt you ever." She took her hands and squeezed them. "What are you afraid of? Why won't you let John in?" Abigail touched Elizabeth's cheek.

She smiled weakly as her friend tucked some hair behind her ear. "I know you're right. I know I should just push it aside, but it's so difficult. I would give anything to have John take me in his arms, but..."

"Goats butt. Go tell John you want to talk to him and let nature take its course," she said, lifting her eyebrows and winking at her.

"Abigail!" Shocked at what her friend just stated.

They both started laughing when Abigail suddenly grabbed her stomach and nearly fell off the log she and Elizabeth were sitting on.

"Oh God! Elizabeth, my water broke." Abigail panicked, taking her hand, and squeezing it.

Jessie stood up and grabbed his wife before she fell over. Abigail bent, holding her stomach as another contraction hit her.

"Shamus, go get Doc. Go." Jessie yelled as he held her close.

"We need to put her in the back of your wagon. I'll be right back." Elizabeth picked up her skirt and ran as fast as she could over to Buck's wagon, panic overtaking her every thought. She spotted John telling Lucas and Aengus a dirty joke.

"And then he said, 'Surprise, that wasn't my finger.'" Lucas and Aengus let out a bellowing laugh when John spotted Elizabeth racing up to them. He jumped up and grabbed her arms when he saw the look of fear on her face. "Beth, what's wrong?"

"Abigail… she's in labor. We need you, Lucas and Aengus to move stuff out of Jessie's wagon so Doc has room to work," Elizabeth said, her voice cracking.

"Come on men, let's get to work." John and his crew ran over to the wagon, Elizabeth at their heels. When she got there, she saw Abigail hunched over in severe pain.

After about an hour, Abigail lay in the back of the wagon, dressed in a nightgown, breathing heavily. Dr. Grant sat on one side, Elizabeth on the other. Abigail insisted she stay, wanting a friendly face she could count on.

"Thank you, Elizabeth. I need… Oh…" She squeezed Elizabeth's hand.

She took a cool towel and placed it on Abigail's forehead. "Shh, just breath."

Doc lifted Abigail's nightgown and checked her. "She's beginning to crown. Abigail honey, it's time to push. I need you to bare down and push. Elizabeth, get behind her and help her."

She sat behind Abigail and straddled her, lifting her up so her head rested against her chest. "Abby, push. I'm right here." Elizabeth gently pushed her forward while Abigail bared down.

She let out a scream as she pushed. Tears streamed down her face as the baby's head started crowning. "God help me. Elizabeth, oh it hurts. Get it out," she screamed again.

Elizabeth placed another cool rag on Abigail's forehead, wiping away the sweat. She couldn't believe it, she was witnessing the miracle of life. She smoothed her friend's wet hair and rubbed her shoulders while Abigail waited for another contraction. Elizabeth was so happy for her friend, but wished she weren't in so much pain.

"It will be over soon. Tell me the baby's name." Elizabeth dabbed the sweat off Abigail's cheeks.

"If a boy, Jessie." She said through gritted teeth. "If a girl, I want Clementine." She tossed her head in pain and grabbed Elizabeth's hand, held her breath and pushed.

"Breath Abigail. That's right. You're doing great. I'm so proud of you." Elizabeth leaned over and kissed her friend's forehead. Doc pulled the nightgown up, so he could see the baby's progression. Elizabeth looked at Doc and smiled. Everything was going as planned.

∞ ∞ ∞

John grabbed Jessie when he tried to climb into the wagon. They heard Abigail scream.

"Whoa there, Jess, let Doc do his work. Lucas go get a bottle of whiskey, I think Jess here needs a stiff one," John said forcing Jessie to sit.

Lucas got up and made his way to Buck's wagon while John patted Jessie on the shoulder. A few minutes later, Lucas popped the cork and handed it to Jessie. He took several swigs, sitting with his elbows on his knees. He heard Abigail scream again and looked into John's eyes.

"I hate how much pain she's in. I wish she could just have the baby and be done with it," Jesse drawled, taking another swig.

She screamed again, and Jessie stood up and started to pace in front of the campfire. "I can't stand it. Make it stop." Jessie tried to cover his ears.

"Jessie, it's a part of life. It'll be over soon. Have patience," John said with a smile. He took the bottle from him and took a sip.

"John, she's in so much pain. And there's nothing I can do to help her." He sat back down and rested his elbows on his knees and stared at the ground.

John nodded and took another sip. "I know, Jess. But just think, in a little while, you'll be holding your son or daughter. You're a very lucky man."

Jessie gazed at John and smiled. "You know, you could be standing in my shoes in a year or so, if you would just take Elizabeth to wife."

"Right now, let's think about Abigail and the baby," John said, taking a long swig. He loved Elizabeth, but did he love her enough to marry her or even father a child with her? *Am I even father material?*

Several hours passed and everyone in the encampment walked on eggshells. They went about their chores but kept an eye on the wagon. John and Jessie sat near the fire drinking coffee, the empty whiskey bottle long forgotten.

"What's taking so long?" Jesse asked, standing up and shoving his hands in his pockets.

"Jess calm down. Doc would have told us if something was wrong." He looked at the wagon. He, too, was getting worried but couldn't tell Jessie that.

John sipped his coffee, staring at the fire. Elizabeth was still in the wagon lending a hand. He was so proud of her. As he sat there, he noticed how quiet it had become. Darkness had fallen, and the only sound was the crackling of the fire and the wind blowing through the trees. Abigail had stopped screaming. He gazed at the wagon, fear gripping his chest. He hoped, for Jessie's sake, everything was alright.

Suddenly he heard a baby cry. Jessie and John stood up and stepped over to the wagon. The canvas flap of the wagon was pulled, and Elizabeth emerge holding a little bundle.

"Jessie, come meet your daughter," Elizabeth said, gently patting the baby's bottom. The little head was covered in thick blonde hair.

He looked at John and smiled then rubbed his hands on his jeans and held out his arms.

"Mind her head," Elizabeth said placing the baby in his arms.

"Abigail? Is she…." Jessie asked.

"She's just fine. She did great." Elizabeth grinned as she watched Jessie coo to the baby. He slowly rocked his arms, looking at his baby daughter. He walked over to John, so he could take a peek. John moved the blanket and touched the baby's hand and she responded by clutching his large finger.

"She has a good grip," He moved his finger up and down.

"Alright, Papa, let me take her back to her mother." Elizabeth took the baby and laid her gently in the crook of her arm.

John walked up to her. She had never looked lovelier then she did right now. Part of her hair had fallen out of the bun, she had dark circles under her eyes, and she looked completely wiped out, but her, standing there holding that baby, she was an angel.

She smiled up at him, then, with his help, climbed back into the wagon.

"She's beautiful, isn't she?" Jessie said, looking at his hands.

"She sure is," John said watching Elizabeth disappear behind the flap.

About an hour later, Doc and Elizabeth emerged from the wagon. Doc stood, cracking his back, and rubbing the back of his neck. Elizabeth wiped her brow with her sleeve.

"Jessie, you can go see Abigail and the little one now." Doc poured himself a cup of coffee and stretched again.

"I don't know how to thank you, Doc. I'm so glad you were here to help Abigail and the baby." He took Doc's hand and shook it.

"My pleasure, Jessie." Doc took a sip of his coffee.

Jessie hopped in the wagon, it shifted from side to side. John looked over at Elizabeth as she swayed to and fro, her eyes barely open. He nodded to Doc and put an arm around her shoulders, leading her to her wagon.

"You look exhausted," John said, they strolled along the edge of the campsite.

Elizabeth smiled up at him. "Abigail wants to name her Clementine. Most beautiful baby I've ever seen."

John pulled the blanket aside and helped her into the wagon. "Get some sleep, we'll start back on the trail tomorrow."

"Thank you." She smiled, and he dropped the blanket in place.

John walked over to Buck's wagon. Sitting near the campfire, he poured himself a cup of coffee. He ran his fingers through his hair and yawned.

"It's been a long day," Buck said fixing John a plate. He handed it to him then wiped his hands on a towel.

"Yeah, it has." John sat the plate down on the ground and rubbed his eyes.

"Eat up, boy. That there is the best Chinook ever cooked," said Buck, pointing to the fish cooking over the fire. The whole camp was busy finishing their dinners and working on their chores. News of the birth spread like wildfire, and many gathered around Jessie's wagon offering their congratulations.

John smiled, ate his dinner, and handed Buck back the plate. "You can be a real son-of-a-bitch, you know that?" He stood up, cracked his back and waved goodnight, then went to his bedroll near a fallen log. Before he fell asleep, his mind drifted off to Elizabeth holding the baby in her arms and a smile curled his lips.

Chapter Twenty-Five

Elizabeth awoke with a fright. She didn't know if it was a dream or a sound from outside. She sat up in her bedroll and listened. Except for a few crickets, all was quiet. She pushed the blanket aside, noticing it was still dark and climbed out of the wagon, stepping silently into the woods to relieve herself. She just returned to camp, when she heard something move in the woods near the Mulligan wagon. She slowly made her way across the encampment, when a big grizzly bear walked out of the woods. She stopped, frozen in her tracks. Her teeth chattered, her legs shook, and her body told her to run, but her mind said to stay put.

The bear wandered around the wagon sniffing the air. Elizabeth looked to her right and spotted John sleeping about twenty feet from where she stood. The bear started pawing at the side of the wagon, so she dropped to her knees, slowly crawling over to him. Without thinking, she put her hand over his mouth.

"John," she whispered. Suddenly she found herself on her back with him on top of her and a gun pointed at her head.

"Beth, I could have killed you," he said, pulling the gun away.

She put her fingers against his lips. "Shh." Her frightened eyes stared up at him.

He smiled at her, bent down, and whispered against her lips, "I've missed you." He cupped her head and pulled the yellow ribbon, undoing her nightgown.

She placed her hands on his bare chest and turned her head away. "John, bear." Her eyes grew large, and she stared at the animal. It was starting to tear at the wagon.

John followed Elizabeth's gaze, his lips brushing against her cheek. "Oh, Shit," he whispered and rolled off her. "Get behind this log and stay down."

John slipped into the woods and made his way to Lucas' bedroll near Buck's wagon. She watched him sneak up to his friend and give out a bird call. Lucas sat up and gazed around him, seeing John nearby. He suddenly saw the bear make its way to the back of the Mulligan wagon. Lucas crawled out of his bedroll and over to his saddle where he kept his rifle. John crept up beside his friend and spoke in muffled tones. Elizabeth couldn't hear what they were saying, but knew they were discussing what to do next.

"Hey, what the hell's going on?" Robert Mulligan stuck his head out of his wagon. The grizzly reared up on its hind legs and let out a roar; saliva dripping from its mouth. It swiped at Robert, knocking the man out of the wagon.

When it roared again, the camp began to wake. People looked out to see the giant bear growling and roaring. As Robert lay there, Elizabeth didn't know if he were alive or dead. John and Lucas ran to the middle of the encampment as the grizzly went down on all fours and began to maul Robert. The bear bit and swiped at him and he began screaming. Elizabeth could hear Mulligan's bones shatter as the grizzly's teeth crunched down on him. She turned away as the bear took Robert's head in its mouth and crushed it like a walnut.

"Hey, over here!" John waved his arms and whistled.

Lucas knelt on one knee while the bear snarled, blood covering its muzzle, and started walking toward John. It shook its massive head side to side, growling while making its way toward the big man. Its black eyes piercing, and its giant paws crossed the ground, ready to tear John apart. Elizabeth bit her knuckle as she watched it terror as the grizzly reared up and roared, standing to its full height. She watched John distract the animal, at the same time Lucas aimed his Sharp rifle and fired. The explosion echoed though the camp and the fire that shot out of the barrel, lit up Lucas' face. The bear stumbled back and fell on its side with a loud thud.

Elizabeth watched it take its last breath and closed its eyes.

She ran from behind the log into John's arms. Aengus, Jed, and Buck walked over to the bear.

"Boy, he could have killed you!" Buck scolded and kicked the carcass.

Doc jumped out of his wagon and ran over to Robert. John followed, signaling Elizabeth to stay put. The men kneeled and looked at each other. John gazed at Elizabeth and shook his head. She covered her mouth, terror filled her eyes.

"Why did it come into camp in the first place?" Jed asked.

John stood and stepped to the back of the wagon. He looked around and found dried blood and fish remains on the tailgate. He stood there shaking his head. "That damn fool. He led the bear right in."

"What do ye mean?" Aengus asked marching over to John. His hand was no longer sore, but several of his fingers were permanently crooked.

"I told all the men to clean their fish down by the river. Mulligan didn't listen. The back of the wagon is covered in blood and fish guts. The smell led the bear right in." John said crossing his arms.

Elizabeth started to walk toward John when he shook his head. He reached in the wagon, grabbed a blanket, and threw it over Robert's body. He stepped away from the gruesome sight and walked over to her.

"Lucas, Aengus, Jed, take the bear into the woods. Lucas," he stopped in front of him and slapped his friend on the back, "thanks. I thought I was a dead man."

"Do you want the meat?" Lucas asked. John nodded and took Elizabeth back to her wagon.

"I can't thank you enough, Beth. You saved the camp." He rubbed her shoulders.

"I didn't save Mr. Mulligan," she said sadly, looking at the covered body.

"No, you're right. But if he had heeded my warning, the bear would never have come into the camp." He tucked a strand of her hair behind her ear.

"John, I..." She looked deep into his eyes. She wanted so much to feel his body pressed against her. Her lips quivered at the thought of his mouth on hers. She wanted him in every way possible, but she didn't dare, not after what happened with Billy Ray. "Thank you for saving my life." She started to turn.

"Beth, don't push me away." He grabbed her arms.

"John, please, don't do this. I'm not good for you. Forget about me." She tried to pull out of his grip.

"Never." His fingers tightened. "I love you."

"Let me go!" She pulled away from him and climbed into her wagon, laid down and cried herself to sleep.

∞ ∞ ∞

As John stood there listening to her crying, he clenched his fists wishing Cobb were still alive, so he could kill him with his bare hands. Anna walked up to John and looked up at him.

"Mr. Evans don't give up, she'll come around. She loves you," she said, placing a hand on his arm.

He nodded and walked away toward Buck's wagon. Grabbing his knife, he stomped off into the woods. He couldn't kill Cobb, but he could take his frustrations out on the bear. Tomorrow he'd help Lucas make jerky out of the meat and tan the hide. They were going to leave, but with the new birth and the bear attack, John felt that maybe one more day near Salmon Falls wouldn't hurt.

Early the next morning, before anyone was awake, John had made his way to the falls to wash the blood and smell of bear off him. He stood, waist deep, under the falls, the water rushing over his naked body. He ran his fingers through his hair then stepped out, only to see Elizabeth hang her towel on a branch. Her back was to him, and she pulled the pins from her hair, letting her hair fall in gentle waves over her shoulders and down her back. He licked his lips when her nightgown fell to the ground in a pile around her feet. His body throbbed, and he watched her step into the cool water.

Her body shone in the early dawn. She had a slim, wild beauty and her fine hips and shapely thighs waded through the water. She ran her hands up her stomach and across her plump breasts causing the nipples to harden. Reaching down, she cupped the water, bringing it to her throat and letting it run down her body. She obviously thought she was alone. *Did all women bathe like this*? he thought. He watched the cool water drip from her nipples then leaned her head back and closed her eyes. She ran her hand up her inner thigh, when suddenly she stopped and looked around. *Could she hear my heavy breathing*? Her head turned toward him, as he left the falls and came up behind her. He placed his large hands on her shoulders, caressing her skin with his thumbs.

"John." She tried to pull away, but his arm went around her waist.

He kissed her neck and nibbled her ear. Turning her, he claimed her with ravenous, wild kisses, their tongues tangling in a crazed dance.

He held her up as ripples of pleasure as he slowly looked her over seductively, his gaze dropped from her eyes to her shoulders to her breasts. Claiming her lips, his tongue explored the recesses of her mouth, and he crushed her to him. He reveled in the beautiful curving lines of her sensuous back. Her mind swam as he kissed her. She needed to escape, to run away, but his hard chest felt so good against her breasts. She could feel his member throb and she wrapped her arms around his neck, giving in to him. He picked her up in his arms and left the water, laying her gently in the grass, near a dark wooded area. She felt him pull away and looked up at him.

"I want you so bad I can barely breath," he whispered in her ear as he cupped her swollen breast.

Elizabeth gripped his hair and leaned up and kissed him. "John, make love to me." Her eyes full of desire.

"Beth, I love you."

She whispered against his lips, "I love you, too. Do it now," she grabbed his buttocks, pushing hard.

He plunged into her, and she felt a burning pain, but the discomfort passed quickly then the pleasure was pure and explosive. She saw a smile cross his lips as he looked down at her. She exhaled her breath and watched him love her.

He rolled over, pulling her to him, their bodies naked and still moist from their lovemaking. She looked at him, his eyes closed, his breathing soft and steady.

"I love you." She gently kissed him then rose and quickly dressed.

She left and watched the sun creep over his sleeping form. Leaning against a tree, she smiled. He truly was a sight to behold. She slowly turned and made her way back to the encampment, no longer the same woman she was just an hour ago. For the first time in quite a while, she felt safe and loved.

Chapter Twenty-Six

John awoke to the sudden sensation of a bucket of cold water being dumped on him.

"What the hell?" He sat straight up and eyed his attacker. The fat man standing in front of him glared at John with anger in his eyes.

"Where the hell have you been, boy? Get dressed before the women see you." Buck threw John's clothes at him. "Everyone's been out looking for you."

"Since when is it a crime to take a bath?" John asked stepping into his pants.

"Just get dressed and get your ass back to camp," Buck scolded and waddled away.

Suddenly he became aware that Elizabeth wasn't with him. He quickly slipped his shirt and pants on, pulled on his boots, and headed up the hill. He made his way to the encampment and saw the women carrying baskets of laundry to the river. As he passed, he made sure his hand touched Elizabeth's. She smiled and batted her sultry eyes when she went by. He stopped and watched her hips sway to and fro, taunting him. Before he became too aroused, he grinned and walked into camp.

Jed ran up to him and grabbed him by the arm. "Where have you been? We were about ready to send out a search party."

John looked around and saw the horses saddled and ready. "I fell asleep near the falls." He went over to Buck's wagon, snatched his bag, and pulled out a clean shirt and jeans.

"Fell asleep?" Jed questioned, watching his brother put on a clean shirt. "And what's that on your shoulder? Is that a bite?"

"It's nothing." He said buttoning it. "Where's Lucas?" He finished getting dressed, grabbed a cup, and poured some coffee.

"He's making jerky. John…" Jed began.

"Better go help him." John handed him the empty cup and marched off. Jed followed close behind.

"You were with that slut of a whore? When people in Ocean City find out she's not a virgin and unmarried… John, she'll ruin you," Jed said, his hands moving in a pleading gesture.

John whirled around and pointed a finger at him. "Shut your mouth lil' brother, or by God, I'll shut it for you!" he seethed, and for a moment looked as wild as the bear itself.

"She's soiled goods. John, listen to me," he pleaded.

John made a fist, swung back, and hit Jed's jaw so hard, his body flew backward and fell over a fallen tree. John then rushed over and grabbed Jed's collar, pulling his face to his. Jed struggled to gain his feet, but his brother held him down.

"Now you listen to me, you little bastard. Cobb didn't rape her. I know for a fact, he didn't. If I ever hear you speak ill of her again, I'll kill you. You hear me?" He shook Jed, rattling his teeth.

"He didn't? But I thought…." Jed stared into his brother's eyes and noticed truth shining back. John's eyes glittering with a fierce light that was extremely unsettling.

"You thought wrong." He shoved Jed to the ground, stepped over him and stomped into the woods.

Chapter Twenty-Seven

Several weeks later, the wagon train came to the Snake River Cutoff. By taking this route, John and the train bypassed the Three Island Crossing, which would have the emigrants cross the dangerous and swift waters of the Snake River three times. Here, they only had to cross once. John signaled Aengus and Jed to make camp.

Except for work, John and his brother spoke no more than two words to each other. Elizabeth hated seeing them so at odds. Jed no longer helped her with her team, so between John and herself, the work had to get done. She sat near her campfire, gazing at the flames. The nights were starting to get cooler, and she hoped John would get them over the Cascades before the first snow.

Abigail walked up, her arms cradling a sleeping, Clementine. "Elizabeth, are you okay?"

She looked up at her friend and smiled. "I'm fine, just tired."

"Come to our fire and have dinner with us," Abigail said, slowly rocking the baby.

Elizabeth shook her head. How could she tell her friend that food was the last thing on her mind?

She was afraid she was getting sick and didn't want the camp to know that she may be contagious. They'd tell her to leave the train and then where would she be?

"Thank you, Abigail, but I think I'm just going to bed." Elizabeth smiled again, trying not to show her illness.

"Alright, but if you need anything, just ask." Abigail rubbed Elizabeth's shoulder and headed back to her wagon.

Elizabeth slowly got up and walked away from the encampment. She held her stomach, her hands were clammy, and her body felt hot. As she made her way to a bush, John came running up behind her. She fell to her knees, grabbed her stomach, and retched. John rubbed her back as she dry heaved.

"John, why are you here?" She coughed, covering her mouth.

"Abigail's worried about you. Why haven't you told me you weren't feeling well?" he asked as she threw up again.

She sat up and wiped her mouth with her apron. "I drank from the river. I'm going to die, aren't I?" Tears filled her eyes while she shook from the chill. Her face and lips were pale, she felt hot one minute and cold the next; she was very dizzy.

"Not on my watch." John took off his jacket and wrapped it around her then picked her up in his arms and quickly headed back to camp. He carried her past several wagons before coming up to Dr. Grant's. A few people watched as they passed.

"Doc." John called, knocking on the side of the wagon.

The doctor climbed out of his wagon and looked at John then Elizabeth. "What's wrong?" He walked up to her, touched her forehead, a frown crossed his face.

"She's really sick. Help her." John sat her down and handed her over to him.

Doc helped her in the wagon and followed her. John began to pace back and forth, shooing everyone away. Buck walked up to him with a bottle of whiskey and a cup. John grabbed the bottle and took a long swig.

"She's so sick." He shook his head and took another swig.

"Probably something she ate." Buck slapped him on the back. "Buck up. Come on, son. Let Doc do his job" He took John's arm and led him to his wagon. John took one last look at the Doc's wagon and walked away.

$$\infty \quad \infty \quad \infty$$

Elizabeth laid on Doc's bedroll, a bucket near her. She felt awful. She covered her eyes with her arm. Doc had taken her temperature, palpated her belly, took her pulse, and asked all kinds of difficult questions.

"Elizabeth, tell me the truth. Have you been intimate with John?" Doc asked, raising his eyebrows.

She swallowed hard. If she answered yes, what would he think of her? How could she tell him that she and John had become lovers, making love as often as they could? Just the thought of him caused her heart to beat fast and her womanhood to throb.

She looked away and nodded. "Yes," she whispered shamefully.

"Honey, you aren't going to die, you're pregnant," he said patting her leg and started to climb out of the wagon. "You and John have a lot to talk about."

"No, he mustn't know. Please don't tell him. Please." She took his hand, her eyes wide with shock.

"Alright. If that's what you want." He gripped her hand as she nodded. He gave her a sad smile and left the wagon.

Elizabeth looked up at the bonnet of the wagon gently blowing in the wind. *What am I going to do*? If she told John, he'd want to marry her, but would it be because he loved her or out of obligation? She loved him with her whole heart, but did he feel the same way? She curled up, put her hand over her stomach and cried.

She awoke to the sound of John's voice just outside the wagon.

"Doc, what's wrong with her?" he asked.

"Just an upset stomach. She'll be just fine. You can go see her," Doc said.

Elizabeth cringed at what Doc had said. She wasn't ready to see John just now. *What am I going to tell him?* She felt the wagon move as he climbed in and sat next to her.

"You feeling any better?" he asked, smoothing her hair.

"Yes, thank you." She smiled at him. His fingers slowly combed through her beautiful locks. She closed her eyes, enjoying his touch.

"You really had me worried. So many things were running through my head. I even thought you might be pregnant," he snickered, relief on his face.

"John, I'd like to go back to my wagon now," she said, sitting up and frowned.

"Here, let me help you." He climbed out and helped her down and slowly walked her back to her wagon.

Elizabeth sat, sadly watching him start a fire then filled her tea kettle with water and placed it on the embers.

"You forgot to add the tea," she said getting up and went to the back of her wagon. Grabbing her tin of tea, she made her way back to the fire. She took the kettle, sprinkled in the right amount of tea, and returned it to the fire. She stood looking at the sun disappearing in the distance.

"Beth, you, okay? You seem distant this evening." He pulled her into his arms and kissed the top of her head.

"John, what's to become of us when we get to Oregon City?" she asked.

"I thought you wanted to open your tea shop like the one you had back home. Is that still your plan?" He rubbed her back.

"Yes, of course, but what about you?" She looked up at him sadly.

"Well, I was planning on giving this job to Jed, but I don't think he wants it. So, after I finish here, the boys and I will head back to Missouri with or without him, hire more men and lead another train in the spring."

"Oh, I see. So, you just can't wait to be on another wagon train." She moved away from him and took the kettle and poured herself a cup. She sipped it, her back to him. "Have you had many others while on the trail?" She took another sip.

"Others? What are you talking about?" he asked, stepping toward her.

"Oh, come off it, John. Don't tell me I'm the only girl you've had on a wagon train." She spun around and eyed him.

Elizabeth's anger grew as she watched him from over the rim of tin cup. How could he be so relived over her pregnancy? He looked so happy at the thought of her not with child. She was so infuriated, she could have punched him in the nose. Without thinking, she began to pace.

"What? Girl, I think you're getting too big for your britches. Yes, I've kissed a few, but until you, I never bed any of them. What's this all about, anyway?" he questioned, stepping back.

"Bed? Is that what you call it? So, you bed me then just dump me off in Oregon City and go without so much as a by your leave because maybe the next wagon train will have someone even better." Tears blinded her eyes and choked her voice.

"I don't get you! What the hell is going on?" he shouted.

"Just leave. We'll be in Oregon soon and then you can go bed someone else." She angrily held back tears of disappointment. She grabbed the tea kettle and poured it over the fire then tossed it at his feet, climbed into her wagon and collapsed in a heap, tears streaming down her face.

"Fine." She heard him shout and stormed off.

∞ ∞ ∞

John sat at Buck's fire, his elbows on his knees. He stared at the flames trying to figure out what had just happened. Buck handed him a cup of coffee.

"You got something a little stronger?" he asked, looking up at his friend.

"Sure." Buck tossed out the coffee, went to the wagon and poured John some whiskey. He returned and handed it to him.

John took a sip and leaned back. "That's better."

Aengus and Lucas sat next to him. "Can we join ye, lad?"

"Be my guest." He raised his cup and took another swig.

After all the men had their drinks, they gazed at John, who was staring at the fire once again, a frown plastered on his face. *Why was Elizabeth acting that way?* His brain was numb from being verbally accosted and being accused as a womanizer. He loved her so much, how could she say such things about him, especially since none of them were true. He took another gulp, slouching and sighing with utter disappointment.

"Want to talk about it?" Lucas asked.

"About what?" He poured another drink. "Oh, how about Elizabeth accusing me of bedding every woman I meet. Or how I'd rather be on the trail fucking rather than be with her." He downed his whiskey and poured another then went to the wagon and grabbed another bottle.

"What prompted that? This is your last wagon train…isn't it?" Lucas asked.

"I thought so, too, but I had a talk with Jed, seems he doesn't want the job anymore. He wants to go off to California." He finished his cup and gave himself another.

The headache he once had was starting to fade, but the world began to tip. Buck leaned over to take the bottle, but John got up and stumbled backward, glaring at the men.

"I love that little gal." He pointed at Elizabeth's wagon. "I was planning on giving her my name. But…" He tossed the cup and took a swig from the bottle. "She accuses me of screwing anything with a skirt." He spread his arms out. "Me, John Evans." He stumbled toward her wagon. Lucas got up and followed him.

"John, come on, let's sleep it off." He grabbed John by the arm and started heading toward his bedroll.

"No!" He pushed Lucas away. "I need to see her." He threw the words at him like stone. John stumbled, almost fell, and tried to walk in a straight line. He stopped and drank, then continued his mission.

People started coming out to witness the disturbance. They saw John stagger to Elizabeth's wagon, stop and took another long swig.

"John. Come on, leave her be," Lucas said, his hands on his hips

"Hey, Beth!" he yelled and took a swig of whiskey. "I wanna talk to you." He wiped his mouth with his sleeve.

They saw a light and then her head peeking out. She looked around and then focused on John. Her mouth twisted in annoyance as she stared at him. *What the bloody hell was he doing?*

"What do you? … John, you're drunk." She climbed out of the wagon. "I don't want to argue with you."

John walked up and pointed at her. "I loved you." He swayed back and forth. "I chose you. I wanted only you." He finished the bottle. "You're the only one I've ever took to my bed," he yelled. A sudden thin chill hung on the edge of his words.

Elizabeth's mouth dropped open then she slapped him hard across the face. "How dare you, you bastard." She whirled around and climbed back into her wagon. "Go away, John Evans. I don't ever want to see you again," she cried.

"Sorry lady, but you're stuck with me till Oregon," he yelled, throwing the bottle against her wagon. It crashed against the wood frame.

Abigail ran up to him as he stomped toward his horse and began saddling Joy. The young woman grabbed his arm. "Mr. Evans, you can't treat her like that, not when she's…."

"Leave me alone." He mounted Joy and took off across the river. He had to get away, away from Elizabeth, away from everyone.

Chapter Twenty-Eight

Elizabeth climbed out of the wagon, the sun barely above the horizon. She looked around the camp, her eyes burning from crying all night. Most everyone was still asleep except Abigail, who was sitting in the shadows feeding Clementine. She walked over to her friend and sat on a log near her.

"Elizabeth. So good to see you." She smiled, patting her hand.

"I know you saw what took place last night. I'm sure everyone did." She put her hands to her face. "Oh Abigail, how could he?"

"Now, now. It'll be alright. You mustn't get excited, for the sake of...." Abigail stopped herself.

Elizabeth looked at her friend, horrified. "How, how did you find out? Did Doc tell you?"

"No. Elizabeth, I'm a woman and know about such matters as babies. You showed all the classic signs." She rocked the baby as she nursed.

"Oh, God, what am I going to do? What should I do about John?" Her voice cracked, and she started to cry. Her whole body felt numb as she sat near her friend.

"You haven't told him? Oh Elizabeth, you must. He must know," she stated, switching the baby to the other breast.

"I can't. If I tell him, he'll want to marry me." Elizabeth shook her head while clutching her hands.

"What's wrong with that? I thought you loved him?" Abigail placed Clementine in the cradle then came and sat next to Elizabeth. It was obvious her friend was in trouble.

Elizabeth began to bounce her knee, panic gripping her heart. What was she going to do?

"I do. I love him very much, but he doesn't love me. You heard him last night." She wiped away her tears and sniffed. "Now I'm with child and no man to give him a name."

"He was drunk. He probably doesn't even remember what he said." Abigail took her friend's hands and gripped them. "I've seen the way he looks at you and when Billy Ray hurt you, he was insane with fear at the thought of losing you. Tell him, he deserves to know."

Elizabeth nodded, thanked her friend, and went back to her wagon. She started breakfast and did her chores. When she returned from washing the dishes, her team was hitched up and ready to leave. She wished she knew where John was, so they could talk. An hour later she was sitting in her wagon, snapping the reins, and watching the train move forward. No one had seen or heard from him.

They approached the river, Aengus rode up and stopped her. He dismounted, tied his horse to the wagon then climbed up next to her. He gave her an apologetic smile then snapped the reins.

"I'm real sorry aboot how John treated ye, lass. If I ken where he was, I'd box his ears." His nostrils flared with fury.

"Thank you, Aengus," she said sadly and stared in front of her, her hands in her lap.

"Hold on, it can get pretty rough," Aengus ordered.

Elizabeth grabbed the side of the wagon and prayed they'd make it across without tipping. The water rushed past the wheels and started rising. Aengus whistled and shouted, snapping the reins, trying to push the mules forward. Elizabeth bit her lip and closed her eyes, trying to will the team to move.

"She's stuck!" he called to Lucas, who was on the other side of the river. "Get some rope, we're gonna have to pull er' out." He looked at Elizabeth. "You doing alright, lass?" She nodded. "Good. We'll be outta here in no time."

After Jed and Lucas hitched several teams together and tied the ropes to Elizabeth's wagon, the men whistled and smacked the mules' rumps. Aengus stood up, snapped the reins, and yelled at the team. Elizabeth watched as the mules across the river, dug their hooves into the dirt, trying to pull her wagon out of the rut. Suddenly, the wagon jutted forward and slowly moved through the river. It shuttered back and forth, the supplies shifting with every bump in the riverbed.

"We got it, lass. We're almost there. Get on, you filthy bastards," shouted Aengus, snapping the reins again.

Elizabeth looked down at the river and wished John were seated next to her. A tear dripped into the water as they made their way across the Snake River. Soon they would arrive in Oregon City, with or without him. She didn't mean what she had said and the thought of never seeing him again or feeling his touch; to never love him and or have him inside her tore at her heart.

"John, where are you?" she whispered.

∞ ∞ ∞

John rolled over and groaned, shielding his eyes from the sun. His head felt like someone was bashing it in with a two by four. He slowly sat up and looked around, his horse was grazing nearby.

"Oh, my head." he groaned, grabbing it with both hands.

He slowly stood up and staggered toward Joy. Gripping the reins, he leaned his hot forehead against the saddle. *What the hell am I doing out here?* He remembered the argument with Elizabeth and drinking two bottles of whiskey, but everything seemed a bit fuzzy after that. *Dear God, what have I done?*

He placed his foot in the stirrup and slowly pulled himself up. After mounting, he looked around. He was in the Grande Ronde Valley near the Blue Mountains. He kicked Joy and loped toward the area he knew the wagon train would be. If he was right, they had crossed the Snake River that morning and were heading right toward him.

As he rode, he thought about Elizabeth. What had gotten into her? Since her illness, she had become someone he didn't recognize. She seemed afraid of something and wished he knew what it was, so he could help her. His life had changed since that little gal had entered it and wasn't about to give her up.

John came over a ridge and gazed down, shielding his eyes from the bright sun, he watched the long wagon train follow the southern edge of the Snake River canyon. It was a much rougher trail with steep descents and ascents.

John saw Lucas and Jed up front and Aengus riding behind the last wagon. He gazed around and spotted Elizabeth driving her team like a pro. She wore that pretty, yellow dress he loved and the cream-colored bonnet covering her beautiful, raven hair. God, what he wouldn't give to run his fingers through it.

He gave Joy a little kick and cantered down the ridge toward Elizabeth's wagon. He needed to know why the sudden change in her and by God he was going to get the answer whether she wanted to tell him or not.

Chapter Twenty-Nine

Elizabeth sat watching the wagon in front of her. Her mind wandered to the first night she and John had made love as the mules slowly made their way along the trail while the harnesses jingled to the rhythm of their hooves. Was that the night she became pregnant? John rode up next to her while she sat driving her mules.

"Beth, I need to talk to you," he said trotting alongside her.

"I thought I told you I didn't want to see you again," she replied, staring straight ahead.

He dropped the reins and jumped from his horse and onto the wagon. He climbed aboard and sat next to her, reached over her lap, and took the reins.

"Get off my wagon," she said folding her arms across her chest and pierced her lips.

"Not until we talk. Beth, I want you to know that whatever I said or did last night, I am truly sorry. When I drink, I can get a little belligerent."

"A little?" She glared at him. "I have never been so humiliated in all my life. The camp heard you. How could you say those things to me?" Her breath burned in her throat.

"Um… well I," he rubbed the back of his neck while giving her a sheepish grin.

"You don't even remember, do you? Well let me enlighten you, you Wanker, and I quote 'You're the only one I've ever taken to my bed'," she sneered at him. She had a fiery, angry look that was unfamiliar to him.

"Oh." He looked down at his knees. Guilt roiled unpleasantly in his stomach; he worked to shake it off. "I know I don't deserve your forgiveness," he gazed at her solemnly, "but I am sorry. I never meant to hurt you."

"Well, you did." She looked away, staring at the mountains in the distance.

John put the reins down, turned in his seat and took her hands. "Beth, how many times do I have to say it?"

Elizabeth looked at her hands wrapped in his and couldn't help but feel warm inside. He had apologized but did he do it because he loved her or because he just wanted to bed her.

"I'm scared," she whispered, looking away from his handsome face.

"Of what? Beth, what's going on?" He pulled her into his arms. "Talk to me."

"I'm afraid you'll leave and never come back." She cried on his shoulder.

He put his hands on either side of her face and gently kissed her. "I love you. I'll always come back.

Is that what's bothering you? Girl, you can't get rid of me that easily." He smiled at her then kissed her forehead.

Aengus trotted up beside the wagon, holding the reins to John's horse. "John, Lucas needs you."

He nodded and gave Elizabeth a quick kiss on the hand then jumped on his horse and rode away. She wiped her eyes and picked up the reins, snapping them against the mule's rumps. He loved her, but was it enough? Would he stay if she asked him to and if he did, would he hold it against her? And what about the baby? How will he feel once she told him? Tears started to well in her eyes as she placed her hand to her stomach. She needed to tell him and soon.

Hours passed, and they finally stopped for the evening by the Blue Mountains. Tomorrow the train would tackle them, but for now, they had time to rest. Elizabeth started a fire and put on her stew and tea kettle. She sat stirring the pot when John walked up to her and smiled. He was so handsome, standing there with his hands in his pockets and his hat pushed back. She wondered if her baby would look like him.

"Evening, Beth," he said happily.

"Please, won't you join me for dinner? I need to speak with you." She dished up the stew, handing him a plate and utensils. She poured two cups of tea, added some sugar, and gave him the cup.

He made a face but stopped when he looked into her eyes. "Okay." He smiled then took out a flask and poured a small amount. "If I'm gonna drink tea, I might as well get some enjoyment out of it." He took a sip and nodded.

"Tea and whiskey." She shook her head and grinned.

After dinner and the dishes were cleaned, Elizabeth took his hand and walked him away from the wagons. When they reached an area of large rocks she sat down, placing her hands in her lap. He sat next to her, eyes full of questions.

"How much do you love me?" She asked, her eyes sparkling in the moon light.

"What kind of question is that?" he said, taking her hand.

"Answer the question." She gazed up at him.

He took her in his arms and lavished kisses on her eyes, cheek, and neck. She could feel his hot breath against her skin, and it tingled throughout her body, feelings she thought she'd never have again.

"I love you more than life itself…. I'd die for you. There will never be anyone but you." He leaned over and kissed her. He tasted like chamomile and whiskey.

"What about you're leaving when we get to Oregon City?" she asked.

"Oh that. Well, don't worry. You get your tea shop up and running and I'll be back next September when I can marry you properly. You make all the…"

She frowned and looked away. "That will be too late."

John put a finger under her chin and turned her head. "Look at me. What do you mean too late? What aren't you telling me? Has it got something to do with your illness?"

She put her hands to her face and began to sob. He pulled her hands away and shook her gently. "Tell me, dammit!"

She took his hand and placed it on her stomach. "I'm expecting your child." Elizabeth replied with a smile, which faded as quickly as it appeared.

John had looked expectant, then confused, then worst of all --- wounded and angry. He pulled his hand away, stood up and turned his back to her. He took off his hat and ran his fingers through his hair then began to pace. *A child? What had I done to her?* Stopping in front of her, his face drenched in sweat though it was a cool night and rubbed his beard.

"You're… pregnant?" He looked up at the heavens. "I can't believe this is happening."

"John," she stood up, "I thought you'd be happy about this. You said you loved me."

"Happy? You think I'm happy about this? Damn me, what have I done?" He shook his head and stomped back to the encampment.

"John?" Air whooshed out of Elizabeth's lungs, her pulse hammering out a disquieting beat. She fell to the ground and yelled, pounding the dirt with her fists. "No. Oh God, no."

Chapter Thirty

John marched up to Buck's wagon and threw his hat at it then went over and punched a tree until his knuckles turned bloody. Jed, Aengus, and Lucas sat there in utter shock. Buck waddled up to him and grabbed his shoulders.

"Don't touch me," John seethed. He went to the wagon, grabbed a bottle of whiskey, and stomped into the woods. As he left, he heard Elizabeth yelling near where he left her.

Dear God, pregnant, she was pregnant. Now what am I going to do? His wagon train business was in trouble, Jed was going to California, and now he was going to be a father. He hadn't planned this nor taking her maiden head before they wed, but she was so damn irresistible that he couldn't help it. The thought of her standing in the water touching herself, made his britches very uncomfortable. God, what had he done? As he reminisced about her and their situation, he heard a twig snap behind him.

"What do you want, Lucas?" John asked, popping the cork off the bottle, and taking a long swig.

"This is two nights in a row. Plan on getting pissed tonight as well?" Lucas leaned against a tree, folding his arms across his chest.

"What's it to you?" he asked, gazing at the bottle.

"Give me the bottle, John. Whatever it is, this won't solve it." Lucas stretched out his hand and John complied, placing the bottle in his friend's hand.

John slumped on a log, his elbows on his knees and stared at his boots. Lucas came over and sat next to him and rubbed his shoulder.

"We've been friends for a long time, and I've never seen you like this. What the hell is going on?" Lucas asked.

John put his hands on his head and groaned. "I fucked up and I'm not sure what I'm going to do about it." He began to pale as he took a deep pained breath and closed his eyes.

"What'd ya do?" Lucas gazed at his friend.

"Beth's pregnant." He looked at Lucas and frowned.

"Damn. Now what?" he asked as John stood up and kicked at the dirt.

"Hell, if I know. With Jed leaving, I'm one man short. I was going to give the business to him, but now I gotta take you guys back to Missouri and somehow find a fourth man. If I leave, what happens to Elizabeth and the baby?" He hit his leg with his fist.

"Well first, you have to marry her." He stood up and whirled John around. "You have to take responsibility for you mistake."

"Don't you think I know that. But what about the business? I can't let it run into the ground. I worked too hard to let it falter. I put ten years of my life into this wagon train." He pointed at himself. "This isn't a good time, Lucas. I've got a lot on my plate including getting these greenhorns over the mountains before the first snow. I don't need this right now."

"I know, John. I've watched you build your business from the ground up. But now you have to think about Elizabeth."

"There's not much I can do about it until we get to Oregon City. Besides, there's no one in the party who can marry us." He began to pace while rubbing his injured hand. "I've got a job to do. I can't think about this right now. She's just going to have to wait until we get to Oregon City."

"John…" Lucas began.

"I appreciate your opinion, but this job is too important. I have to think of everyone, not just Elizabeth, and how to get the rest of the wagons safely to the coast." He frowned, piercing his lips.

"You're my best friend, but sometimes you can be a real asshole." Lucas stomped through the woods, heading back to camp.

John watched him go, regret clutching his stomach. What he couldn't admit to Lucas was that he was scared and angry. He knew how to be a trail boss, give orders, find his way in the wild, fix broken wagons, deal with Indians, handle livestock, but had no idea how to be a husband or a father.

∞ ∞ ∞

Elizabeth continued to beat the ground until Abigail grabbed her, pulling her into her arms. "Honey, stop, stop." She held onto her while Elizabeth cried hysterically.

"I told him," she hiccupped. "He was angry, and he stomped off. He doesn't love me. Oh God, what am I going to do?" She cried on her friend's shoulder.

"First things first, we need to get you cleaned up then you're going to get some sleep. We'll take each day as it comes." Abigail helped Elizabeth to her feet and slowly walked her back to her wagon.

Bridget and Anna came running up to the pair as they made their way to Elizabeth's wagon. The two women busied themselves around the campfire while Abigail wrapped Elizabeth in a blanket and held her close. Though she had the support of her friends, she felt utterly alone.

"How can I go it alone with a child on the way?" she whispered, curled up in Abigail's arms.

"You won't be alone." Bridget sat next to her. "You have us. Don't despair. lass." She smoothed down Elizabeth's hair.

Anna handed her a cup of tea and smiled. "Ya, you have us. Don't you ever forget it."

After the water heated up, the women took Elizabeth behind the wagon, helped her wash, and dressed her in a clean nightgown. While Bridget and Anna tended to her, Abigail began to pick up around the wagon when she saw John over by Buck's wagon. She dropped the blanket and marched over to him.

"Mr. Evans!" she spat out the words contemptuously and glared at him with burning, reproachful eyes.

"Yes, Miss Pritchard?" He looked at her.

Before he could react, Abigail swung back and slapped him across the face. "You don't deserve her, you… you…Oh, I can't say it, being a Christian woman. Stay away from her." She was breathless with rage. She turned on her heel and stomped away.

He rubbed the side of his face, he deserved it. John looked up to see Anna and Bridget helping Elizabeth into the wagon. Abigail finished the chores, put out the fire and climbed into the wagon.

Though it was crowded, Elizabeth was glad they were there. Abigail ordered her to lie down and covered her with an Indian blanket.

"Get some rest, my dear. We will see you in the morning. Come ladies, let us take our leave." Abigail, Bridget, and Anna climbed out of the wagon and went to their own fires.

Elizabeth lay there listening to the crickets and she tried to doze off. All she could see was John's face after she told him. She curled up, tears rolled over her nose and down her cheeks. Would there ever be a day that she might smile again?

The next morning Elizabeth did here normal chores then went to her team of mules. She placed the harnesses on them when a hand reached out and took them from her. She gazed up to see Jed helping her.

"Miss Elizabeth, I'm so sorry for the way I've behaved toward you. Can you ever forgive me?" he asked.

She smiled sadly and nodded then started gathering her team. Her hands shook as she grasped the harnesses.

"No Ma'am, I'll do it." He took the reins and pulled the mules toward the wagon.

Elizabeth walked back over to her wagon and finished putting her breakfast dishes away, folded the blankets, and poured water over the fire. After everything was in order, she climbed onto the wagon, took a seat, then grabbed the reins and waited for the call to start.

She looked at the mountains they were to tackle that morning and saw her life where those mountains stood. She needed to be brave and climb out of the rut she was in, over the tribulations and into the valley of a new life. She was no longer sad and mouse-like, she was stone-cold pissed, and she'd be damned if she let John hurt her again.

"Wagons ho!" She heard John call and the wagons lurched forward.

She snapped the reins and set her wagon in motion, making herself emotionally ready for the long climb ahead.

Chapter Thirty-One

John and Lucas rode ahead locating the trail. *Put her out of your mind. She's not your only responsibility and you've nothing to feel guilty about.* But try as he might, he couldn't stop thinking about Elizabeth or remembering the stricken expression on her lovely face after he'd refused her.

"Lucas, go back and tell the boys, they want the right side of the fork, then let Jed know I want to see him now, before the train catches up."

"You got it, John." Lucas wheeled his pony and kicked the pinto into a steady run.

John took a deep breath and closed his eyes. His hands tightened involuntarily on the reins and his horse slowed its gait. Soon, they'd be at the Barlow Road. Though it was a toll road, it was the quickest way around Mount Hood from the Dalles that led to the Willamette Valley and Oregon City. He felt it deep in his bones, he was almost home. He looked around at the mountains when he heard a rider come up behind him. He turned in the saddle and saw Jed pull his horse to a stop then walked him to John's side.

"Lucas said you wanted to see me?" Jed asked.

"You see that trail to the left?" John pointed to a rough looking dirt road full of rocks and potholes.

"Yeah, what about it?" His eyebrows came together as he frowned.

"It leads to California. I'm letting you leave the wagon train. You can grab your stuff and leave right now." John leaned his arms on the horn of his saddle.

"Now? You want me to leave now?" Jed asked.

"Well, you said you couldn't wait to get away from me and this damn train, so be my guest." John waved his arm toward the fork in the trail.

"I'm not leaving, John. I need to finish the job I signed onto." He situated himself in the saddle and leaned on the horn. He would complete this journey, see his promise through to the end.

"Then you start listening to me. I'm still Captain on this wagon train and I'm not going to put up with anymore of your bullshit. If you can't agree to this, then go," John spat.

"What's got into you lately? You're not the same man you were when we left Independence. You've changed and not for the better." He heard jingling of harnesses and turned to see the wagons making their way up the hill. Jed kicked his horse and loped up to ride alongside the wagons.

John sat and watched the wagons roll past him. Five months ago, he started out with eleven wagons in his charge, now he only had seven. So many lost. Maybe it was time to retire, to hand the business over to someone else. But who? He sat thinking when he suddenly noticed Elizabeth pass by. She was staring straight ahead, lips pierced into a scowl. She didn't even look at him when she rolled by.

John kicked his horse and rode to the front of the wagon train, following the trail up the Blue Mountains. Lucas wandered up to him and walked alongside him.

"We're almost there, John. Another week or so and we'll be pulling into Oregon City." He grinned from ear to ear. "I sure can't wait to get a decent bath and sleep in a real bed."

John groaned then looked at Lucas. "Don't get too comfortable. If I can't get Jed to take over the business, you and I will be heading back to Missouri after we unload this train."

"What about Elizabeth? You planning on marrying her?" Lucas asked.

"I don't know. She doesn't want anything to do with me right at the moment. Maybe it's best if we just separate for a while. I'll send her money whenever I get a chance," John said, frowning.

"She doesn't need money, John, she needs you. You love her?" Lucas gazed at his friend.

"Yes, I do," John declared.

"Then what's the problem?" Lucas rested his horse.

John pulled on the reins and stopped. He looked out over the beautiful country. The mountains were covered in trees, so thick that it looked like a canopy. Moss covered nearly every rock and tree and ferns blanketed the ground. They both stepped off their horses and started walking.

"Lucas, I'm... I'm not father material. As long as I can remember, I've been on the trail. What am I gonna do with a baby?" John walked off the trail, letting go of the reins and leaned against a tree.

"You raised Jed and he turned out alright. John, whether you like it or not, this baby is coming." Lucas patted him on the shoulder then mounted his pinto and rode away.

John walked over to his horse and grabbed the reins. Joy shook her head, bent down and continued grazing. He patted the animal's neck, climbed onto the saddle, and rode up the hill toward the wagon train.

"Mr. Evans?" Joe Callahan called after him.

John trotted over and walked alongside the wagon. "Yes, Mr. Callahan?"

"Is it true that in less than two weeks we'll be in Oregon City?" he asked, and John nodded.

He couldn't wait to get there so he could talk Elizabeth into marrying him. A child needed a father as well as a mother. He knew she was angry with him and wanted nothing to do with him, but the marriage had to happen, even if it was for convenience and nothing more. He loved Elizabeth and he hated himself for putting her in this situation. The best thing for both was to marry her and then leave for Missouri after the wedding was over.

"Mr. Evans, you alright?" Bill Callahan asked.

John was pulled from his thoughts of Elizabeth only to find his horse nearly collide with the team of mules. He nodded to the Callahan brothers then loped past several wagons, spotting Jed riding alongside Elizabeth's wagon. He was talking, and she was laughing. It had been quite a while since he had heard her beautiful laugh. As he rode past her, he looked at her and their eyes met. He missed gazing into those beautiful, violet eyes.

"Ma'am." John tipped his hat to her and trotted past before she had a chance to respond. He made his way to the front of the train and planned on staying there until they stopped for the evening.

∞ ∞ ∞

Several days past and they rode by Whitman Mission near Fort Nez Perces. Many of the settlers asked if they would be able to pick up supplies there, but John informed them that it was no longer a mission after the Whitmans were killed by Indians in 1847. The trail continued through the Cascade Range toward The Dalles. Before 1846 the settlers would either give up their wagons or disassemble them and put them on boats or build rafts to sail down the Columbia River. Now they would take the Barlow Road, which carved a trail through the forests and up around Mount Hood.

Elizabeth sat on her wagon, counting her money. To use the Barlow Road, she would have to pay five dollars for her wagon and ten cents per animal. Jed came up beside her.

"You have enough?" he asked.

"Plenty. Jed, are we getting close?" She paid the man standing by her wagon before he went to the next wagon down the line.

"Very close." He smiled. "I hear you'll be staying with Jesse and Abigail once we get to Oregon City."

"Yes. They're going to help me find a place for my tea shop. You still thinking of going to California?" she said, putting her money in a bag behind her.

"Yep. I thought maybe I'd try and find some of that gold everyone's talking about." He grinned and winked at her.

"What about John and the business? He told me he wanted to leave it with you," she said.

"I never really wanted it. I stayed around cause he's my brother, but it's time to try something else." The horse began to move impatiently. "Miss Elizabeth, do you love John?"

"Yes, I mean no…I don't know. I thought I did, but lately he doesn't want anything to do with me. Jed, love isn't supposed to hurt, and he tore my heart out. What am I suppose do?" She looked down at her hands.

"I'm sorry Miss Elizabeth, I truly am." He frowned and shook his head.

"Wagons ho!" Elizabeth heard John yell.

"A few more hours and we'll stop for the evening," Jed said. They began to move forward and started down the Barlow Road.

She nodded and entered what looked like a tunnel of trees. Everyone had to go slow and single file. At times, Elizabeth wasn't sure if the wagons could make it on the narrow trail. It was beautiful. Everything was green with large cedars and Douglas firs, ferns covered the ground and moss grew on every tree. It was the most beautiful place she had ever seen. She looked around and could hear birds singing in the shadow of the trees, and there standing near the trail she saw a family of deer.

Later in the day, it started to rain, but not a down pour that they had on the prairie. It was a misty rain that brought the temperature down to the point that Elizabeth reached behind her and grabbed a blanket, wrapping it around herself. The weather reminded her of England, maybe that was why she began to love this area and wanted to call it home.

An hour or so later, she noticed the wagons were slowing to a stop, so she pulled her own wagon to a halt; the mules nickered and stamped in protest. For the last few hours, she had not felt well and gave a sigh of relief that John had called for a rest.

She wrapped the reins around the brake then stood to stretch out her aching back. Suddenly, a shooting pain gripped her abdomen. She grabbed her stomach and she fell back against the wagon seat. The pain was so intense, it took her breath away.

"Miss Elizabeth?" Jed's smile turned to panic when he saw the pain etched on her face. She was pale as tears rolled down her cheeks. "Oh Lord. Don't you fret none, I'll go get John." He kicked his horse and darted to the front of the wagon train.

Elizabeth screamed and crumpled to the floor of the wagon. She stared up at the dark, grey clouds as the misty rain dampened her face…as it dampened her spirits. *God, please don't take my baby.*

Suddenly, a familiar face came into view. "Elizabeth, honey?"

She reached up and gently touched John's stubbled chin as a slow smile crossed her white lips and she felt her body being lifted out of her wagon.

The last thing she saw was John's tear-filled eyes before she slumped in his arms and darkness took her.

Chapter Thirty-two

John stood outside Elizabeth's wagon, fear gripping his heart. What was to become of her or the baby? He watched Abigail climb out of the wagon, grab some hot water, and rushed back to the wagon.

"Don't worry, John. She'll be fine." Lucas patted him on the shoulder.

"When I heard her scream and fall clutching her stomach, I thought my heart was going to stop. I've been such an ass." He took off his hat and ran his shaking fingers through his hair. His regret for his past actions sent his stomach in a whirl wind. He felt sick and hoped he wouldn't retch.

"Don't tell me, tell her." Lucas leaned against a tree, arms folded.

Doc pulled the blanket aside and climbed out of the wagon. He frowned at John then walked over to the fire and poured himself a cup of coffee.

John quickly stepped over to him. "Doc is she going to be alright?"

He took a deep breath and let it out slowly. "It was touch and go, but she'll be alright."

"And the baby?" John asked.

"We're just going to have to wait and see. She's been under a great deal of stress…She could still lose the child." Doc tossed out the coffee and handed him the cup. "Take heed, Mr. Evans."

John looked at the wagon then at his friend.

"Well, what are you waiting for?" Lucas asked.

John pushed back the blanket and peered inside.

Abigail was helping Elizabeth to sit up and placed a pillow behind her shoulders. She handed her a cup of tea and tucked a patch-work quilt around her legs.

"Is there anything more I can do for you?" Abigail asked.

"Thank you, no. You've done so much for me already." Elizabeth said taking a sip of tea.

"Goodnight, then." She kissed her cheek and left.

Elizabeth looked up and saw John poking his head in. "May I speak with you?" He looked so crestfallen as his eyes swept her up and down.

"If you must," she said, taking another sip. The wagon moved from side to side as he climbed in and sat next to her.

"Beth, are you alright? I mean…," he asked, a lump forming in his throat as he took off his hat.

"I'll be fine. Is that why you came here?" She sat her cup down.

"Yes, I mean no. I need to speak with you," he said curling the brim.

There was a strange pause between them.

"Well?" she asked.

"Oh, um…I've been thinking, and I believe it would be a good idea if we got married." He smiled.

"Really?" She crossed her arms and cocked her head.

"Yeah. Look, I've been a real ass and I want to make it up to you. If we got married, then with the money I have, we could get your tea shop and the baby would have a father…a name." He took her hand and caressed it. Her skin was so soft, it sent electrical pulses shooting through him.

She took his hand and dropped it in his lap. "Mr. Evans, I don't need your money or a marriage proposal. The baby and I will be just fine without you, so why don't you finish this job and then set out for Missouri. Now, I'm rather tired, so if you'll excuse me, I'd like to go to bed."

John's mouth hung open as he climbed out of the wagon. As he closed the blanket, he heard her crying. He sadly walked over to Buck's wagon and sat down on an overturned log. Lucas came over and sat next to him.

"So, when's the wedding?" he asked.

"There won't be no wedding," John said, dumbfounded. He couldn't believe she turned him down. He thought she loved him. *That woman is driving me crazy.* He leaned on his knees and shook his head, bewilderment crossing his face.

"What'd you say?" Lucas gazed at his friend.

"I told her we should get married. That with my money, I could help her with the tea shop and that the baby would have a father." His voice sounded strange to his ears.

Lucas smacked him upside the head. "You got shit for brains! Did you apologize? Confess your love? Get on your knees and beg to come back?"

"No! I mean she knows I'm sorry and that I love her." He rubbed his head.

"Does she? I think Abigail's right, you don't deserve her." Lucas stood and walked away.

John watched him go, then gazed at Elizabeth's wagon. How was he going to fix this? He got up, grabbed his bedroll, and walked over to her wagon, laid down and stared up at the stars. Two months ago, if he had asked her to marry him, she would have jumped at the chance, but now she didn't want nor need him. *What happened?* He closed his eyes, covered his face with his hat, and fell asleep.

Chapter Thirty-three

Several days past and the wagon train began to head down into the Willamette Valley. Elizabeth sat in the back of her wagon while Jed drove. John didn't want her doing anything that might cause her to lose the baby.

When they stopped for their afternoon meal, Bridget and Abigail busied themselves with Elizabeth's lunch. John walked up to them, a bowl in his hand.

"May I see her?" he asked Bridget.

"Don't upset her. Doc says she needs to stay calm." She placed her hands on her hips.

John nodded and walked to the back of the wagon. He pulled the blanket aside and peeked in. "May I come in?"

"Yes," she said, trying to grasp her brush that was out of her reach.

He climbed in, sat the bowl down and handed her the brush.

"What's that?" She pointed at the bowl.

He picked it up and handed it to her. "Berries. Huckleberries, Salmon and Blackberries. They're native to this area. I thought you might like to try them."

She picked up a berry and popped it in her mouth and smiled. "Thank you, John. It was very thoughtful of you."

He reached over and took the brush, sat next to her, and started brushing her hair. It felt so silky and soft in his big hands. He brought a handful up to his nose and inhaled. It smelled of roses. He heard her sigh when he massaged her scalp. It felt good to be this close to her again.

He bent over and brushed his lips against her cheek. "Beth," he whispered.

She pulled away and looked at him. "Thank you, John, but no." She stared into his face, disappointment etched in his handsome features. *If only he loved me enough to apologize and ask me to marry him properly.*

Abigail poked her head in. "Lunch is ready."

John took the plate from her and handed it to Elizabeth, then climbed out. "Take good care of her."

"I will, John," she said, patting his back.

He nodded and walked toward Buck's wagon, wanting to get some lunch before they started up again.

∞ ∞ ∞

While Elizabeth ate, she stared at the brush. She could still feel his fingers running through her hair. She still loved him, but she couldn't be with any man who only wanted to marry her out of obligation. She needed to know he really loved her and their child.

Tomorrow Jed said they would be in Oregon City. She was excited and heartbroken. After they arrived, John would leave for Missouri. Jed told her that his brother, Lucas, and Aengus along with Buck would head south and then east through warmer country before heading north to Independence in late March.

Tears welled in her eyes, knowing that he would be on another wagon train the same time as the birth of their baby. She touched her stomach. Would he look like him? Would she have her eyes? A hot tear rolled down her cheek and she wiped it away. "I'm sorry you won't have his name," she whispered.

Abigail pushed the blanket aside and climbed in. "All done? We'll be leaving soon." She stared at her friend. "Oh Honey, don't cry. Everything will be alright. You'll see." She wiped a tear away with a napkin.

"I can't help it. Once we get to Oregon City, John's leaving. I just want him to apologize and tell me he wants and loves this baby as much as he said he loves me," she said, her lower lip quivering.

"He's a man. They don't express their feeling like we do. And it's very hard for them to admit when they're wrong. But if he loves you, like I think he does, he'll come around. Just give it time. Get some rest." Abigail collected the dishes and climbed out of the wagon.

Elizabeth laid down and curled up, placing her hand on her belly and closed her eyes. As she fell asleep, she pictured John holding his child in his big, strong hands, a smile crossing his face.

An hour later the wagon jutted and moved forward, causing Elizabeth to awaken. She sat up and propped the pillow behind her. She looked out of the opening at the head of the wagon and saw John driving. He was dressed in a rain slicker and his hat was pulled tight on his head. Thunder rolled in the distance and the rain poured down in buckets. She pulled the blanket around her and felt bad that while she lay safe and dry, John was getting soaked to the bone. She reached over and picked up *Pride and Prejudice,* the book John had bought her, found the page she was at and began reading. The rocking of the wagon was soothing, while she read about her name's sake and Mr. Darcy.

Several hours past and Elizabeth felt the wagon come to a halt. She looked out the opening and saw John hop down and unhitched the team. It was still raining, but not as hard. After a few minutes, John returned and walked to the back of the wagon.

"Beth, you doing alright?" he asked.

"Yes, except I need to go to the necessary."

"Let me help you out." He took her hands, helping her then put the slicker around her, took off his hat and put it on her head. "Looks good on you."

"John, I can't take your slicker." She started to take it off.

He stopped her. "Leave it on, I'll get another one." He took her hand and kissed it. "So beautiful." He put his arm around her waist and slowly walked her to a bunch of trees and turned his back.

Elizabeth went behind them and did what needed to be done. After she was through, she wiped her hands on the hem of her dress and stepped out. She walked over to John and looked up at him. The rain had soaked him to the bone, his shirt stuck to his rock-hard che and she longed to feel his body close to hers. She missed him terribly.

"John, is it true, will we be in Oregon City tomorrow?" she asked.

"Yes, around dinner." He placed a finger under her chin and caressed her cheek with his thumb.

"It's been a long, agonizing trip, hasn't it?" She looked into his eyes.

"Very agonizing." He cupped her face.

"Once we get there, I have so much to do. Find a place to stay, find the best location for my tea shop…have the baby." She touched his hand. "Oh John…"

"Let's get you back to the wagon." He took her arm and helped her to the wagon. She climbed in and removed the slicker and his hat. "I'll be back to check on you in a little while." She nodded and replaced the blanket, listening to him walk away.

With the rain, it made starting a fire nearly impossible, so for dinner she would have jerky, hard tack, dried fruit, and water. As she gathered her dinner, she listened to the rain falling on the bonnet of her wagon. It was soothing to the soul. She spread out her blanket, placed the food on a plate and filled her cup and sat down to eat her meal.

While eating, she thought about John and how she was going to fix her problem with him. When she tried to talk about the baby, he changed the subject and couldn't wait to get away from her. He was angry and ashamed of her, and she knew he couldn't wait to leave.

Without hope, without love… without John, Elizabeth felt her life was nearly over.

Chapter Thirty-Four

John awoke to a pair of Steller Jays singing right above him. He groaned and sat up, rubbing his face. He hated sleeping in the rain, even though he had a slicker and his hat, he still woke up drenched. He stood up and walked to the back of Buck's wagon, grabbed his bag, and pulled out some dry clothes and a towel.

He walked over to a group of trees and hung his things on some branches and started to undress. Suddenly, he heard a woman humming. He peeked through the leaves to see Elizabeth picking wild berries. Smiling to himself, he watched her put several in her basket and then popped a few in her mouth. He finished getting dressed, hung his wet clothes out to dry and walked over to Elizabeth. She was still humming when he reached in her basket and stole a berry.

"Oh." She jumped and whirled around, prepared to hit the thief with her basket.

He started laughing. "Whoa, careful there, Beth." He put his hands up.

"John, you scared me." She punched his arm.

He smiled and took another berry. "Sorry, but I couldn't resist. You looked so cute in your blue cotton dress, bare feet and picking berries. A real pioneer girl." She was so beautiful standing there with the wind gently blowing her ebony hair and her blue dress. Her cheeks were flushed, and her eyes sparkled. He wanted so much to hold her.

She smiled at him. "Today's a big day." She started walking toward her wagon, John fell in step with her.

"You still planning on staying with Jesse and Abigail?" he asked as she put the basket in the back of the wagon.

"Yes, at least until I find a place of my own. I would like to find a building where I can live above my tea shop. I don't want to be a burden to them, so I plan to find a place as quickly as possible."

Jed walked over and started harnessing the mules to her wagon. "Morning, Miss Elizabeth."

"Good morning, Jed and thank you," she said.

"Beth, would you like my help looking for a place?" John asked, rubbing the back of his neck.

"I thought you were leaving as soon as we got to Oregon City?" She sat on her stool and put her shoes on.

"Not for at least a week." He stood there gazing down at her.

She stood up and looked at him. "John, why are you doing this, to you, to me? It's obvious you don't want to be with me, and I don't understand. You say you love me, but when I talk about this pregnancy, you either change the subject or walk away." She stepped over to him and took his hands. "I can't tell you what to do. Stay, go, do what you want, but do it because it makes you happy." She touched his cheek. "I love you, but please, John, stop torturing us." She turned and climbed up on her wagon, waiting to leave.

John stomped over to his drying clothes, grabbed them, and threw them in the back of Buck's wagon, went over to his horse, saddled her, roughly cinching her up and mounted then rode to the front of the wagon train. Lucas trotted up to him.

"Everyone's mounted up. Last day, John. You ready?" Lucas asked.

"Yeah, I guess so." He frowned, rubbing his jaw. "The sooner we get to Oregon City, the better." He shifted in the saddle, stood up and yelled. "Wagons ho!" John watched the wagons pass him. Elizabeth looked at him, sadness in her eyes.

She loved him, and he loved her, but could he be the husband she deserved and the baby, what kind of father could he be to a child he never meant to bring into this world? He felt so ashamed. Why didn't he marry her before he took her to his bed? He took advantage of her, taking her in a moment of weakness. He kicked his horse and rode ahead of the wagon train, Lucas following close behind.

As the hours passed, John and Lucas finally rode up a ridge and looked down at the town of Oregon City. It was a beautiful sight. Stores, lumber mills, saloons, houses all settled along the Willamette River beseeching the wagon train to end their long journey and put down roots of their own.

Lucas smacked John's arm and grinned. "We made it." He turned his pinto and raced back to the wagons to let Aengus and Jed know.

John wished he could be excited, but he knew once they rode into town, the journey would be over and so would his relationship with Elizabeth. As long as they were on the trail, he could be near her, but now they would go their own separate ways. He hung his head as his horse slowly made its way down the ridge.

Chapter Thirty-Five

Elizabeth's excitement could hardly be contained as her wagon entered the bustling town. She let out a deep sigh and bit her lower lip as she followed the wagons to a clearing just outside of town. She parked her rig and jumped down. Abigail, Bridget, and Anna ran up to her. They all hugged her and cried tears of joy.

Jed walked up to the women. "Miss Elizabeth don't worry about your wagon, I'll take care of it for you." He climbed up and took the reins.

"Thank you, Jed." She watched her wagon roll by. She put her hands on her hips and took a deep breath; she was home.

John trotted over to her and dismounted. "Ladies, welcome to Oregon City."

"Thank you, John for getting us here safely. We couldn't have done it without you." Abigail smiled and wrung her hands in her apron.

"You're welcome. I better see to the wagons. Ladies." He tipped his hat and walked away.

Elizabeth's heart was breaking. If only he would have the nerve to apologize and ask her to marry him properly. She shook her head and followed the women to Abigail's wagon. Tomorrow she would go into town and start trying to find a place of her own.

The next morning, Elizabeth was busying herself with breakfast and tea, when John walked up to her.

"Beth, I need to talk with you, would you join me for dinner tonight?" He took his hat off and rubbed the back of his neck.

Elizabeth smiled as she watched him. She always loved his little quirks when he was upset or nervous. "I don't know, John. I'm going to be looking for a place today…"

"Please Beth, I really need to talk with you." He gripped his hat tighter.

"Alright. Have you eaten? Would you like some tea and biscuits?" She got up and went for another cup.

"I'd like that, thank you." He sat near the fire, the mornings were growing colder.

She sat on her stool and poured him a cup of tea adding a pinch of sugar. "No whiskey?" she asked, handing it to him.

"Too early." He looked at the liquid and smiled. "Look what you're having me do, choosing tea over coffee. Soon you'll have me speaking with a British accent."

■■

She started laughing, her eyes twinkling with merriment. He reached over and touched her hand, stroking it gently, little shivers tingled up her arm. She covered his hand with hers and smiled.

While they ate their breakfast, he looked up to see Jed and a stranger walk up to them. John stood up as they approached.

"John, this gentleman wants to speak with you," Jed said, a frown crossed his face.

"Alright. What about? If you're looking for a job, I'm sorry, I'm not hiring," John said, putting his hands on his hips.

"Oh no, I'm looking for someone. A young woman, by the name of Miss Elizabeth Cornwall." The stranger's British accent was very eloquent.

Elizabeth started coughing and dropped her cup. John patted her back, but she waved him away. She whirled around and stared into the stranger's hazel eyes, questions reflecting in her own.

"Ellis?" she asked, dumbfounded. She found him vaguely disturbing. *What the bloody hell was he doing here?*

"Elizabeth, darling. Is it really you?" He grabbed her and pulled her into his arms, kissing the top of her head.

"Darling?" John mouthed to Jed, his eyebrows raised.

She gently pushed him away. "What…what are you doing here? How did you find me?"

"It's a long story. I'll tell you over a proper breakfast." He looked down at the campfire and wrinkled his nose. "Come my dear, let us get you out of this...place and to the hotel where you belong. There, you can take a bath and rest, later I'll take you shopping so you may purchase some proper attire." He touched her faded blue dress with a small tear in the sleeve. He placed his hand on the small of her back and began to walk away.

"Wait just a damn minute," said John, stepping in front of Ellis. "She's not going anywhere until I get a few answers. I don't know you from Adam and *I'm* responsible for Elizabeth. Who the hell are you and what gives you the right to just take her away?"

"Oh, I'm sorry, forgive my prudence. My name is Ellis Hawkins." He extended his hand, John refused to take it. "I'm a very good friend of Elizabeth's."

Elizabeth smiled meekly, and she gazed at John. She could see he was extremely upset by the way he stood, blocking Ellis from leaving.

"That still doesn't explain why you're here," John said, crossing his arms and sneered at him.

"Yes, how did you get here before me? And why are you here? I thought I told you back in England my feelings for you." She stepped away from him.

■■

"How rude of me. As soon as you left, I sold everything and took a boat here to Oregon City. What a horrendous trip that was. I arrived two weeks ago and have been looking for you ever since. Every wagon train that has come through, I've asked for you and well, here you are."

"Ellis, why? I told you I needed a fresh start. To get away from England and the memories it held." She shook her head, tears wetting her eyelashes.

"I don't think this is the time nor the place to be having this conversation. Come along, Elizabeth. Let me take you away from here." He took her arm and escorted her away from the campfire. "If you would be so kind as to bring her things to the hotel." He looked at Jed and nodded, then walked away, Elizabeth on his arm. She turned to look behind her and saw John kick the ground and hit his hat against his leg.

"Ellis, I really don't think…," she began.

"That's your problem, you don't think. I can't believe you went along with this plan of yours alone. Well, don't worry, I'm here, everything will be taken care of." He quickly walked down the street and to the hotel, Elizabeth in tow.

She decided to keep quiet until she was safe in her room. He walked up to the front desk and began to talk with the clerk. Elizabeth wandered around the lobby looking at the beauty of the place. It was bright, painted white and cream and wall to wall carpeting. The windows had yellow curtains and a beautiful chandelier hung from the ceiling. In the middle of the lobby sat a circular cream-colored settee.

"Elizabeth," Ellis called. She walked up to him, and he guided her up the stairs and to her room.

While walking down the carpet covered hallway, her mind went to John and what he might be doing now that Ellis was in the picture. Stopping in front of her door, she reached out for the key. "Thank you, Ellis."

He smiled, unlocked the door for her and opened it. He walked in and tossed the key on the dresser. "Very nice. Now Elizabeth, we need to talk." He strolled over to one of the two blue chairs and sat down. She shut the door, stepping over to the other chair and sat across from him.

"Ellis, why did you come?" she asked, placing her hands on her lap.

"I had to. I was so worried about you." He took her hands and squeezed them. "Elizabeth, I still love you and I want you to be my wife. We can make a life here in Oregon City, together. Please Elizabeth, I love you," he pleaded, kissing her hand.

"Oh Ellis, you don't want me." She shook her head and pulled her hands away.

"I don't understand." His hazel eyes questioning her.

■■

"I've done something that...Ellis believe me. Please, go back to England." She shook her head and closed her eyes.

He got on his knees and touched her face. "There is nothing you can do or say that will stop me from loving you. I'd make you a good husband. I'd love you, protect you, take care of you for the rest of my life."

"Ellis, I don't love you in that way." She took his hand away from her face. A tear fell from her eye and ran down her cheek. "I wish I did, but I don't." She sadly glanced at her lap.

"We could learn to love one another," he said.

"Ellis, I love someone else. My heart belongs to him," she said as he stood up and walked around the   room.

"From the wagon train I expect?" She nodded. "You've known him for only a few months, how can you love him? You've known me your whole life, and I've loved you for that long. How can you...?"

"I'm pregnant," she said gravely, clasping her hands on her lap.

He stopped dead in his tracks and gazed at her. "Oh Elizabeth, how could you? What would your parents think?" Disappointment echoing in his voice. He went back and sat near her.

"It takes two to make a child, Ellis." She frowned at him.

■■■

"Do not mock me in the ways of conceiving a child, Elizabeth. This is a serious discussion. Does he love you?" He leaned back and crossed his legs, covering his eyes with his hand.

"I believe he does," she said.

"Has he asked you to marry him?" He covered his frown with his fingers.

"Well, I wouldn't actually call it a marriage proposal, per say." She got up and walked to the window, wringing her hands.

"So, no. What are your plans?" He got up and walked up behind her, placing a hand on her slender shoulder.

"I'm going to find a nice building to open my tea shop and hopefully live on the top floor. I need…," she began.

"You need a husband to help take care of you and give your baby a name. Who is this man you claim to be in love with?" He turned her around and looked seriously at her.

"It doesn't matter. He'll be leaving soon, and I'll probably never see him again." She started to cry, putting her forehead against his shoulder.

"Oh Elizabeth, you poor girl." He wrapped his arms around her.

As she cried, there was a knock at the door. She stepped away from Ellis, wiped her eyes and opened the door. Jed and John stood looking at her, their arms filled with her things.

"Miss Elizabeth, we brought you your belongings." Jeb held several bags.

Elizabeth moved aside, and the two men walked in, placing her belongings on the floor.

"Thank you, it was very thoughtful of you," she said.

Jed smiled and tipped his hat. "You're welcome and if you need anything else, just let me know. John let's go."

"Meet me downstairs." He nodded at his brother to leave. Jed waved nervously and left, shutting the door behind him.

John and Ellis glared at each other while Elizabeth sat on the edge of the bed. John took his hat off and rolled the brim.

"Ellis, this is John Evans. He's the wagon master." She smiled at him and batted her eyes.

"Yes, we've met." Ellis crossed his arms over his chest.

"Beth, about dinner…I," he began.

"We're still on for tonight, are we not?" she asked, her voice trembled.

He looked deep into her eyes, wanting to take hold of her and kiss her until he took her breath away and Ellis be damned. "Well, you have company now, I'm sure you two would rather dine together. I just came to bring you your things. Mr. Hawkins. Good afternoon, Beth." He put his hat back on and slammed the door as he left.

■■

Elizabeth stood up, her lower lip quivering. She slumped in the chair and covered her face with her hands. "Oh Ellis, what am I to do?"

"Come, let us leave this so-called room for the afternoon and begin looking for a place for your tea shop." He took her hands and pulled her up. He put his arm around her waist, and they left the room.

Elizabeth was being torn in two. She was in love with John, but he seemed to not want to marry her. Ellis wanted to marry her, but she didn't love him. Should she choose John and hope he changed his mind or choose Ellis and live in a loveless marriage, but know she'd be taken care of?

■■■

Chapter Thirty-Six

John stood at the bar, Jed leaning next to him. He stared in the mirror, his reflection showing a man who seemed to have lost everything.

The saloon was much smaller than the one in Missouri. It had a small bar with one window and two swinging doors. Hurricane lanterns hung all around the room while only a few tables and chairs sat throughout, most were occupied by men drinking and playing poker. The place smelled of booze and cigarette smoke and an older gentleman played a piano in the corner near the bar.

"Whiskey and leave the bottle." John threw several coins on the bar. He poured himself a glass, threw back his head and drank it, then poured another. He looked in the mirror again and saw tears glistening on his eyelashes. His vision was still gloomily colored with the memory of Elizabeth with Ellis.

"John, talk to her. She loves you," Jed said, taking a hold of John's arm.

"Shut up, Jed and leave me the hell alone." A saloon girl in a bright red dress wrapped her arms around John, rubbing her hands on his shoulders.

Jed turned away and finished his drink. He knew John would need him after a few bottles, so he decided to stay. He waved down the bartender. "Beer." After getting his drink, he walked over to a table in the corner and waited.

John didn't want the girl's company and tried to ignore her. He poured himself another drink and stared in the mirror. *Elizabeth didn't need me, she had Ellis*. He had traveled all the way from England to be with her, giving up everything just for her. John took a swig and shook his head. *What had I done for her? Nothing*. When she needed him most, he had walked away.

The saloon girl laughed in his ear and her hand ran down his back. "Come on, cowboy, buy me a drink."

He signaled the bartender for another glass and poured her a drink. "Take your drink and git," John slurred and threw back another.

"But honey, I can show you a good time if you let me," she said, running her fingers down his bearded face.

John pulled away from her and poured another drink. "Go bother someone else." He took a swig and finished the bottle.

She leaned against him and put her arm around him. "She must have done a number on you. What'd she do, cowboy, kick you out?" She laughed and smacked him on the back.

He grabbed her by the arm and pulled her face close to his. "I told you to leave me alone." He shoved her down the bar then turned back to his drink.

"Hey, that's no way to treat a lady!" said an older man, stepping up to John and whirling him around. The man was a few inches shorter than John, but larger in size. He wore cream-colored shirt and brown trousers with a tan, leather vest. He had a fat, round face, and beady eyes. His meaty hands clenched, and he stared John down. John swayed, scoffed at the man, and turned away.

"You owe her an apology, cowboy." The man said.

John ignored him and ordered another bottle. The man tapped him on the shoulder as John poured another drink. He stood against the bar, sipping his whiskey when the older man whirled him around, balled up his meaty fist and hit John square in the jaw. John spun around and landed hard on the wooden floor. He shook his head and grabbed his jaw, then slowly stood up rocking back and forth, tackling the older man. As they started throwing punches, they suddenly heard the cock of a gun. They looked over to see the bartender holding a shotgun.

"Not in my bar. You two, get out." The bartender waved the gun toward the door.

John let go of the older man and stepped back. "Alright." Blood ran down his chin while he threw some coins on the bar, grabbed the bottle, and staggered out. Jed followed close behind, knowing he would have to help John back to the encampment after he passed out in some alley.

They stepped out of the bar, looked across the street and saw Elizabeth and Ellis, arm in arm, walking toward a restaurant. John threw the bottle on the ground and marched across the street toward the happy couple.

"John," Jed called after him.

He walked up in front of Elizabeth and glared at her. She stepped back and gazed at him.

"John, I thought you went back to the wagon train. I didn't know you were still in town. Would you like to join us for lunch?" Elizabeth asked.

John swayed on his feet. He looked Ellis up and down and curled his lip. "So, this is the kind of man you want?" He smacked Ellis in the chest. "Well, I hope you two will be very happy, you English hussy."

"Wait just a minute." Ellis grabbed John by the collar. "You have no right speaking to her in that manner."

"Ellis, please." Elizabeth put a hand on his arm.

John grabbed Ellis and punched him in the stomach. Elizabeth stepped back as he hit Ellis in the face, sending him in the street. John jumped on him, and they rolled in the dirt, throwing punches. Horses whinnied and stepped out of the way as the two men wrestled on the ground. Elizabeth went to break up the fight, but Jed grabbed her around the waist.

"Jed, stop them." She watched the two men battling it out, terror in her eyes.

"I thought all women loved having men fighting over them." He smiled at her. She scoffed at him, then turned her attention back to the fight. "Boy, does John love you," Jed yelled.

She looked at him and smiled as the two men fell at her feet before getting up and attacking each other once more. Her features became more animated and her heart sang with delight. She was blissfully happy, fully alive. *John was fighting for me.*

A large crowd surrounded the men, yelling and taunting as John hit Ellis in the nose then Ellis punched John in the mouth. As they threw punches, the sheriff ran up and fired his gun in the air.

"Knock it off, the both of you. What's going on here?" The sheriff looked at the two men.

John and Ellis looked like hell. They stood covered in dirt, hair a mess, torn shirts and jackets, and blood covering their faces and hands.

"Just a personal dispute, constable." Ellis said, wiping his bloody nose. "I apologize for the disturbance."

Jed walked up to John and grabbed him by the arm. "I'll see him home."

"Sorry, son, but I gotta lock 'em both up. Come on you two." The sheriff marched the two men toward the jail. John glared at Ellis then he picked up his hat and followed the sheriff down the street.

"Jed, do something. They can't be incarcerated." Elizabeth gripped his sleeve and shook it wildly.

"Miss Elizabeth, there's nothing I can do, besides this might be a good thing. After John cools down, they can talk things through. Come on, I'll buy you a cup of coffee…I mean tea." He laughed, and they walked toward the restaurant.

Chapter Thirty-Seven

John awoke and grabbed his head. "Oh, God," he said. His body felt like a herd of horses had run him over. He slowly opened his eyes and noticed the bars. Looking around, he saw Ellis sitting in the cell next to him, smiling.

"Good morning, Sleeping Beauty?" Ellis rubbed his fingers over his mouth to hide a grin. He sat on a cot with his back against the wall.

"Shut up, Ellis." John sat up and bowed his injured head.

"Bloody hell John, you have a wicked arm. I thought I lost all my teeth," Ellis said, grabbing his jaw.

John groaned as the door opened and the sheriff walked in. "Morning boys. Sleep well?" He held a tray with two coffee cups and two plates with hot cakes, eggs, and sausage. "My wife fixed you two some breakfast." He passed the plates to Ellis and John then left, John heard the clinking of the jail keys on the sheriff's hip.

John put the plate aside and drank his coffee. "I wasn't myself yesterday. I'm sorry, Ellis."

"Are you ready to talk, John?" Ellis walked over to the bars and gazed at him.

"About what?" John finished his coffee and sat the cup aside. He laid back down and put his hat over his face.

"About Elizabeth." Ellis leaned against the bars and drank his coffee.

"I don't want to talk about her." John crossed his long legs and closed his eyes.

"You don't have to talk, but you're going to listen." Ellis threw his cup at John hitting him in the head. John turned around and glared at him. "I've known Elizabeth since she was a little girl. Her father and I were best friends and I watched that little girl grow into a fine woman. It's true, I fell in love with her, and I proposed, but she said no. After her parents' death, I proposed once more and again she turned me down. She doesn't love me. When she left, I came out here hoping against hope that she would have changed her mind, but she didn't. She told me she loves someone else, that her heart belongs to only him."

"Yeah? And who might that be?" John stood up and crossed his arms.

"You, you Wanker." He hit the bars, making a loud bang. "She loves you. She and I are merely friends. I don't want to step on any toes. You belong with her."

"I can't. You don't understand." He sat down, rested his elbows on his knees and bowed his head.

"You don't love her?" Ellis asked.

"No…I mean yes, yes I do, but look what I did to her. I took advantage of her and got her pregnant. How can she love a man like me? I wouldn't make a good husband or father. How can she forgive me? She deserves someone better, someone she can depend on to make her happy." John hung his head.

"John, I don't believe that. She told me all the things you did for her and the way you saved her life when that Mr. Cobb fellow attacked her. You are a damn good man, John, and you deserve her. She has forgiven you. All she wants is an apology and a proper proposal."

The sheriff walked in, keys jingling. "It's been twenty-four hours, guess I gotta let you go. No more fighting in the streets, you hear?"

"Don't worry, constable. There shan't be. We have a clear understanding, do we not," Ellis said, walking out of his cell.

John grabbed his hat and the two men ambled out of the jail. Ellis clapped John on the back, and they stopped and looked at one another.

Ellis extended his hand. "Friends?" John nodded and took his hand. "We need to locate Elizabeth and tell her there are no hard feelings."

Ellis looked around and spotted Jed. "Is that not your brother?"

John turned and saw his brother rushing toward them. "Jed, what's going on? Where's Elizabeth?"

Jed had to catch his breath before answering. He bent over and gripped his knees, taking several deep breaths. "She's…she's at the bank."

"The bank? What is she doing there?" Ellis asked, putting on his jacket.

"After the fight and you two were taken to jail, Elizabeth was mad as a hornet, so she ordered me to help her find a place for her tea shop. We spent all day and was about to give up when she saw this place next to the general store. The bank owns it, so this morning she went over there. She's still there now." Jed pointed down the street.

The three men quickly made their way to the bank. They approached as Elizabeth stepped out and closed the door. "Oh, afternoon gentlemen. How was your time in jail?" She smiled and snickered at them.

"Most amusing," Ellis said. "If you will excuse me, my dear, I believe I shall go retire and clean up before our next meeting." He leaned over and kissed her cheek. "Gentlemen." He nodded and walked toward the hotel.

"Oh John, I just bought the perfect place for my tea shop. Come on, let me show you." She took his hand and the three walked to the general store.

Just past the store on the left, stood an empty building with two large windows on either side of the entryway. She put the key in the lock and opened the door. When they walked in, John noticed a long counter and several shelves around the room, perfect for a tea shop. He looked around and saw stairs leading to the second floor where Elizabeth would have her living quarters. There was an area in the back that looked like the storeroom.

"Isn't it perfect. Oh, John, my dream is finally coming true." She wrapped her arms around him, pressing her head to his chest.

"I'm gonna go back to camp. I'll see you two later." Jed left, closing the door behind him.

"Beth, we need to talk." John picked her up and sat her on the counter.

"Of course. What's wrong?" she asked, crossing her ankles, and swinging her legs.

He took off his hat and curled the brim. He walked around the room, his boots echoing on the wooden floor. "Beth, I…I'm sorry I've been so angry and left you to deal with this all on your own." He walked up to her and placed his hat on the counter. "I never meant to hurt you. I love you, Beth." He touched her face, leaned in, and kissed her.

"I love you too, John." She wrapped her arms around his neck and hugged him.

"Listen, I got some stuff to do, so I'll see you tonight for dinner, alright?" He helped her down off the counter, kissed her forehead, grabbed his hat, and left.

Elizabeth stood in the quiet stillness of her new tea shop. It was all hers and one day it would be the grandest shop in Oregon City. She stretched out her arms and spun in several circles, her shoes clicking on the floorboards as her skirt billowing with every turn. She was so happy. Her mother was right, good things come out of bad situations.

Chapter Thirty-Eight

Elizabeth brought the rest of her things from the hotel to her new place. She carried them up the stairs and placed them in her bedroom then came out and looked around. It was a quaint little place with two bedrooms, a living room, kitchen and eating area. She couldn't wait to start decorating and painting not only here, but downstairs in the shop. Unfortunately, the necessary was out back behind the storage room.

She walked down the stairs into the empty store and smiled. Her mother and father would have been so happy to see this. A tear dripped from her eye, and she walked over to the counter. As she moved around it, there was a knock at the door. She stepped over to it, looked out the window and noticed it was Ellis. He was holding a large, wrapped package.

She opened the door and let him in. "Ellis, it's rather late."

"I wanted to bring this to you. I knew you would want it. I brought it all the way from Seaford." He laid it against the counter. "Open it, my dear"

She strolled over to it and ripped the brown paper away. "Oh Ellis, thank you." She hugged him then looked at the gift. It was the portrait of her mother that hung in the house back in England.

"You look so much like her." He smiled. "Well, like you said, it's late, so I will take my leave. Goodnight, Elizabeth." He kissed her cheek and left.

She sat on the floor in front of the picture and touched her mother's face. "I miss you so much. I wish you were here, I need you." She touched the small bump on her stomach. She heard the door open, and John walked in. She smiled, rose, and ran into his arms.

"What's this?" He asked handing her a bundle of wildflowers. He looked at the portrait and then at her. "Is that you?"

"No, that's my mother. Ellis brought it with him." She smelled the flowers then laid them on the counter. "John, I want to name the baby after my mother or father."

"That would be wonderful. I think they would have been very honored. Are you hungry? Would you like to go to dinner?" he asked, touching her face.

"Yes, please. Let my just get my wrap." She run up the stairs and grabbed her wool shawl. As she came back down the stairs, she heard John talking.

"And I promise to love your daughter with all my heart," he said to the portrait. Turning, he smiled sheepishly at her. "You ready?"

She nodded and took his arm. "I love you."

He patted her hand. "And I you."

∞ ∞ ∞

For the past week, Elizabeth worked harder than ever to get her living quarters in order. John, Jed, Lucas, Ellis, and Aengus helped with the heavy lifting while Elizabeth, Abigail, Anna, and Bridget concentrated on the cleaning. Little Clementine slept in a basket while Rachel played with her doll near Bridget.

"Elizabeth?" said Rachel.

"Yes, sweetie?" Elizabeth squatted down next to her.

"Are you going to have a baby? Mommy said you're going to have a baby like Abigail." She sat cuddling her doll.

"Yes, Rachel. I am." Elizabeth smiled at her.

"I hope it's a girl like me," she said.

"I do, too." She replied, picking up Rachel and twirling her around. The little girl squealed, holding her doll tight while Elizabeth held her close. At that moment, Elizabeth felt her heart was full of love and laughter. She had a wonderful man that she loved and friends whom she could cherish. However, things were to change once John left in a week.

∞ ∞ ∞

Elizabeth needed to keep working, it kept her from thinking about John leaving. He said he'd only be around for a week or so and the week was coming to an end. As she cleaned the window in the kitchen, she looked out and saw John and Jed lifting part of her new bed out of a wagon and onto their shoulders. Tears dripped from her eyes as she watched them. Soon he would leave and there was a chance she may never see him again.

"Are you alright, Elizabeth?" Anna asked.

"Yes, I'm fine. I just got some dust in my eyes." She continued washing the window.

Later John came into the kitchen to get a drink of water from a bucket. He took a sip and looked around at the sparkling room and smiled. Elizabeth stood gazing at him.

"You're so beautiful," he said with a smirk.

"I'm a mess. Look at me," she said. She was covered in dirt, smudges on her face and her hair had come out of its bun.

"I am." He walked over to her, pulled her into his arms and kissed her.

Jed walked in and cleared his throat. Elizabeth pulled away and turned around, covering her face with her hand. "Miss Elizabeth, could you come take a look at the bed? We need to see where you want it before we put it together."

Elizabeth nodded and quickly left the room, John and Jed followed. She entered the room, and she couldn't help but blush; five men stood in her bedroom.

John caught her looking at the bed and leaned against her back and whispered. "There's room for two."

She elbowed him then proceeded to tell the men where to put the bed, dresser, and armoire, then glared at John and walked out. She went into her living room, heard John snicker, and couldn't help but smile.

"John, could you hang my mother's picture over the mantle for me?" she asked.

"Sure." He grabbed a hammer, some nails and a step ladder and went over to the fireplace. He measured where the nail should go, then hammered it into the wall. Elizabeth handed him the portrait and he hung it above the mantle. He stepped down off the ladder, wrapped his arm around her and looked up at her mother. "She was a beautiful woman… like mother, like daughter." He kissed the top of her head and rubbed her back.

"Stay here," she said and went downstairs to the corner of the empty store where the men had put her belongings and opened her carpet bag. She pulled out the teacup, saucer, and plate and went back upstairs and walked over to the fireplace. She stacked the plate,
saucer and cup and placed them on the mantle, just below her mother's portrait.

"There, now she will be with me always." She faced him, leaning against his body, and gazed up at him. "Thank you, John, for everything."

"You're very welcome, Beth," he said, smoothing her ebony hair. "Well, I better get back to work." He turned and went back into the bedroom to help the men put the bed together and place the furniture where Elizabeth wanted it.

The week went by, and her living quarters were finished. She walked around gazing at all the lovely things John and his men had set up. The two easy chairs sat on a beautiful rug in front of the fireplace, a cedar eating table with a vase of flowers he had picked for her, and the bed with the carved headboard he had had made especially for her. She smiled as she ran her hand over it. It had ivy and flowers all around it and in the center, was a teacup with a saucer and a shot glass of whiskey.

"Tea and whiskey." She whispered and fell on the bed crying. Today he was leaving, and she knew if he left, she'd never see him again.

∞ ∞ ∞

John sat at the table drinking his beer, a frown shadowing his bearded face. Lucas and Aengus walked into the saloon and pulled up a couple of chairs and sat with him.

"Well, have you made up your mind?" Lucas asked as a saloon girl brought over two beers.

"Yeah, afraid so." John looked down at his drink and scowled. "I have no choice, Jed's leaving for California."

"I'm sorry, John." Aengus took a sip of his beer.

"So am I." John finished his beer and stood up. "I'll see you back at camp." He walked out of the saloon, mounted his horse, and rode out of town.

Later that afternoon, Lucas, Jed, and Aengus stood at the back of Buck's wagon. Everything was packed and ready for the long trek back to Missouri. Jed took the paper John was filling out on the tailgate and signed his name.

"You understand that you're selling your half of the company over to Lucas?" John asked.

"Yes. Don't worry, John, I know what I'm doing," Jed said as Lucas handed him a stack of money. He put it in his saddle bags then grabbed Aengus and gave him a big bear hug. "You know, you're welcome to join me. We could be partners."

"I ken, but John needs me." Aengus shook Jed's hand. "Take care, my friend."

"You, too." He turned and shook John's hand. "See you later, big brother. Take good care of Miss Elizabeth for me." He smiled, punched him in the arm and mounted his horse. He tipped his hat and rode out of the encampment.

"Take care, little brother," he said watching Jed fade into the distance.

"Are you sure this is what you want, John?" Lucas asked.

He nodded and got on his horse. "I better go tell Elizabeth." He kicked his mount and rode toward town.

Chapter Thirty-Nine

Elizabeth sat in the big easy chair staring at the fire in the fireplace. The wind blew violently, and thunder clapped outside her window; her mood matching that of the weather. She wiped away her tears, soon he would be there to say goodbye. She loved him, but it wasn't strong enough to keep him. She curled up and wept, knowing that after today, she would never see him again.

As she sat there, she heard a knock at the door and her heart went to her throat. She slowly rose from her chair and went downstairs. Crossing the empty room, she saw him standing, a smile across his face. She turned the lock and opened the door.

He quickly stepped in and shut the door. "Whoa, it's cold out there."

"Let me make you some tea," she said sadly as they climbed the stairs to her living room.

She went over to the fireplace and hung the tea kettle over the fire as he took off his jacket and began to warm his hands by the fire.

"Beth, you've been crying," he said, gazing at her. Her eyes were puffy and red, her nose was a dark pink and streaks of dried tears ran down her cheeks.

He walked over to her when her lower lip began to quiver.

"Oh John," she walked away from him, pacing the floor like he did when he was upset. "I know why you're here, what you're going to say…"

"You do?" he questioned, rubbing his beard.

"Yes, and I told myself that whatever you want, I'd except. I know I frighten you, and I know that sounds strange that I would frighten you, but I do. I was ignorant to think you would be happy here in a tea shop when you could be out on the trail under the open sky."

"Are you going to stop and let me talk?" John asked, stepping up to her.

She turned her back to him. "No John, that's what frightens you, that I'd be an anchor around your neck and when you got tired of this life, you wouldn't be able to leave, and I made up my mind that when you came here today, I'd tell you that whatever you want John…"

He spun her around and gazed into her violet eyes. "Will you marry me?"

"What are you saying?" She looked up into his rugged face.

He reached into his front pocket and pulled out a diamond ring. "I'm asking you to be my wife and help me be the father our baby deserves. I love you, Beth," he touched her belly, "you and the child you carry."

"Oh John." She hugged him. "Yes." He took her hand. The ring was lovelier than anything she ever expected. It was silver with tiny carvings and in the middle was a beautiful diamond shimmering in the fire light.

"I hope it fits," he laughed as he slipped the ring on her finger.

She gazed at it and smiled. "It's lovely." She looked up at him, shock in her eyes. "Does this mean you're not leaving?" A tumble of confused thoughts and feelings assailed her.

"Wild horses couldn't pull me away. No, I gave the job to Lucas. He, Aengus, and Buck are going to Missouri and hire up a few more men. Looks like you're stuck with me."

"Oh John, I love you." A cry of relief broke from her lips. She wrapped her arms around his waist and laid her head against his chest.

"And I you." He picked her up in his arms and carried her to the easy chair. As they crossed the floor, she smiled and laid her head against his herculean shoulder.

Her life was complete, she had everything her heart desired and for once she was truly happy. She hugged him tightly and kissed his lips. All her dreams had come true and as he placed her on his lap, she couldn't wait to see what the next adventure lay in store for them. Gazing at John, she placed his hand on her belly and smiled. He leaned over and brushed his lips against hers. As she drank in the sweetness of his kiss, blood pounded in her brain, her body melted against his and she exhaled a long sigh of contentment.

"Are you ready for our next big adventure, Beth?"

"As long as it's with you, always." She touched his lips with her fingers. "Together…"

"Forever" He gazed into her beautiful violet eyes. *I can't believe how blessed I am. What did I do to deserve such a woman*?

She pulled him to her and kissed him with a fierce want, tears glistening on her lashes; her heart had finally found a home.

The End

Appendix

Aff: Off
Ah: I
Arse: Ass
Aye: Yes
Bairn: A young child
Blighter: Person or thing to be re-
garded with contempt
Canna: Can not
Clarty: Dirty as a clarty bastard
Cood: Could
Cowp: Knock over
Dinna Fash: Don't worry
Doona: Do not
Dunderheid: Idiot
Glaikit: Stupid
Jist: Just
Ken: Know
Knobber: Stupid, irritating person
Oaf: Off
Pish: Piss
Shite: Shit
Wanker: Despicable person

Wee: Little
Ye: You
Yer: Your

Made in the USA
Middletown, DE
07 August 2022

70771306R00203